THE

Goodbye
Girls

THE
Goodbye Girls

Putting the *fun* in funerals

a novel

JULIET DOMVILE

House of Miles Books

Copyright © 2022 by Juliet Domvile
All rights reserved.

Published by House of Miles Books, Victoria, BC
www.thegoodbyegirls.ca

Edited and designed by Girl Friday Productions
www.girlfridayproductions.com

Cover design: Emily Weigel
Project management: Reshma Kooner
Editorial production: Jaye Whitney Debber

Image credits: cover © iStock/homeworks255, Shutterstock/ Ljupco Smokovski, Shutterstock/xpixel

ISBN (paperback): 978-1-77835-106-8
ISBN (ebook): 978-1-77835-107-5

Chapter 1

Life is a gravel road that requires constant maintenance. Ignore the potholes, and they can become sinkholes—that swallow you whole. Aislin was in a sinkhole.

Her rolling suitcase spun on its remaining wheel, the handle banging into her bum, twisting her arm and wrist as she bounced it over the cedar roots pushing through the cement path. She bumped along to the front of the house, pausing a beat before humping it up the steps.

The front mat, a gift to her granny years ago, greeted her with "Go Away." It was supposed to be a joke, a comment on the chaos of her childhood. Everyone was welcome. Aislin rarely had a meal alone with her grandparents. There was always someone in need of their advice or a meal, or to share a piece of good or bad news or pure gossip. Their door was always open. It was never even locked. Not at night, not when they were in the backyard, not even when they were out. But after her husband passed, her grandmother developed a pantomime of unlocking the door in a nod to her vulnerability. She kept an imaginary key under the mat.

Aislin paused at the mat. The words mocked her. She turned and looked back at her car. The lyrics from the Clash song "Should I Stay or Should I Go," which had been on a near-continuous loop in her mind for the last few days, restarted. The thought of dragging her suitcase all that way back convinced her to stay. Sighing, she reached under the mat for the imaginary key.

"Gran? It's Aislin. I've come for a visit," she called as she walked down the hall to the kitchen, straightening the pictures as she went. She pushed open the swing door. Plates, bowls, and mugs stacked precariously covered the counters and filled the sink. Teabags sat in their cold little puddles of stain. Gardening magazines lay open on the table, tacked to the melamine with mug rings and dribbles of honey. Aislin's shoes stuck to a mystery sheen as she crossed the floor to the fridge, where a sliver of light shone from the cracked-open door. She elbow-jabbed it closed.

The sound of a car pulling up drew her back to the hall. She watched the two women walk up the path, chattering away.

"Elaine, the key is under the mat."

"Yes, Letty, I know," said Elaine.

Aislin listened to the key ritual play out, rooted to the spot. Every fibre of her body screamed at her to grab her suitcase and bolt out the back door.

"Surprise! It's me, your long-lost granddaughter! I've come for a visit."

"Oh, honey, I didn't know you were coming. I would have stayed home, but Agnes from down the street passed away last week, and Elaine kindly offered to drive me to the celebration of life. It was so crowded. I didn't know she had so many friends. I always thought she was a bit broody and dour. But the sandwiches were light and lovely. And the devilled eggs were perfectly moist. Not like the eggs at Betty Anderson's service last month. Did you know she had passed? Heart attack. Those eggs were dry. I could hardly swallow. I was so grateful when someone offered me some wine. Not nice wine, mind you, but it did wash down the egg. So, honey, how long are you staying? Elaine will stay and have tea with us."

"Thank you for offering, but I'll leave you and Aislin to catch up. Nice to see you, Aislin. How long will you be in town this time? Longer than your usual forty-eight hours?"

"Not sure. Let me get the door for you. Bye now."

"I'm surprised Elaine wouldn't stay. Her husband is not very good company lately. Quite grumpy and dim. But then he was always a bit . . . you know. . ."

Aislin knew precisely what Ed was. Ed had always creeped her out.

His hugs were just too tight, and his hands always dropped from her back to her bum. After every encounter, she regretted not kneeing him in the crotch and letting everyone know he was a dirty old man. She wondered how many other women in Ed and Elaine's family and social circle suffered in silence.

Aislin was not sure how tea could be considered an option in the kitchen chaos. Letty didn't seem embarrassed by the mess, as Aislin had expected. No apology. No explanation. Letty idly picked up mugs, peered inside, and rejected them. She looked out the window at the garden in the watery dusk. Aislin gave her an awkward sideways hug.

"How about you sit down while I tidy up and make the tea?" She pulled out a chair and removed the magazines. Letty sat gratefully.

"I'm worn out after all the singing and talking. The same people seem to be at every service. No one had anything new to say. Same old news about their kids and grandkids. I, of course, had nothing to share."

There it was—the dig. Aislin looked at the clock. Less than ten minutes into the visit. A new record. Tea was not what Aislin wanted. She wanted a long, cold beer.

"So, Gran, about these dishes. Is the dishwasher broken or something?"

"No, it's not broken. I ran out of those tab things and just kept forgetting to buy more. I tried to use the dish soap, but that made such a big mess. Suds everywhere. I had to crawl over to turn it off because the floor was so slippery."

Aislin filled the sink and collected the silverware as she listened. Wings of panic beat against her ribcage. She focused on breathing as she washed and rinsed the cutlery. The warm, sudsy water was oddly comforting. Having grown up with a dishwasher, doing dishes by hand was a dreaded last resort. She tackled the stack of plates next. Letty instructed her to change the water before the mugs and glasses. As she worked through the dishes, her grandmother gossiped about her friends.

Order restored, Aislin looked in the fridge and quickly closed it again. The cupboards didn't offer much in the way of options for dinner. She looked sharply at her grandmother and noticed how thin her face had become. She had always been slim, but now she had a new angular look, her skin hanging loosely from her jawbone. Aislin opened the fridge again. Half-empty Tupperware containers with lids askew, a creamer occupied by a solidified lump of milk, some hardened, half-wrapped cheddar, an open egg carton with three eggs, sad lettuce and limp parsley in the crisper. And the remains of a bottle of pinot gris. Taking out the wine, she turned to Letty. "How about we skip tea and have some wine?" Not waiting for an answer, she emptied the bottle into two glasses. "Gran, let's order Chinese food for dinner. When was the last time you had delivery?"

"Oh, that's so expensive. I'm sure there's a can of tomato soup somewhere," said Letty, getting up stiffly.

"Nope, I'm ordering Chinese. My treat. I'm assuming Jack's is still the best in town."

Aislin went to the hall for her purse and dug out her phone. Without checking messages, she found Jack's number and placed her order. She felt compelled to order quite a few dishes to make it worthwhile for the driver. And, hopefully, to cover lunch tomorrow. She could scramble the eggs for breakfast.

"Gran, I'm going to bring in my things from the car. Back in a jiff."

She carefully slid out an aquarium. Her arms just barely reached around the sides. Once on the porch, she nudged open the door and edged in sideways, inhaling deeply so she and the tank would fit.

"Sorry, buddy. You must be freezing. I'm going to get you warmed up, don't you worry," she cooed.

"Who are you talking to? Is the food here already?" called Letty. "I've opened more wine. Let's eat in the kitchen. The dining room is a bit dark. I hardly ever go in there. You know, since Frank . . ."

"Sounds great. Hope my glass is the biggest. I'm just going to put my things in my room." Aislin struggled sideways up the steep stairs. She had forgotten how narrow the staircase and halls were. Apart from updating the kitchen structurally, the house was unchanged from the day it was built in 1957. After her years in condos with skylights, open floor plans, and oversized windows, it felt dark and crushing.

Aislin flicked the light switch with her elbow, then carefully placed the tank on the dresser. She plugged in its light and stroked the shell of the small turtle.

"Sorry about all that, buddy. You'll be fine once we get you warmed up. I'll be right back with some water and food."

She hurried to the kitchen, filled a water jug, grabbed the parsley, picked off the worst of the saggy sprigs, rinsed it under cold water, and vigorously shook off the excess.

"Back in a jiff."

"What's going on, Aislin? Who are you talking to, and where are you taking the parsley? Did you bring a rabbit home? I detest rabbits. They're nothing but vermin. They ruin my garden."

"Nope, not a rabbit. I'll tell you all about everything in a bit."

Aislin hurried back up the stairs. She filled the water bowl, tore off parsley chunks, and dropped it in the cage. "There you go, little buddy. You'll feel better after some food and water. I'll be back in a little while."

She saw the delivery car pull up behind hers, so she raced downstairs and opened the door.

The delivery boy looked about ten. Since when did young people look so young? She hadn't noticed that phenomenon before. Maybe it was being back home, which always seemed to exist in an alternative universe. Nothing ever seemed to change. Stuck in a time warp. Still able to order the family's favourite foods from Jack's was bizarre but oddly comforting. In Vancouver, the selection of restaurants was endless, with a constant churn of new ones opening and favoured old ones closing.

Letty had put the dishes away, set the table, and topped up their wine. The aroma of food was warm and calming. The floor was still sticky, but that could wait. Aislin ladled out the food, and they both settled down gratefully.

"Cheers," said Aislin, with a crooked grin, hoping the firing line of questions would not begin right away.

"Cheers," said Letty, drinking deeply. "Ah, I think I needed that—such a long day. Elaine wears me out. She's always dragging me to this funeral or that celebration of life. And some of the holy rollers don't serve wine with the food. It can be quite tedious sitting through all the singing and praying, so I look forward to a decent glass of wine afterwards."

"Jeez, Gran, how many of these things do you two go to? Why are so many of your friends dying? Is that normal, you know, for people your age?"

"My age? I am only seventy-four," she snapped. Aislin raised her eyebrows, and after a beat, they both laughed.

"Sorry. It just sounds as though you've been going to a lot of funerals, so I'm curious. That's all." Aislin dropped her eyes to tackle the almond chicken, which challenged her skill with chopsticks.

"You're not the only one who's curious. Why are you here? You didn't let me know you were coming. It would have been nice to have known in advance instead of being surprised in front of Elaine. She's such a gossip; I'm sure half the town now knows you're here with no warning. I haven't heard from you for weeks, and suddenly you're here with a bunch of suitcases. What's going on, Aislin? Are you in some sort of trouble?" Letty's voice was hitting that querulous tone that had always signalled an impending litany of complaints and judgments about Aislin's shortcomings and frequently triggered her earlier-than-planned departure.

Aislin quickly popped some bright-red sweet-and-sour pork balls into her mouth and awkwardly moved the food as she worked the meat off the bone with her tongue. She took a long drink of wine and focused on breathing before looking up and answering.

"It's a bit of a long story. I'm in a bad spot. It's work-related, not relationship-related. I'm not quite ready to talk about it. I'm still processing, so can we please just eat our dinner, enjoy our wine, and maybe watch some television? What shows are you watching these days?"

"You can't throw me off that easily. At least tell me how long you're planning to be here."

"I don't know. I came home to regroup, and I don't know how long regrouping takes, as I've never been in this situation before. I burnt some bridges at work. With my editor. And with someone who was a good friend, roommate, and coworker, and with a colleague from another paper. And with the guy who's the paper's major advertiser. Who has a ton of clout in Vancouver and in every town in the province that publishes a newspaper." She looked up at her gran and saw soft sadness, which made large, hot tears of self-pity spring from her eyes.

"Look up at the ceiling."

"'Scuse me?"

"If you look up at the ceiling, you can stop the tears before they start pouring down your face. I learned that in a *Grey's Anatomy* episode. It works. I do it all the time when I'm out with Elaine. Last thing I want is for people to see me with twin freeways of mascara running down my face."

Aislin tipped her head, stuck out her chin, and looked up.

"Not like that! Just look up—raise your eyes, not your chin. Your chin isn't about to blubber."

Aislin pulled her shoulders back, settled her chin over her centre line, and raised her eyes. "Like this?"

"Yes, much better. And see? Tears gone. Mascara intact. You're wearing an awful lot, you know. Your eyelids look as though they've trapped a couple of caterpillars."

"Gee, thanks. It's a new look I'm trying. I don't wear much makeup, but thought I could make my eyes pop some more. You always said my eyes were my best feature. Too much?"

Letty snorted. "You look ridiculous. The lashes are the only thing you see. Big enough to be awnings. Makes you look hard. And older. I'm sure Elaine noticed."

They sat back and looked at each other—Aislin with a comfortable grin, Letty with an appraising frown. Aislin had dodged the questioning. For now.

She got up and began clearing the table, scraping plates, closing up the food containers before storing them in the fridge.

"Why don't you go find us a show?" Aislin asked while she worked.

No answer. She turned and looked at Letty, who was fiddling with her napkin in her lap.

"I have a TV in my room now. I rarely go into the living room. In the winter, I go upstairs right after dinner. Get ready for bed, and then watch a show or two until I'm ready to sleep. In the spring and summer, I'm in the garden."

"Okay, well, you go do that, and I'll join you when I've finished here. And when you're tired, I'll leave. Are you watching anything funny? Or at least light? I don't think I can take anything with subtitles and dead bodies."

After tidying up, Aislin paused at the door before turning off the

light. Concern about the mess she found earlier was sinking in. She
had come home to escape her problems, not take on new ones.

Letty's door was open; she was in bed, remote in hand, and patted
the spot beside her. Aislin plumped the pillows and leaned awkwardly
against them. Not quite ready to lie down. Not quite relaxed.

Letty turned on a show, gave Aislin an outline of the plot, and
they sat in companionable silence, Letty watching intently, Aislin just
watching. Flickers from the past week—the email from her boss, her
roommate's hostility, her decision to bolt for home, the rush to pack,
the crowded ferry, the drive, the state of the kitchen and what that
might mean, Letty's weight loss—were all fighting for top billing in her
mind. But she was suddenly too tired to care.

"I'm going to bed, Gran. I'm pooped." She gave Letty a peck on the
cheek. Letty put her warm, wrinkled hand on Aislin's cheek and gave
it a gentle pat, her rings jangling. "Whatever mess you're in, we can
sort in the morning. Sleep tight. And be sure to wash your face. I can't
think straight looking at those things."

"Yes, Gran, off to kill the caterpillars. See you in the morning."

Her room was unchanged. The same floral duvet cover and matching
curtains. The chest of drawers still had her soccer uniform from her
last season. In the closet were her cleats and her music stand. And her
grad dress. Unworn. Memories floated up of how desperate she had
been to leave town. The need to be free, anonymous, alone, and away
from home where everyone knew everything about everyone.

Despite the all-consuming desire to get away, when the time came,
guilt and anxiety had washed over her. To leave Letty and Frank, who
had raised her since she was three. But her desperate need to go was
greater than her guilt.

First to Ryerson for a degree in journalism. The anonymity of a
large campus suited her. She was Aislin Fitzgerald, a student on track
to a career. Just like everyone else. New beginning. No backstory, no
baggage. Over the four years, she became friends with a core group but
maintained a certain distance. One brief boyfriend compared her to
a venetian blind—closed or open with conditions. Her female friends
were so wrapped up in their own dramas they never asked much about

her, so they knew little more than that she was from a small town on Vancouver Island.

She rarely went home, preferring to stay in Toronto and work. And journalism was a good fit for her, as she always asked questions. She had an insatiable "need to know," as Frank called it; "nosey" was Letty's description.

While she loved the four years at Ryerson, she did not love the four Ontario winters. She hated the snow and the cold by the final term and became sentimental about the coast's long, wet springs and falls. And the smell of the sea. She was offered an ideal position on a paper in the prairies but settled for an internship with a community paper in Vancouver. It was supposed to be a stepping-stone to a full-time job with a bigger paper, but the newspaper business was struggling, and that next step never arrived. Papers, and opportunities, were shrinking. She eventually grew comfortable with her beat, bonded with her few colleagues, and reluctantly accepted that advertisers were deities and reporters were not.

When Frank died of a heart attack, Letty, pitched into the lonely vacuum of widowhood, asked Aislin to move home. She refused, and the chasm between them deepened and widened. Her visits became even more infrequent and short—obligatory visits for holidays and sometimes a long weekend.

The bathroom was small, with little surface or storage space. This room also needed a good cleaning. She hung her makeup bag on the hook on the door. Aislin scrutinized her face in the medicine cabinet mirror above the sink as she brushed her teeth. She smirked as she recalled Letty's description of her new look. Maybe her eyelashes did look a bit like fuzzy caterpillars. She wiped her eyelashes clean and appraised her face. "Unremarkable" came to mind. Sighing, she turned out the light and went across the hall to her room. She anticipated a sleepless night, her mind a muddle of emotions.

But sleep came fast and hard. Unexpectedly so. She awoke early, not to the sound of garbage trucks banging and crashing their way through the service alley but to the frenetic chirping of robins as they began their day. She didn't remember them sounding so bossy and manic.

She knew she should get up and check on Secretariat, but her bones felt too heavy to move. Her thoughts returned to the past seven days. She questioned, again, her call to her mentor and the subsequent betrayal. If she hadn't made that call, how differently things would have unfolded. If she hadn't been walking down the hall past Lara's bedroom at the exact moment Lara slid off her blouse, she never would have seen the bruises.

Lara had painfully tried to pull her blouse back up when she heard Aislin's gasp. When she looked up at Aislin, her eyes were bloodshot, her face grey and drawn.

"Victor?"

Lara nodded.

"The first time?"

Lara shook her head.

"Is this the worst?"

A nod. And a deep, shuddering sob.

"Jesus, Lara, what the hell? Why would you let him do this to you? Twice?"

"I didn't *let* him! He's six four. What chance do I have? He got so mad so fast. I didn't see it coming. I couldn't talk him down. And it's been months since, you know, the last time. It's not Victor's fault. His dad beat him all the time. And I spoiled his soccer game by laughing with Tim Oakes. Victor hates Tim. Thinks he's flirting with me all the time. He missed the goal kick because he saw us together and couldn't concentrate. I shouldn't have stopped to talk to Tim, but I had to pass him to get to my seat."

"Are you kidding me? You're taking the blame for Victor beating you up? Oh my God, that's textbook victim-speak. Why haven't you told me about this?"

"Because I knew you would interfere. You always think you know best. And Victor's never going to let me leave. He told me that after the first time I told him we were done, that I was leaving town. He said he would find me. That we were meant to be together. That he needed me. That I was the only person who had ever loved him. That he was sorry. And tonight, I told him that was the last time he ever touched me. That I was going to lay charges. You know what he said? 'Good luck with that,' and laughed." Deep sobs shook her thin, bruised body.

"Victor beat you up. More than once. That's a chargeable offence. We need to go to the police; we need to find you a lawyer and a place to stay. And I think we should do a feature on the silence of abused women. We need to write about this. We owe it to other women. And their kids."

"No! We are *not* writing about this. You have to promise. This can never get out. And look where we're living. This place belongs to Victor's dad—you know that. If this gets out, he will crush us so badly neither of us will ever get another job. That's what Victor said. He said I better not tell you because you would go ballistic. His dad will go after us both and the paper if this gets out. He's our main advertiser. I'm stuck."

"Nope, not stuck. In a really horrible place but not stuck. We can get you away from Victor. But we should tell Jack. He'll agree with me. This can't be ignored. You're in danger. Thousands of women in this city are probably in the same situation. When Jack finds out Victor hurt you, more than once, he's going to be all over this."

Lara was staring at her in horror. "Are you nuts? This is exactly why I didn't tell you. This isn't 'news'—this is my life. Do you even care what happens to me if this gets out? And don't you dare tell Jack. It's unprofessional. He's our editor, our boss, not our friend."

She dropped her voice to a whisper. "Victor will kill me. I know he will. I saw it in his face tonight."

Aislin looked away. This was not going to be dropped. Her instinct was to push for details, but Lara's terror was genuine. She had never seen raw terror before. And there it was all over Lara's face. But behind it there was also resignation that made Aislin's insides go cold. And she had seen Victor angry. The rage flashed up with no warning. It was short, intense, and powerful. She remembered Lara's inertia. Aislin was poised to bolt out the door, but Lara just sat there, looking down at her hands.

All the signs had been there. Lara was missing deadlines at work. And she was never available for after-work drinks or morning jogs. She was either with Victor or in her room. Had lost a freakish amount of weight. Jumped whenever her phone pinged. She only ever answered her phone in her room. Her outrageous sense of humour was gone.

She dressed differently, too. She had begun wearing looser clothing, and generally, it was black on black. Gone were the insane colour combinations that only ever seemed to work when Lara put them together. Aislin had always envied her style.

She had missed every single sign that Lara was being abused. The weight of her failure as a friend crushed her.

The house was still. She looked at the clock, just past eight. Usually, Secretariat would be shuffling around his tank by now, eager for his breakfast, but his room was quiet. Reluctantly, she got up, crept down the hall and slipped into the spare room. No reaction. She turned on his light, reached her hand into the tank and traced her fingers around the markings on his shell.

"Morning, little buddy. How're you feeling? Want some brekkie?"

When Secretariat didn't move, she gently picked him up. She fought the instinct to juggle and jiggle him like a baby or sway back and forth. Why she felt like doing that was a mystery; she didn't like babies and actively avoided contact with them. Her friends always tried to thrust their progeny at her as though it was their right and her duty. She typically feigned a cough as an avoidance technique, which generally resulted in her being quickly shooed from the room like a plague-bearing rat.

Secretariat's head was firmly tucked in, and when he was in that mood, there was no getting him to come out. She put him back in his tank, changed his water, and looked for droppings. But the parsley was untouched, and there were no new droppings. She heard Letty moving around, so she went downstairs to put on the coffee, praying her gran had not switched to tea. Tea before noon was just wrong.

Letty shuffled in in her housecoat, feet bare, her short, white hair sticking out wildly in all directions. Frank used to tease Letty that her bedhair was a crime against humanity. Aislin smiled at the memory.

They exchanged nonsensical morning greetings as they waited for the coffee. The milk was a solid lump in the creamer. Aislin poked through the cupboards and discovered three cans of evaporated milk. She pulled one out and waved it at Letty.

"Well, that's a bit rich, isn't it? I've been taking mine black."

"Oh. When did you switch?" asked Aislin, hoping to put a date stamp on the lump of milk in the fridge and some insight into how long Letty had been letting things slide.

"I don't know. And I don't even know why I decided to switch. Not important. However, what is important is you filling in some details on what you told me last night."

Aislin tilted her head and looked at Letty. She had been dreading this moment ever since she turned on the ignition and drove away from Kitsilano, her car jammed tight with her life. Time was up. How her grandmother was going to react was a wild card. She was hoping for the best but expecting the worst.

Looking at her hands and fiddling with her coffee cup, she began. "My roommate and colleague, Lara, was beaten up by her boyfriend, who is the son of a prominent entrepreneur in Vancouver and one of our major advertisers. I wanted to do a feature on abuse, but Lara said no. I wanted her to press charges, but she said no. I wanted to call our editor, but she said no. So, I called my mentor from Ryerson and told her the whole story and asked for her thoughts on how I should handle the situation. Was I an enabler if I knew someone was being abused? Didn't I owe it to all women in similar situations? Should I go ahead and work on the feature but without names? She grilled me. Asked a bunch of questions about Victor, the boyfriend, and his family and their connections. I know I should have been less forthcoming, but I was upset and was looking for guidance. The following week she wrote a huge four-page spread on abused women in Vancouver, and she described Lara and Victor's family so closely the information could only have come from someone close to Lara. I was gutted and terrified for Lara. She blew up at me. Made some harsh comments about me as a person and a friend. Told me to pack and get out of the condo.

"And my boss, Jack, was equally furious but for different reasons. He said I had no right to speak to someone from another paper about my dilemma. That I should have gone to him, which was just one front of his fury; the other front was more dire for him. Victor's dad went apeshit and pulled his advertising from the paper. And coerced his cronies to do the same. The paper can't make it without the advertising income.

"And then I started to get disgusting, misogynist messages on my Twitter account. And on Facebook. Stuff that was beyond sick. I think I know who posted them, but I can't be sure. They just kept coming and coming. So I shut everything down. It was the only way to stop them." Aislin paused and looked up at Letty.

Letty was staring at her in disbelief. "What on earth were you thinking? How could you be so naive? And selfish? Of course you should have gone to your editor. It needed to be contained."

Aislin couldn't believe what she was hearing. "Contained? Abuse by a partner is the most common type of violence experienced by women. It's happening all around us, even in this charming little town. And you think I should have kept quiet? As a journalist, it's my duty to reveal the truth and bear witness. Seriously, Gran?"

"Well, maybe not contained but certainly handled with discretion. If you had thought things through, you might have seen how you were handing this mentor of yours a gift. How well do you know her?" Letty snorted. "Not well enough. She needs to have her professional standards reviewed."

"I wanted to take it to Jack, who's a sweetheart, and I trust him. But Lara didn't. I wanted to write the feature and include resources for women in abusive relationships. I wanted to help. I wanted to contribute to change."

"Well, Aislin, as they say, it's not all about you, is it? This situation was not about you. You violated your friend's trust and thrust her into a worse situation. Have you heard from her? Do you know if she's okay? Does she have family she can stay with?"

"I haven't checked my messages. I just needed a bit of space to sort out what I should do."

"Listen to yourself. There you go again. How could you not check when you know your friend may need you? Although it's unlikely she would reach out to you, if you don't mind me saying."

"Gran, I think you're being pretty hard on me. This has been a horrible, horrible week. All I wanted was to come home and regroup and spend some time with you."

"Suddenly you want to spend time with me? You certainly weren't interested in spending time with me when I needed you after Frank died."

There it was. She had handed Letty the perfect segue to the root of their relationship issues. The volcano of pent-up anger, pain, and resentment had found its fissure. And there would be no stopping the lava.

The eruption was almost a relief. She had been a prisoner of her past for too long. Nonetheless, she felt like her teenage self, coming clean about some misdemeanour. Letty was always formidable, whereas Frank had been the soft one, her human shield.

Aislin knew her gran well enough to know that neither of them would leave the room until every last grievance had been brought into the light, the seams picked open and examined. In detail. Hopefully, after all was said, they could stitch themselves back together.

"Yes, Gran, I owe you a huge, long explanation of every decision I've made since I was about sixteen. But first, can we have some breakfast? This may take a while. And the house is cold. Can I turn up the heat?"

"We can't talk on empty stomachs, so yes, let's eat. I put in a baseboard heater a few years ago because I didn't want to heat the whole house. Just turn it on. And where's the dressing gown I gave you a couple of years ago?"

"It's in my suitcase. I didn't put it on because when I came down to make coffee, I didn't realize I was going to get the third degree." Aislin focused on beating the eggs and resolved not to be drawn into the fray before eating. She got the eggs going, then looked around for something to serve with them. She found a loaf of bread and sniffed it gingerly. She thought she could smell mould but didn't see any blue fuzz, so she dropped two slices in the toaster. The jar of jam was fine, as was the butter. She sniffed the jam, hoping for that evocative smell of fresh berries that always reminded her of hot, sticky August mornings with Letty presiding over steaming pots of jelly.

When the eggs were ready, she divided them between two plates. Letty had busied herself setting the table and putting away last night's dishes. They worked in silence. Sun rays warmed their backs. Aislin moved her chair over to Letty's side of the table so she, too, could enjoy the warmth. She wrapped herself in Letty's stretched-out gardening sweater that always hung on the door. She sniffed it, too, and found the flashback she needed. It smelled of Gran, soil, roses, and cedar.

They ate in silence, and when they were both finished, she dragged her chair back to the other side of the table, topped up their coffee cups, and reached for Letty's hand. It wasn't a comfortable connection for either of them, so she applied a little pressure to keep Letty from pulling back.

"You're right. I have been avoiding you. I love you, Gran, have always loved you. And Frank." She paused. "But when he died, I didn't know how to exist without him. He was my rudder. And whenever I tried to think about how you could ever live without him, it just hurt too much. I couldn't bear your sadness. I couldn't bear *my* sadness. I am an emotional coward."

Her voice dropped to a whisper. "I think I should have had counselling. To, you know, deal with their death." She looked up at the ceiling. "I don't even remember them. Not really. I just have a vague vision of Mum's hair and the gold stripe on Dad's uniform. And that's probably because I know there's a gold stripe on RCMP officers' pants. So it's probably not even a genuine memory of him. But I have his leather jacket. I always wear it when I'm anxious. It's my shield.

"You and Frank were everything to me, and you gave me everything. I know how hard you worked to make sure I felt 'normal.' You were ready to retire and enjoy life before they died. You had to change gears to take care of me. Your life imploded. And you had no time to grieve because I was here—a three-year-old who wouldn't talk.

"My earliest memory is of being scared. Too scared to ask where Mum and Dad were and when they were coming back. And the longer I held my words in, the less able I was to let them out. I remember hearing you crying. And I saw Frank crying in the garden. I didn't understand grief. I thought it was my fault you were so sad.

"But you know all that. What you might not know is that later, growing up, I felt smothered. I was drowning in cotton balls of compassion because everyone loved them and missed them except me. Everyone assumed I loved them. But I never even knew them. How could a kid that young love a memory? I've always felt guilty for not loving them.

"I couldn't be normal. I wasn't allowed to be normal. Everyone watched out for me, kept tabs on me. I was Larry and Cathy's poor little orphan girl. I was 'special.' And the fact that I look so much like my dad must have been and continue to be hell for you.

"I couldn't skip out or go to parties with my friends or do the stuff they did because I was always afraid of getting caught and disappointing someone's memory of them.

"And then one time, I did sneak out. Do you remember? Ed saw me running down Chester Street, on my way to meet Sam and Sarah. And then followed me to the party. And then told Frank where I was. And Frank told the cops after he dragged me out. Then the cops came and busted everyone for drinking. Do you have any idea how that went over? That was the last time I was invited anywhere.

"Jim Thompson and his nasty little bunch of thugs blamed me and made my life a living hell. That's why I quit soccer. Not because I didn't want to play anymore. I loved soccer. But the rest of the team shut me out, were horrible to me when no one was looking. And it's why I didn't go to grad. I was scared. And that's why, when I saw the bruises and the fear in Lara, I thought I could do something to help. To stop a bully."

Letty pulled her hand back and wrapped both hands around her mug. "I had no idea. About the bullying. You told us you didn't want to go to grad because you, Sam, and Sarah were boycotting it. We believed you at the time. But the grad photos were in the paper. We saw Sarah and Sam in the pictures. We never pushed you for an explanation. You had become so closed off. We thought it was just typical teenage moodiness. I wish we had pushed. We could have gone out of town, to Vancouver for a nice dinner and some shopping or something. You spent grad night in your room.

"I am so sorry, honey, about the bullying. I should have noticed. I do remember being worried about your weight loss. I talked to Dr. Church about it. He said to bring you in. But I didn't."

She looked up at the ceiling, blinking hard. "I don't think I wanted to know. I just hoped you'd get over it. Whatever it was. And then you left so suddenly. We had no idea what your plans were after graduation. We didn't even know you were applying for university. Or wanted to go into journalism. Like Frank. He was so honoured but so hurt that you didn't talk to him."

"I've made so many stupid decisions, mainly because I'm so impulsive. Of all the messes I've made, it's how badly I hurt you and Frank that eats at me. I wish I could go back and do it all over. If wishes were horses, I would have such an enormous herd."

"He knew you loved him. He understood you because you were so much like your dad. Talk about impulsiveness. Your dad was the living definition!"

They both held their breath.

"Let's get on with our day," said Letty, getting up, breaking the ice. "Elaine's picking me up at eleven. A distant cousin up in Ladysmith passed, and there's a service today. What're you going to do?"

"Wow, another one. Do you, like, have a whole separate wardrobe of funeral-going clothes?"

"Don't be cheeky. It's unbecoming." The sharp reprimand flooded Aislin with relief. It felt normal. Balance restored.

"Gran?" Aislin was about to ask if she could stay with Letty until she sorted her next steps but quailed at the thought of rejection.

"Yes? What's on your mind?"

"Nothing, never mind."

"Suit yourself," Letty said before leaving to get dressed.

Aislin tidied the kitchen and made a shopping list of immediate essentials. Including dishwasher tabs and rubber gloves. Her hands were already feeling dried out.

She stayed in the kitchen until she heard Letty leave with Elaine. Elaine was bursting with questions, but Letty neatly dodged them. After they left, Aislin checked on Secretariat. He was still tucked in his shell. And hadn't eaten or touched his water. She wasn't sure if he was sick or just out of sorts because of the move. She stroked his shell.

"Come on, buddy. I know it's been a rough few days and I'm sorry. Why won't you eat? We've been through lots of moves together and you've never gotten sick. I really need you. You're my only friend."

Lara flashed into her mind. The bruises. The fear in her eyes. Aislin shuddered as she relived the avalanche of events triggered by her reaction to those bruises and fear.

"Nope, not going there," she muttered as she poked through her purse for her phone. "I can't undo the mistakes I made, but I am not going to lose my turtle over it."

Chapter 2

There were two vets in town. One ad stated Veterinary and Taxidermy Services—Either Way, You Get Your Pet Back. Interesting side hustle. The other was Nick de Vries. Nick. A big part of her life growing up.

"Nick speaking."

Aislin was surprised he answered the call. She was expecting a receptionist. "Hi, Nick. It's Aislin Fitzgerald. I'm calling because my turtle's sick. Can I bring him in for you to assess? That is, if you treat turtles." Her words tumbled out in a rush.

"Aislin Fitzgerald. There's a name I haven't heard in a while. How the heck are you? Are you back in town or just visiting? I never pegged you as a turtle owner or having any sort of pet, now that I think about it. I don't remember you guys having pets when you were growing up."

"Nope, no pets. Just me. I was the family pet. The turtle is a bit of a long story. Can I bring him in? My schedule is pretty open, so whatever works for you works for me."

"Okay. Let me get some details. My receptionist is out, and if I don't get the right info, she will make my life a living hell. Turtle's name?"

"Secretariat."

"Oh my God. The perfect name for a turtle. Symptoms?"

"He's lethargic."

Aislin could hear the struggle in his voice to remain neutral and not laugh. Finally, someone who got the joke. She grinned.

"He's lethargic? Sorry. But how can you tell he's lethargic? He's a turtle. Lethargy is what they do best."

"He's just not himself. He's usually got a bit more pep than he has right now. Not that he's high energy or anything. Maybe he's just depressed."

"Depressed?" Another snort. "Not pining for the fjords, is he?"

Aislin started laughing. "Yes, depressed. And no, not yet pining for the fjords. He's just hiding in his shell."

"As opposed to galloping laps around his tank?"

"Exactly."

"Well, I can see why you're concerned," said Nick, still struggling. "It sounds pretty dire for poor Secretariat, so you better bring him this afternoon. It looks as though I have an opening at one thirty. My office is at 1701 Spruce on the corner of Cottontail."

Aislin swallowed her laugh as the Aesop fable came to mind.

"You're in the book." Nick paused, then added, "Looking forward to seeing you and catching up."

Aislin was grinning as she ended the call. She tried to think of the last time she had seen Nick. He had been her secret crush from the moment she met him. Almost. He was twelve, and she was ten. He was on the soccer team Frank coached. When Nick's dad died suddenly, Nick's world collapsed. His schoolwork plummeted, as did his self-esteem. He shrank into himself.

Then Nick quit the team. When he came by the house to drop off his jersey, Frank sat on the front porch and asked him about his decision. It was then that Frank learned of the family's financial hardship. Frank didn't try to change Nick's mind about soccer or offer to cover the cost. Instead, he offered him a job helping with the garden on the weekends and delivering flyers three times a week after school. The bond between them was instant and mutual.

Aislin's world changed dramatically. Frank now had two apples of his eye. She was not willing to welcome the intrusion in any way, shape, or form. They both had dead parents in common, but that did nothing to warm her to Nick. Fury boiled within her every time he was at the house. Standing on the toilet in the bathroom, she spied on them as Frank showed Nick the intricacies and rituals of gardening.

During one of her obsessive spying binges, Aislin saw her

opportunity. Frank had just shown Nick how to thin the luscious, thick rows of new carrots. She waited until Frank was elsewhere, then strolled up to Nick and, in her best little curious girl voice, said, "Hey, Nick, Letty needs some carrots for dinner. Could you please pick out a dozen of the largest?"

Nick eyed her and then the pale threads of new carrots he had just pulled out. She held her breath. "If Letty says so," he said and studiously went to work pulling out all the carrots and arranging their anaemic little corpses in order of size. Aislin hurried back to her position on the toilet and waited.

As Nick shook the dirt from the last of the carrots, Frank came around the corner of the house.

"What the hell?" he exploded. "I asked you to thin them, not rip the whole bloody garden apart. What part of thinning did you not understand?"

Nick's face flamed deep red. He started to say something, then stopped, grabbed his gloves, and ran out of the garden. Frank called after him to come back, but the kid was gone. Letty came out and spoke to Frank, then they both turned and looked at the bathroom window. Aislin ran into her room, jumped on her bed, and picked up a book.

She cringed at the memory. Not her finest hour. The fact that Nick never did rat her out had made an impression on her juvenile self. He suddenly became a prince in her eyes. But he had nothing to do with her from then on.

She chewed on that snippet of her history as she picked through her clothes. In the week since her life had imploded, she had taken to wearing day sweats and night sweats. She pulled on her grey day sweats and topped them off with a grey hoodie. She glanced at herself in the mirror, and a pale face with dark half-moons under her eyes stared back. She grinned as she thought back to Letty's comments about her mascara. She still felt the dramatic lashes lent interest to her face, but perhaps they weren't appropriate for a visit to a vet in her small hometown. More of a big-city look. She gave her lashes just a light brush of colour. She shrugged on her dad's leather jacket, picked up Secretariat's tank, remembering at the last minute to act out the key pantomime.

As she drove into town, she tried to remember what news she had had of Nick in the decade-plus since high school. She had not kept up with anyone, so the information was all secondhand from Letty. And after Frank passed, news about Nick stopped.

Frank had been working on an article about Nick the night he had his heart attack. He had gone back into the office after dinner to finish it up. When he hadn't returned hours later, Letty drove to the office to check on him. It was she who found him and called the ambulance, although she knew he was gone. Aislin had never asked about that night but had overheard conversations at his service and had obsessively read his obituary. The author wrote about his contributions to the community, gave a light touch to the circumstances of his death, and went into detail about the death of his son and daughter-in-law. Letty had asked Aislin to write his obituary, but she had refused. Driving the wedge deeper between them.

Being back home and finally facing her actions was uncomfortable. She struggled to avoid indulging in self-reflection. It was always about tomorrow, not yesterday. Now she was immersed in all the yesterdays of her life, all the mistakes, all the poor and selfish choices. Not her comfort zone, but there was no more avoiding it.

And here she was, driving to an appointment with someone who had featured large in their lives for many years. And had featured large in Frank's death. If he hadn't been in the office polishing the piece on Nick, he would have had his heart attack at home. He could have lived. Letty never forgave Nick. As irrational as that was.

Aislin pulled over a block from Nick's office. She looked at Secretariat. He was still in his shell, which wasn't unusual when he was in the car. She called Nick's office, hoping his receptionist would answer so she could cancel without questions. What she had not expected was his mother answering the phone.

"Dr. Nick de Vries Veterinary Services, Elspeth speaking."

"Hi, Mrs. de Vries, it's Aislin Fitzgerald calling. I'm afraid I have to cancel my one-thirty appointment for this afternoon."

"Aislin. This sort of short notice is inconvenient. It's unlikely we will fill the spot. That's unbillable time. Our policy is to charge for cancellations within an hour of the scheduled time. But, as you are not a client, it won't apply, so we have to absorb that loss. Are you rescheduling?"

Aislin flushed with embarrassment. Nick's mother had always been a sharp-tongued, brittle woman. She had not changed. "Nope, won't be rescheduling. And sorry about the short notice."

Her heart was hammering up high in her throat, threatening to choke her. She took long, deep breaths, slowed it down, drank some water, put the car in gear, and drove to a park by the water. There weren't any dog walkers or children in sight, so she put Secretariat on the grass in a sunny spot and sat down beside him, hugged her knees, and wrapped herself in her dad's jacket. The ground was a bit damp, but there was warmth in the sun and just a light breeze. The water shimmered and glistened. She watched a small metal boat zoom past, heading north. It looked as though there were four people on board. No sign of fishing gear, so maybe they were just out enjoying themselves. Nice for them.

"Well, little buddy, what the hell are we going to do with the rest of our lives? I think this is what it means to be at the crossroads of one's life. Or is it a dead end? I'm back home. I may have alienated my one relative, alienated my one friend, lost my one job, and have no future job prospects. I'm actually behind where I was when I left. Not everyone can regress as well as I do. I'm the winner of losing. I should be damn proud!"

Secretariat stuck his head out and swung it from side to side. Aislin held her breath. He sniffed, then nibbled the grass. Tears stung her eyes. She looked up, trying to stop the flood, but the sun was so bright she had to look down. And let them flow. She tucked her head into her dad's buttery-soft, worn, brown leather jacket and gave way to all the sorrow and anger and fear that had been welling up in her. Tears soaked her face and the front of her hoodie. Her nose ran. She cried to the bottom of her well of sorrow and back up. She fished around in her pockets for a tissue. Nothing. She used the cuffs of her sleeves to wipe her face. She untucked herself and looked for Secretariat. Gone.

She had been hugging her knees so tightly the circulation was slow to return. She lurched a bit as she straightened up, calling for him. Not that he came when called.

A woman walking by with a small child stopped. "Aislin? Is that you? Wow, it's really you! Have you lost your dog? Can we help?"

Aislin's first instinct was to run. Abandon Secretariat and run for her car. She did not want to see Sarah. Or anyone. Not today. Not like this. Staggering around the park like a day drinker. Her face was blotchy, her nose red and swollen, her mascara streaming down her face. Not like this.

"Oh, hi, Sarah. Nope, I haven't lost a dog. I've lost my turtle. He was here nibbling grass, and then he wasn't. Believe it or not, turtles can move pretty damn fast. He won't survive a night here. It's too cold, and there are lots of predators."

"You have a pet turtle? You never struck me as a turtle owner. I don't remember you guys having pets. Why a turtle?"

"Long story. No time to get into the details. If you and your son want to help, that would be great. Otherwise, can we catch up another time? I am desperate to find him." Aislin was shocked to see Sarah with a child. Had never pegged her as the maternal type.

"We'd love to help, wouldn't we, Fitz? What's your turtle's name? And what does he look like?"

"Like a turtle? Small, about three inches high, brown shell. It's not like there are a bunch of turtles out here, so you don't have to be worried about catching the wrong one. And his name is Secretariat, but he doesn't come when called. He's probably gone under some bushes, maybe those along the fence. You could look there while I do a quick scan of the field."

As much as she appreciated the gesture, the very last thing she wanted was Sarah, her former best friend, probing her for details about her life. Not now. She needed to contain the outflow from this meeting, or it would be all over town that Aislin Fitzgerald was acting drunk in the park and ranting about a lost turtle. But first, she desperately needed to find her soul mate.

The spring grass was long. Not wanting to step on Secretariat, she drew on her tai chi training. Leaping and then balancing on one foot, she began to work a grid pattern across the grass. From the corner of her eye, she saw Sarah watching her. And she could hear her lecturing

Fitz to be very careful not to touch needles or any garbage. The kid looked quite game to get right in the bushes, but Sarah hung onto the back of his jacket. A turtle hunt was something new and exciting. With apparent practised ease, Fitz slipped out of his coat and dove into the bushes.

Sarah ran along the front of the bushes, yelling at him to come out or he was going to be sorry. Her yelling and Aislin's prancing attracted the attention of an older couple on the beach, walking a sizable German shepherd.

"You better get your kid out of the bushes. Full of needles. If he gets stabbed by a dirty needle, he'll get AIDS and die," the man called.

His wife smacked his chest. "Don't say things like that. It makes you sound like an old fuddy-duddy. Put Herman on his leash."

Calling out to Sarah, the woman asked if they could help. Sarah pointed to Aislin, who had stopped prancing and was looking anxiously at the dog.

"My turtle has bolted, and I desperately need to find him before dark. He is afraid of dogs, so could you maybe not bring your dog onto the grass?"

"Bolted! I've never heard anything so ridiculous in my life. And who has a turtle as a pet? They carry diseases like salmonella. You can die from salmonella. Filthy things."

Sarah increased her beseeching of Fitz to get out of the bushes and not touch needles, garbage, or turtles.

"If you have the scent of the turtle, Herman can track him. He's trained for this," offered the woman. "He won't hurt him; he'll just track him, sit, and bark when he's found him."

"Oh, brilliant. Here's my jacket. I was carrying him in my right arm. Is there enough scent there for Herman? And I was sitting just about here when he took off."

The woman, taking charge, held the jacket to Herman's nose and instructed him to find it. Herman, tail wagging, nose down, tracked back and forth and then picked up a ziggety line to the beach, towing the woman along. He stopped at a log just at the verge of the grass, sat, and barked.

"He's found him!" called the woman.

Aislin, Sarah, and Fitz ran to the log. Aislin could see turtle tracks in the sand leading straight to a shallow well under the log. She reached in and lifted the little turtle out. Cradling him to her chest with one hand, she patted Herman on the head with the other. She looked up at the sky, swallowing hard and trying to control her breath. She kept her eyes up until she was sure she could speak without sobbing.

"What the hell are we looking at now?" demanded the man.

Sarah, Fitz, the man, and the woman looked quizzically at the sky. Herman had his great long nose resting against Aislin, pointing up towards Secretariat, fascinated by the unusual scent.

"Thank you all so much for helping. I can't thank you enough. And Herman, you are a superstar. My hero. I don't know what I would have done if you hadn't come along when you did. Suppose I hadn't found him. It's way too cold at night for him to survive a night out."

"Why the hell would you let it loose? Dirty thing. Who has a turtle as a pet? Do you have proof of purchase? There's a massive trade in illegal exotic pets." He would have gone on, Aislin suspected, but his wife smacked him again on the chest, and he stopped. A well-used and respected communication tool.

"Never mind Jim. He's retired RCMP. Can't leave the job behind. As if you couldn't tell."

Aislin went white. Sarah looked at her. And then they both looked closely at Jim.

"Sgt. Brownlee?"

"I am. And who are you? You don't look like anyone I arrested. Domestic violence? Bored housewife doing some light-fingered shop-lifting? Day drinking and driving?" Another slap was delivered to his chest, this time with more feeling.

"No, you haven't arrested either of us. It's Sarah Quinn and Aislin Fitzgerald."

"Larry's little girl?" Jim's face softened. "I thought you'd left town, gone to be a bigshot reporter. Haven't heard anything about you for years and years. It was such a tragedy. You know, everyone in town loved your dad and mum."

"Thank you and Herman so much for helping me. Would love to catch up but have to get this little guy into his tank before he scratches me to death." Secretariat, unhappy with Herman's nose so close, was batting his way up Aislin's chest with his stubby legs. His sharp little nails were digging through her hoodie and T-shirt.

"And thank you, Sarah and Fitz. Will call soon so we can catch up."

"How long are you in town? Are you staying at Letty's?"

"Not sure how long I'll be here. Plans are up in the air. Chat soon." And with that, Aislin bolted for her car.

"Wash your hands after you've handled that beast," called Jim. "Salmonella's a killer."

Aislin waved and ran to her car, afraid Jim would follow her up to the parking lot listing all the ways a person could die from turtles. She untangled Secretariat from her clothing and tucked him into his tank. Trembling, Aislin started the car and pulled out with just a hint of squealing tires. Looking back, she could see Jim watching her with his hands on his hips.

She drove back into town to get groceries. The randomness of meeting not just Sarah but Jim Brownlee of all people shook her notion that coming home to regroup was a good idea. Before going into the store, she flipped her hoodie up and pulled on sunglasses.

The store smelled the same as it had when she and Sarah worked there during high school. The layout hadn't changed either. She shopped rapidly and without a plan. Her cart looked as though she was preparing for a zombie apocalypse. The late afternoon pre-dinner rush was on, and the lineups at the checkout were quite long. She picked the one closest to the exit and kept her head down as the line inched forward. She didn't think she could bear to bump into another familiar face.

After loading the groceries into the back of her car, she walked quickly next door to the liquor store. She found the aisle with British Columbia wines and chose a mixture of whites and reds. Twelve. She added sherry, vodka, beer, and cider. At the till, the young cashier tried to make small talk by asking her where the party was but received stony silence for his efforts. She grabbed her receipt, banged her way out the door, and almost ran to the car with her cart. She was shaking violently as she transferred her purchases to the back seat. Despite her urgent need to get home, she returned the cart to the cart station. After her years of working at the store and collecting carts from

all corners of the parking lot, she believed those who randomly abandoned their carts deserved a special place in hell.

By the time she pulled up to Letty's, the adrenaline had drained
from her body, and she was limp in its void. She looked at the time.
Had it only been a couple of hours since she left the house on her way
to the appointment with Nick?

In her state of emotional and physical exhaustion, the distance
from her car to the house was daunting. She turned and looked at the
small mountain of plastic bags, the box of wine bottles, the cases of
beer and cider. She hadn't eaten anything since breakfast, so she dug
in her purse for a power bar. Looking at her hands and reliving Jim's
premonitions, she decided to just pull the wrapper partway off. She
nibbled at the exposed bar, which tasted like compressed cardboard.

She worked out her strategy for moving the bags and tank to the
house. She wasn't sure if the neighbours were all the same from when
she lived there or if there were any newbies. She surveyed the homes
across the street. They showed little evidence of renovations. Same
old same old. Which meant eyes active behind curtains and gossiping
tongues to go with them.

Pulling her hood back up, she got out and raced around the car,
opened the passenger door, grabbed the tank and her purse—one
quick trip to the porch to deposit the first load. Back at the car, she
hung three grocery bags on each forearm and raced back to the porch.
Two more trips did the trick. Before opening the door, she remembered to fish out the key from beneath the mat, sure that every move
was being scrutinized.

Pushing open the door, she called to Letty as she slung the bags,
tank, and purse inside. She slammed the door and leaned against it,
then whipped it open, used her remote to lock her car, and slammed
it again. Just as she was going upstairs with the tank, Letty emerged
from the kitchen.

"What's all the slamming and banging about? You're making such
a racket. What on earth is all this food for? Are you having a party?
And for God's sake, what is that?" she demanded as she zeroed in on
the tank.

"I'll explain in a minute. I've had a bit of a hairy day."

"You'll explain everything right this minute. Whatever that is, take it into the kitchen."

"Fine." Aislin went through to the kitchen and placed the tank on the table. Then quickly moved it to the floor, ran the hot water, found the bleach, and wiped the table. She laid down some paper towels, returned the tank to the table, and washed her hands, cursing Jim Brownlee and his dire predictions.

"Okay, full disclosure as soon as I put away the groceries. Would you like a glass of sherry? Or cider? Or wine? I stocked up."

"Yes, I can see that. I'm sure the Bings across the street noticed all the bottles. I think they go out on recycling night and tally up the empties in everyone's blue box. They're very judgy."

"Seriously, Gran? They do that, or you *think* they do that?"

"Well, they always seem to be commenting on so and so's drinking habits. But they should talk. I've seen their blue box, and it's sometimes spilling over with empty Scotch bottles."

Aislin shook her head as she listened and unpacked. And she had found the strata title group at her former condo invasive and nitpicking. They were amateurs compared to this neighbourhood.

"Are you saying you don't want a sherry?"

"I said no such thing. Yes, I would like a glass of sherry. I haven't bought sherry for years. Frank and I used to have a glass before dinner in the winter months. It was our little ritual. A glass each and a small bowl of chips. He wasn't supposed to eat greasy food but decided that he was going to enjoy life rather than endure it."

Aislin poured a sherry for Letty and a beer for herself in the silence. The perishables were put away. The rest could wait. She found the dishwasher tabs and got that running. She sat down heavily and took a long, long drink, willing herself to relax and not relive the day.

"What were you doing in Picnic Park? Elaine called to say she heard you were there and acting oddly. And that you saw Sarah. I miss Sarah. You and she were such good friends. Almost like sisters. She practically grew up with us here. She was always so happy. Slightly odd, but in a charming way. She has a son. Her husband left her a couple of years ago. They lived in Alberta, but she came home when the marriage broke down."

"Oh my bloody God, are you kidding me?" Aislin sat bolt upright and thrust both hands into her hair. "What is with this town? Is there some sort of surveillance channel you all watch?"

"There's no need to be cheeky. Elaine thought I should know. She heard it from Delores Brownlee. Some wild tale about a turtle, which I assume is what this is. Why on earth would you have a turtle? Such an odd pet."

"It's a long story," Aislin ventured, hoping that would put Letty off.

"I have the time. Did you buy chips? I could do with some to sustain me during your explanation."

Aislin opened a bag of chips, silently kissing her brain for throwing some in her cart in her wild whip around the grocery aisles. She normally did not indulge in junk food, but something about being home made her crave the salty familiarity.

"Okay. Gran, meet Secretariat. Secretariat is a box turtle. I've had him, at least I think it's a him, for three years. A boyfriend gave him to me. Just before we broke up. And I'm really fond of him—the turtle, not the ex. So, today, he wandered off while I was at Picnic Park, and Sarah and her son also happened to be there. And then Jim and Delores Brownlee and their dog, Herman, came by, and Herman found him. So weird. Seeing them."

Aislin took another long drink, savouring the taste this time. She crossed her arms and leaned back in her chair. Waiting.

"What kind of boyfriend gives a turtle as a present? They carry a lot of diseases. Like salmonella. Which can be fatal. Was he trying to kill you?"

"Wow, what is it with turtles and death? Jim Brownlee read me the riot act about the danger of keeping a turtle. And now you. I've had him for three years. He does not go to turtle daycare or on turtle playdates. He has not been near another turtle. Pretty sure he's clean. And lots of people keep turtles. It's not that weird."

"Why couldn't he have given you a nice cat? Or a bird?"

"Actually, Gran, he gave me a turtle because he said it was the perfect pet for me. It doesn't require attention beyond the basics of food, water, and clean bedding. And he's right. It is the perfect pet for me. I don't do high maintenance. Or needy. In pets or people." Aislin got up and pulled some raw ground beef from the fridge. She broke some off, crumbled it up, and dropped it in the tank. Secretariat hustled right over and began eating. She washed her hands and sat down again.

"I thought he was sick earlier. He hasn't been himself this past week. All the fighting with Lara, the stress, and the move here. It upset him, so I'm thrilled to see him eating. And today was traumatic for him. He's terrified of dogs."

Letty was staring at her. Shaking her head slowly. "How can you tell if he's upset?"

Aislin studied her gran's face, wondering if she should mention the aborted trip to see Nick. She decided to forgo that part of the story. No doubt Letty would hear about it from other sources.

"He's been super lethargic. Spending more time than usual in his shell." She held her breath, waiting to see if Letty would take the bait.

"He's a turtle! Isn't that what they're known for? Being lethargic? And what else is there for him to do? Cooped up in a glass house. And why do you call him Secretariat? That's such a big name for such a little beast." Letty was looking at Secretariat with a certain softness in her eyes.

"You don't know who Secretariat was? He was that famous race-horse from back in the seventies. He ran the Kentucky Derby faster than any horse ever. His record still stands. He won the Triple Crown!" Letty looked confused. "The Triple Crown is a series of horse races in the States. One horse has to win all three. It rarely happens. It seemed like a perfect name for a turtle."

"I had no idea you followed racing." A hint of a grin slipped onto her face. "That's quite amusing and clever. But you always were a clever girl."

"I didn't follow racing, but my ex did. And he was a huge fan of Secretariat. We watched a movie about him. He was a pretty awesome horse. The ex approved of the name, not that it mattered. My turtle, so I had naming rights."

"May I ask why you broke up? He sounds as though he understood you."

"That was the problem. He assumed he knew me better than I knew myself, which became annoying over time. He became a bit con-trolling, making decisions for me."

"Yes, I can see that being an issue. You never liked anyone doing that. I accepted an invitation to a birthday party for you, can't remember who the girl was, and when you found out, you were quite livid. Apparently, I didn't 'know the whole story' behind the invitation. It was an attempt to keep you away from some boy you both had crushes on."

Aislin just let that sit. She did not want Letty to launch into discussing her flaws. Or take an emotional drive down memory lane. She had yet to process running into Sarah and the Brownlees.

"Is it okay if I stay with you for a while? I don't know for how long. I have to sort out my next steps. I will pay rent, cook, shop, and help in the garden. Whatever you need doing. It could be fun? You could get to know Secretariat. Think of him as your grandturtle."

Stress from the day made Aislin feel reckless. Her relationship with Letty had always been somewhat emotionally erratic. It was a rare occasion for them to tease each other. Letty could flip without warning from warm and loving to harsh and critical. Aislin never really minded, but she was always wary. She knew how difficult it had been for Letty to raise her. Not that she was a problematic child, it was just the circumstances of her grandparents having to raise their orphaned granddaughter—the only child of their only child.

Letty snorted and began putting away the remaining groceries. "Stay as long as you like," she said, her back to Aislin.

Chapter 3

Aislin dumped another bucket of grey, gritty water down the utility sink with satisfaction. She had been a cleaning force for three days. As an unnaturally orderly person, she only ever did a deep clean when moving into a new apartment. She judged her friends who were cleaning martyrs. Her cleaning philosophy was simple. If you don't like cleaning, be clean.

She missed her early morning runs but was not ready for any more encounters of the traumatizing kind. Moving furniture and scrubbing were now her weight lifting and cardio.

She was careful not to vocalize her irritations regarding Letty's sloppiness. Letty had never been particularly meticulous, but there was a vast valley of difference between Letty then and Letty now.

Letty tended to fill her glass or mug to capacity and then wander about with it at a precarious tilt. Aislin had so far resisted snapping at her, grabbing a cloth, and wiping up behind her. It was galling to watch the drippage when she had just washed the floor. She was a cleaning martyr by extension.

She had yet to charge up her phone. Whatever was going on was doing so in a vacuum. Plugging her phone into the charger was the last thing she did at night and checking messages was the first thing she did in the morning. Living without it was inconceivable. But the longer she avoided checking in, the calmer she became.

Her sleep patterns changed, with more prolonged bouts of deep, dreamless sleep and fewer hours of thrashing. She no longer woke up with an aching jaw. Her neck didn't click when she moved her head, and her left shoulder, where she carried her tension, was loosening up and dropping back into its socket.

Aislin developed a habit of sitting on the back porch steps with a glass of wine after Letty had gone to bed. From this vantage point, she had a good view of three kitchen windows across the hedge. Unlike Vancouverites, these people did not fear prying eyes. She wondered if she had some sort of Peeping Tom complex—first Nick and now the neighbours. She found solace in knowing she was spying on them in their kitchens, not their bedrooms.

She had her eye on the Bakers' house, directly behind Letty's. After dinner, Mrs. Baker made quite a few trips to the kitchen to drink straight from what looked like a vodka bottle. She seldom saw Mr. Baker in the kitchen. He moved as though he had mobility issues. Aislin wondered what tales their recycling box told. And did Elaine know? She savoured the thought of having intel that Elaine perhaps did not.

There weren't any more funerals to attend that first week Aislin was home. As Letty put it, there was a bit of a dry patch—a sentiment disturbing for many reasons to a thirty-year-old mind, but not to the mind of a seventy-four-year-old.

Letty and Elaine talked on the phone at least once a day. Elaine was, if nothing else, religious in keeping Letty up to date on all the gossip. Aislin was surprised and grateful when she overheard Letty foiling Elaine's frequent and varied reasons to drop by. Aislin was sure her extended presence was the topic of the week, and Elaine, as Letty's best friend, must have been under some pressure around town to provide details. The untimely dearth of funerals had to be frustrating.

Elaine had never been a fan of Aislin and vice versa. Even as an orphaned, traumatized child, she recognized an adversary. Elaine emanated blame. Blame for disrupting the lives of Letty and Frank and, by extension, of her own. The two couples had spent years dreaming of endless holidays once they all finally retired. When Aislin arrived, the planning and dreaming came to a hard stop. Eventually, Elaine and Ed went on holiday on their own but, judging from the comments and complaints from Elaine, they were just as bored with each other on holiday as they were at home.

On the fourth evening of Aislin's visit, the doorbell rang just as she poured herself a second glass of wine for her evening ritual. Letty was already upstairs in bed. If she didn't answer the door and they rang again, Letty would get up, cross.

It wasn't a pair of Jehovah's Witnesses with Watchtower pamphlets as she had expected. It was Sarah. Repeatedly tucking her exuberant curls behind her ear the way she had always done when anxious.

"Sarah."

"Fitz wanted me to find out if Secretariat was okay. He's crazy about animals, and that was the first time he had ever seen a live turtle. And the whole turtle hunt was super exciting for him. He can't stop talking about it, so I said I would come by and ask. How is he?"

"Right. Well, tell Fitz that Secretariat is fine."

"Okay, will do. Nice to see you. Say hi to Letty," Sarah said as she edged down the stairs. "We should catch up sometime?"

"Yes, we could," said Aislin as she moved to close the door. Seeing grown-up Sarah there on the porch made her feel woozy. So many memories of the two of them playing on it, tearing down those stairs off on some crazy lark dreamed up by Sarah, being teased by Frank, lectured by Letty.

She hesitated, then called, "If you have time now, maybe we could have some wine, and you know, catch up or whatever."

Sarah spun around; her face lit up. "I do! Fitz is with my folks. I didn't want to bring him because I hoped you would invite me in. I can't stop thinking about how amazing it was to see you at Picnic Park." She flung her arms wildly in the air and yelled, "What are the odds?"

Aislin grinned and put a finger to her lips. "What are the odds" was Sarah's stock phrase. It was her get-out-of-jail-free card. It was such a big-person expression for a little kid it had always melted Frank.

"What are the odds! Come on in. Letty has gone to bed, but we can take our glasses out on the back porch so we don't disturb her. So, no more yelling." Tamping down the volume on Sarah was such a familiar pattern they grinned at each other as they walked single file into the kitchen, automatically avoiding the creaky floorboards.

"Red or white?"

"Red, please."

They wiggled their bums into the big comfy deck chairs and clinked glasses.

"You do realize this is the first time we have ever legally had a drink together?" Sarah said.

Aislin nodded and turned to look at her. She took in the darkness under her eyes, her startling white-blonde hair, grown out of its stylish cut, and her pallor, which accentuated the dark circles.

"How's it going?" she asked.

"Great. You?"

"Ditto."

"Dinglehopper!" they said in unison. Dinglehopper had been their code for calling each other out for a lie or "misrepresentation of the truth," as Aislin used to intone, imitating with perfection the voice of their grade five teacher.

"My life is a dumpster fire," Sarah offered with a shrug. "In a nutshell, I made a seriously bad choice for a husband, had a kid with him, left him, moved home, and am trying not to take up day drinking. Your turn."

"Well, mine's in a sinkhole. I made a seriously bad choice about how to handle a situation, lost my roommate, my condo, my job, moved home, and have taken up day drinking."

"You're such an overachiever. I'm just thinking about becoming a day drinker, and there you are, as usual, legions ahead of me."

"Is it deeply doubly weird for you to be back? Because it sure is for me. I did not see this as a scenario on my trajectory. When I left, I was never coming back. How about you? How long have you been here?"

"A couple of months now. It's been good for Fitz. You know, to spend time with Moms and Pops. And they seem to love having him around. God knows they never spent time with me. But they're older now. They seem way older than they really are. I think raising eight kids took a toll."

"Ya think?"

"What am I saying! Raising one kid is taking its toll, and against all odds, he's a good kid. We Quinn kids were not good or easy. We were a bunch of wild little bastards. Neither Moms nor Pops ever seemed to notice. Or care. My brain would explode if Fitz did any of the stuff we did. Sometimes I worry that, being an only child, he's going to miss out on all the normal chaos of a big family."

"There was nothing normal about your family. But, believe me, I get your concern about the absence of chaos. If it hadn't been for you, I would have led a pretty boring life. You were a kaleidoscope of colour in my otherwise beige world."

"Funny. I see you, Frank, and Letty as my sanctuary when I look back. An oasis of calm in a turbulent world. Listen to us! So poetic!"

"Fitz! You called your son Fitz! Is that why? It just hit me. That's just the most lovely compliment ever. I wonder if Letty knows."

"Really? You only just figured it out? How many days ago was it that we saw each other? There was never any other name in consideration. My ex wasn't wild about it, but then he wasn't exactly wild about being a father, so his opinion didn't matter. By the time Fitz was born, it was over."

"Wow, Sarah, that's so cool. I mean the part about his name, not your marriage being over. When I saw you at the park, I was in a bit of a state, as you may have noticed, so I didn't process anything beyond finding Secretariat and getting the hell away from Jim Brownlee."

"Yup. I've dreamt about seeing you again. You were the one who left, who chased and caught their dream. I used to track and read all the articles you wrote. I was so proud of you and so happy for you."

"I did not in a gazillion years ever think I would see you at Picnic Park with so much mascara running down your face you looked like Alice Cooper. And freaking out about a lost turtle. I mean, who could ever dream that up!"

"Oh my God, is that what I looked like? I seriously didn't want to see anyone I knew. I didn't even know you were in town. And then bloody Jim with his bizarre obsession with things that kill. Not a good day. But at least his dog found Secretariat."

"So, what's with the turtle?"

Aislin pushed her hands through her hair. "I feel destined to explain the turtle for the rest of my life. My boyfriend, now ex, was on a trip to Washington with his buddies and saw turtles in a pet store window and let his deranged buddy convince him to buy all four of them. Talk about impulse buying. And then smuggled them across the border. Two in his hiking boots and two in the boots of his buddy, poor things. His buddy used to do this a lot. I cringed when Jim mentioned the illegal trade in exotic pets. He sounded as though he was onto my ex. I was terrified he would do something weird, like report me for having a dangerous animal at large. He was always such a rule follower.

"Anyway, my ex's buddy has quite a history of smuggling turtles. It's his thing. One time, he duct-taped a turtle to his back, and just as he was going through customs, the turtle broke free and was scrambling around in his shirt. They have pretty sharp nails. He pretended he was having an epileptic episode, so the customs agent hustled him through because he didn't want to have to deal with it."

Sarah snorted her wine out her nose. "Who knew your first pet would be an illegal immigrant! That's the best 'how I got my pet' story ever. Fitz will be in awe of you. He already thinks you're the coolest person ever because you have a turtle. And super-cool eye makeup."

Aislin dipped her fingers in her wine and flicked them at Sarah. "Look at us. After all these years. At the pinnacles of our lives!"

"Cheers to us! Takes real skill to turn promising adventures into dead ends."

"So, what did you do between high school and breeding outside of your species?"

Sarah dipped her fingers in her wine and flicked them at Aislin. "I worked for a wedding planner. It was fun. But the high drama got old eventually. I developed a knack for identifying which blushing bride was going to be the proverbial bridezilla. The rest of the team used to place bets on my accuracy for picking a doozie. And boy, did we have some doozies.

"There was lots of money in Alberta. It was going through one of its boom cycles. Big money meant big, splashy, ostentatious weddings. Absolutely ridiculous requests."

"Come on, spill."

"Okay. But this better not end up as a news story."

Aislin flinched and sank deeper into her chair.

"What just happened? What did I say wrong?"

"Nothing. You just hit on the reason my life's in a sinkhole. When I said I mishandled a situation, that's what happened. I put a good friend in physical danger. Her story ended up as a double-page spread. And not in our paper. And I lost my job. Although, I could have fought for it if I'd had the will. I loved working there. But the joy would be gone. The others would have made it deeply uncomfortable for me. Journos rally around when one of their own is the injured party. And I was not the injured party."

"That sounds like we need some more wine. Does your room still have our twin beds? One for me and one for you? We can sit here and yak and drink all night."

"Sorry. While I was away, Frank and Letty decided that I was a grown-up and replaced our beds with a double bed. It was a shock the first time I saw the beds gone. Remember how excited we were when they took us shopping and we could pick out our own beds, and they didn't have to match? You chose that ridiculous one with the canopy and curtains, and I chose the one with drawers underneath. Letty hated that bed because she stubbed her toes every time she changed the sheets."

"My bed was not ridiculous. It was elegant. You slept in my bed more than you slept in yours. We spent so much time with the curtains closed. It was our cave. It was our castle. Remember when we pretended we were prisoners of love? Our master was Jordan. Who never even knew we existed. God, we thought he was so hot."

"Would love to have another glass, but I've already had two. Another would put me over the top. I am too fragile right now for a hangover. But this was nice. Really nice. Thanks for coming by to, you know, check on Secretariat." Aislin grinned at Sarah, who had never been good at the nuances of deception.

"Roger Dodger. I'm so glad to hear you say that. Ever since I saw you, I've been trying to figure out a reason to come by. Let's go out for coffee?"

"Ah, no. I'm not ready for a coffee shop. But I could meet you and Fitz at the park one day. You bring the coffee; I'll bring the turtle. It will have to be a warmish day for Secretariat."

Sarah stuck out her hand. "Contact info required."

Aislin wrote her number on Sarah's palm, realizing it meant dealing with all the messages on her phone. That would be tomorrow's project.

Chapter 4

Aislin finally turned on her phone. To her chagrin, her inbox was almost empty. She anticipated being annoyed by the volume of texts and emails. But not a single message from a single former colleague. Just a couple of notices about upcoming appointments. It was as though her former life had never existed. Or maybe it was she who had never existed to them.

It was deeply disconcerting to feel disposable and forgotten. At the very least, she expected some threatening texts from Victor. She would almost have welcomed them. Something from someone. She had entertained, in the very furthest back pocket of her brain, a faint fantasy that the newsroom, realizing she was vital, would invite her back.

Hurricane-force panic filled her. And with it came the pulsating terror she had been holding at bay with her manic cleaning. She lay on her bed and focused on her breath, trying to establish a rhythm, but every time her mind drifted free, a new panic attack squeezed the breath out of her lungs.

Dragging herself up, she went over to her briefcase to get her notebook, but nausea forced her back to bed. When it had passed, she went downstairs, where Letty was busy making breakfast and carrying on a one-sided conversation with Secretariat. The smell of coffee triggered another wave of nausea. Aislin gingerly sat down, resting her head in her hands.

Letty placed a mug of coffee right under her nose, which Aislin quickly pushed away as soon as Letty turned her back. She got herself a glass of water. Her breathing returned to normal, and her legs steadied.

"Do you have a piece of paper or a notebook I could borrow, Gran? I need to make some lists."

"Yes, in the drawer by the phone. There should be some blank pages at the back. If you're making a grocery list, we're getting low on hamburger for Secretariat. I thought we could see if he would like some kale from the garden."

She looked sharply at Aislin as she set the table. "What's wrong? You look awful."

"I'm not feeling great, so I'm going to skip breakfast. I'm going to stick to water for now. I'll eat later."

"What's going on? What's happened?"

"Nothing has happened. It's just I had a panic attack earlier. I've been avoiding my reality. I don't have a job, so I don't have an income, and I have some bills coming due. I'm okay short term, as I was always good at saving. Grandpa drilled that into me. I just need to figure out the next steps, which means getting a job. But, not sure what sort of reference I could expect from Jack, so I'm thinking my career in journalism is over. I loved what I did; it's all I ever wanted to do. I have no idea what else I can do. It's the only thing I know. I need to reinvent myself. Just not sure as what. Or where."

Letty finished her breakfast, then cleared the table, put the dishes in the dishwasher, and left the room. Aislin expected her to jump right in with opinions about her questionable decisions or provide some suggestions about work or comforting words about there being no need to worry. Some sort of recognition of her plight. She did not expect silence.

She busied herself cleaning Secretariat's tank. He was happier living in the kitchen than in the spare bedroom. At least that was one good thing. And Letty seemed to be softening to him, which was another good thing.

Elaine rang, as she always did right after breakfast. Aislin let it ring through to the answering machine. Which meant the always predictable Elaine would call back within five minutes, which she did. Aislin let it ring through again and then called out to Letty that Elaine was trying to reach her.

Aislin listened to Elaine's message that something had come up, so she was unable to go with Letty to Margery Johnson's celebration of life today, so maybe "if Aislin's not too busy, she could go with you." Aislin registered the covert criticism.

"Gran, Elaine says she can't go to Margery Johnson's celebration of life today. I could go with you if you don't want to go on your own."

Aislin called upon the gods of good fortune to intervene. Going to a celebration of life was at the top of the list of things Aislin did not want to do, but she wasn't sure how comfortable Letty was behind the wheel. It was a topic that had not yet come up, and not one Aislin was eager to raise.

The second day she was home, Aislin had checked out the garage and was shocked by the state of Frank's old white Toyota Tercel. It looked like a rescue from a demolition derby dump. One taillight and the passenger side-view mirror both dangled by their wires like loose teeth, the wheel hubs all bore deep scars, the front bumper was bashed in, and there were multiple gouges across each door panel. The thin veil of dust it wore was a relief.

She remembered driving home from the dealership with Frank after Letty had convinced him to replace his pampered, beloved Acadian Beaumont Sport with a new car. He did not consider a Toyota a man's car, but Letty had wanted something smaller and more reliable. And they were of the mindset that maintaining two cars was financial frivolity. A cold front had blown in and hung around the Fitzgerald household for weeks. It was the only time Aislin remembered her grandparents arguing hotly or speaking to each other through her. Aislin had learned to drive in the Beaumont, so she secretly sided with Frank but lacked the audacity to say so to Letty.

"It would be good for you to go to Margery's service. She always liked you. And there's sure to be lots of people there you'll know. We'll leave at eleven. You can drive; just don't drive as though you're in Vancouver.

There's no road rage here," said Letty. Given the condition of the Tercel, Aislin doubted the accuracy of that statement.

Aislin grimaced and cursed the gods of fate, who were clearly annoyed with her. "Okay. I'm not too keen on reconnecting with people just yet, but whatever." She put some bread in the toaster and leaned against the counter while she waited, tapping one foot, working on an explanation she could trot out to satisfy the ever-inquisitive as to why she was back home.

The short trip to the community hall was filled with admonishments from Letty about Aislin's driving. They arrived, tense and unspeaking, along with a crush of other cars, so Aislin was lucky to find a parking spot. She felt the stares as she walked with Letty to the entrance. She fervently hoped this was an alcohol-imbibing bunch of mourners, as the desire for a drink escalated with every step.

"What are the odds?" rang out across the heads of the mourners. Aislin spun around so fast she almost knocked Letty out of her shoes. There was Sarah, waggling her arms in the air, grinning wildly, much to the chagrin of her mother.

Aislin just had time to give her a thumbs-up before entering the hall. She quickly ushered Letty to a table near the door, then looked for Sarah so she could invite her and her mum to sit with them before anyone else took the vacant seats.

"Hi, Mrs. Quinn, it's been ages. Would you like to sit with us?"

"Aislin! Sarah said you were back in town. Lovely to see you. Thank you, but it looks as though all the seats at your table are taken."

Sarah grinned because Delores and Jim Brownlee were settling down at Letty's table. And Jim was already in deep conversation with Letty. No doubt informing her of the perils and pitfalls of turtle ownership. Aislin pulled a face at Sarah, then sat down beside Letty. She detected an uncomfortable tension. She also caught a strong smell of beer.

Letty turned to her and said pointedly, "I was just telling Delores and Jim how much I enjoy having Secretariat in the house."

"And I was just telling Letty about the illegal trade in exotic animals and how turtles are one of the most commonly smuggled animals. When we saw you at the park, you didn't say where you got your turtle." As he spoke, his beer breath wafted over the table.

"And I was just telling Jim," said Delores, "that it was none of his business."

"Can I get anyone a glass of wine? Jim, nonalcoholic punch?" asked Aislin.

"I don't drink that crap. I brought real beer." Jim pulled a can of Lucky out of an inside pocket in his jacket.

The host took the mic and urged everyone to get a drink for a toast and find a seat but to wait until later to line up for food. Four men already at the buffet tables shuffled off with loaded plates as he said this.

A brief overview of Margery's life had everyone murmuring with memories. Guests were encouraged to step up to the mic and share their memories. Two hours later, against the backdrop of audible stomach rumbles and an occasional soft snore, the host finally cut off further trips down memory lane. There was an instant, collective scraping of chair legs as all the able-bodied in the room surged to the buffet tables.

The only thing that had kept Aislin awake during the sharing of memories was her hunger. She was reluctant to join the lineup, but Letty sealed her fate with a sharp elbow jab and a nod towards the queue. She looked for Sarah, but she was already elbow-deep at the dessert end.

"I'll go with you," said Jim. "You can update me on what you've been up to for the past few years besides getting a filthy turtle."

Aislin looked at Delores to see if there was any help on that front. "Don't let him load either of our plates with pasta salad or bread. We're cutting back on carbs," was all she offered.

Jim took Aislin by the elbow and propelled her to the lineup. She tried to pull free, but his years with the RCMP won, and she did not want to cause a scene in front of seventy-five-plus seniors, many of whom were friends of Frank and Letty.

Jim was her least favourite of all her late father's colleagues. He was like a menacing, ever-present cloud. When Aislin was at soccer, he would slide past in his cruiser; when she was working at the grocery store, he invariably chose her till; he was the liaison officer at the high school; and she saw his cruiser when she was out with her friends. He also dropped in frequently to visit Frank and Letty.

She had talked to Frank about how uncomfortable she found Jim's watchfulness. Frank dismissed her concerns, saying Jim had been her dad's best friend and partner, that they had grown up together, taken training together, and how Larry's death had shattered Jim. Frank believed she should be grateful for Jim's interest in her well-being; it was just his way of making sure the daughter of his best friend came to no harm. And here she was at a buffet lineup with him. Life deals odd hands.

"Hey, Roger, look who's here. It's Larry's girl! She's back in town and staying with Letty," said Jim to a soft-looking middle-aged man.

"Aislin! Look at you, all grown up. We've asked Letty about you from time to time. I can't remember what she said you were doing. You were in Vancouver, I think. Are you here for long? We could have you and Letty and some of the old gang over for a barbeque. We might even invite Jim if he promises to behave," said Roger, giving Jim a fake double punch to the gut.

"Hi, Mr. Languille. Nice to see you. I'll leave you and Jim to catch up."

Aislin deftly slipped out from between the two men and rejoined the lineup at the back. She smiled at a few people who looked familiar but more or less kept her gaze on the bowls of food, and her back angled towards the room. After selecting a few lighter offerings, she returned to the table. Jim was hunched over his meatballs, macaroni, and garlic bread but looked up long enough to glare at her.

"You took your time, Jim came back ages ago," said Letty. "Could you get me some more wine while you're up? These quiche tarts look a bit dry. Weren't there any devilled eggs? I love a good devilled egg."

When she returned with wine for them both, Letty was busy talking to someone Aislin didn't recognize, so she quietly took her seat. She tried not to bolt her food. She didn't care if the quiche tarts were dry or the Caesar salad was limp and drowning in dressing. Aislin was starving, so it was all delicious. And chewing meant she did not have to join the conversations around her. She was just reaching for her glass of wine when she heard her name.

"Aislin is looking for work. She was fired from her job at a paper in Vancouver. I can't remember the paper's name, but I know it wasn't one of the big ones—some small thing. So she's staying with me until she finds something."

"Fired! Interesting. I wonder what she did to get fired. It's hard to get fired with all these unions everywhere."

Letty didn't get the first word of her reply out before being kicked under the table. Aislin narrowed her eyes and gave her a nearly imperceptible shake of the head. Delores was looking at her sympathetically.

"Aislin, what sort of work are you looking for?" Delores asked.

With a grateful smile, Aislin replied, "I have a bachelor's degree in journalism from Ryerson University, so I am interested in furthering my career in that field."

When Letty's visitor had left, Aislin turned on Letty. "Gran, could you please not tell people I was fired? I quit. Big difference. And this is an event to honour the life of your friend Margery. It's not a networking session! I did not come with you today to canvas for a job."

"Why were you fired?" asked Jim, just as the host announced it was time to put chairs and tables away before the next event. The noise level shot up, so Aislin ignored him.

Everyone seemed to slip into a role. Some came around with large garbage bags to collect the paper plates, plastic cutlery, and cups, while others efficiently folded chairs, kicking down the tables and loading them on trolleys. Leftovers were wrapped and returned to the care of their creators.

Aislin flashed back to soccer-awards dinners in the same hall, with many of the same people. It was a community to which she belonged but had never valued. And now she felt like an alien on the outside looking in.

She folded up their chairs, returned their wine glasses to the bar, collected their jackets, and looked around for Letty. She was by the door holding forth to a group. Letty caught her eye and indicated she should join them.

"Theo, this is my granddaughter, Aislin. She recently moved here from Vancouver. She's looking for work here in town."

Aislin raised her eyebrows, as this was news to her. She shook hands with Theo.

Theo was a thin, reedy guy about her age with a pronounced Adam's apple that bounced busily above his bow tie. His hips were wide. Child-bearing wide. He rocked back and forth on his heels, with his hands in his pockets. It was all a bit distracting. She saw Sarah a few feet behind Theo, eavesdropping intently. Alarm bells began clamouring in Aislin's head.

"What sort of experience do you have, and what kind of work are you looking for?"

Not knowing who Theo was or why he was asking, coupled with the racket in her head, Aislin decided on an evasive strategy. "What a lovely celebration of life. Were you a friend of Margery's?"

"Didn't know her at all. I wrote her obit. She didn't have anyone literate in her family. Must have some dough, though, as they didn't want a short one."

"I don't understand. If the obit is already published, why are you here?"

"I'm here to circulate and see if I can drum up some business. Old Otto writes most obits, but we think there's plenty to go around so want some of the action."

Aislin frowned her confusion.

"Oh, I thought you were from here. Otto Lawless. He runs the local funeral home, The Maples. He's done the obits for years, but lately . . ." Theo tapped his temple with his index finger.

"I know who Otto Lawless is, thank you. I'm still trying to fathom the ethics of what you're doing. At the very least, it's shamefully insensitive."

"People are increasingly unhappy with old Otto's writing. He's begun editorializing about the decedents. So we saw an opportunity to build up the obit section. I'm the sales rep at *The Standard*. I just want people to know there's an option other than old Otto.

"Not sure if you know this, but the newspaper business is struggling, so we're looking at any and all revenue sources."

Letty put her hand on Aislin's arm. "Theo is Bob Thunberger's nephew. You remember Bob? He bought *The Standard* while Frank was editor."

"Subscriptions and ad revenue are way down and have been spiralling for years. This is a retirement town, and obits bring in revenue. Seems logical to me. You didn't say what sort of work you did or what sort of work you're looking for."

"No, I didn't." Aislin turned to Letty. "Gran, are you ready to go? I'll get the car and pick you up out front."

Aislin caught Sarah's eye and gave her a tight smile as she veered off to find her car. The drive home was silent. Aislin was fuming at how easily she had let herself become irate. Letty wisely refrained from sharing her opinion about Aislin's driving.

"Are we going to have some supper?" asked Letty as they walked up the front steps. When they opened the door, the phone was ringing.

"No doubt that's Elaine panting for intel about the service." Letty shot her a look as she struggled out of her coat while simultaneously answering the phone.

Aislin went into the garden while Letty gossiped with Elaine. She hoped the late afternoon stillness would be calming, but it wasn't. The conversations from the afternoon buzzed around her mind. Her dislike of Theo was visceral. She couldn't remember disliking anyone so intensely within minutes of meeting them. Was it her or was it something about him?

When she saw Letty in the kitchen, she went back in the house.

"I'm not hungry, but there are some leftovers in the fridge. See you in the morning."

"I don't know why you're so angry. Or why you were so rude to Theo. Your behaviour embarrassed me."

"I embarrassed *you*? How about how *you* embarrassed *me*. Telling people I was fired, saying I worked on a rag, and then introducing me to that twit Theo. Me living here is not going to work. I will figure something out and be gone as soon as possible. Good night."

"I am too tired to get into this with you now, and it's too early to go to bed. I suggest you have a shower and then we'll have some dinner. It's a warm evening; we could eat outside. We don't have to talk about it. But you do need to calm down, or you will work yourself up into a state. I am not so old that I've forgotten your short fuse or how you harbour ill feelings."

Aislin came back downstairs feeling relatively calm after a long hot shower. Letty had set the outside table and was sitting there, absently picking at a hangnail, as she did when upset. She looked tired and sad, which took the remaining edge off Aislin's mood. She filled a tray with their plates, glasses, and a bottle of wine and joined her.

"Here we go. Your crab casserole smells even better today than it did yesterday. Man, I love leftovers. I never did get into a routine of cooking regularly and having the luxury of leftovers. Cheers."

"I think it's a symptom of your generation. And maybe the one following as well. Judging from the commercials, everyone eats takeout on their laps in front of the TV."

"So, Gran, what do you know about the Bakers across the hedge?"

"Not much. They've lived there almost as long as I've lived here, but we've never really talked, beyond discussing the annual pruning of the hedge. She always wants me to let it grow higher, but I don't want it to shade out my beds. She's a bit . . . you know."

"No, Gran, I don't know. Could you maybe put some flesh on that?"

"Why do you want to know?"

"Just idle, nosey neighbour curiosity. I sometimes watch them when I come out here after dinner. She seems to drink a lot more than he does. And straight from the bottle. She opens the cupboard, pulls out a bottle, and chugs. And I've seen her do it more than a couple of times per evening."

Her ruse worked, and Letty launched into a lengthy list of Elaine's and her observations about the shortcomings of the Bakers. At one point, Aislin cautioned her, carefully, to lower her voice. If the Bakers weren't outside, no doubt some of the other neighbours were.

No more was said about their mutual grievances. Aislin had deftly steered the ship away from the rocks, for now.

Chapter 5

Once the theme song for *Downton Abbey* filtered out from Letty's room, Aislin crept downstairs for the Scotch she knew was at the back of the cupboard and the last of a bag of Hawkins Cheezies she had stashed. She thought of the countless nights in the newsroom she and her colleagues had spent drinking Scotch, eating Cheezies, and sharing stories. She mourned her old life. And the camaraderie.

She sent Sarah a text. You up? Want to chat?

Sarah called immediately. "Today was beyond painful. I don't know if I can go to another of those 'celebrations' in this lifetime. I think I've used up my quota. They lack any semblance of organization; people get up to the mic and blather on for ages. And then everyone rushes to the buffet. And there's no coordination on the food. Did you see how many pasta salads there were? Drives me nuts. It would be a shock if someone actually planned these events rather than just let them randomly happen."

"That's your inner wedding planner coming out."

"Right? Margery's poor husband was overwhelmed. I felt so sad for him. I desperately wanted to help him out."

"Want to meet for coffee tomorrow?"

"Yes, but not in the park, which I'm sure is your preference, Ms. Anonymous, but can you just get over yourself and meet me at a coffee shop? It's going to be wet tomorrow."

"Fine. Pick a place and let me know what time. My schedule is still wide open."

Sarah chose the Mugshot Café for their meeting, the favourite haunt of their teenage years. Aislin recoiled but recovered as the happy memories overrode her reticence. When she opened the door, the familiarity of the place hit hard. It looked and smelled as it had all those years ago.

Sarah was sitting in their usual booth, grinning like the Cheshire cat. Fitz was twisting side to side on a stool at the counter, working on a large milkshake. Aislin paused to greet him.

"Hello, Fitz, it's good to see you again. Thank you for helping me when I was looking for my turtle. You and your mum should come by one day so you can play with him."

"Yes, Ms. Aislin, I would like that. My mum's been reading books to me about turtles," said Fitz.

Aislin reached out to tousle his hair but stopped herself. She had never spent time around kids his age, or any age, so wasn't sure about their tolerance for relative strangers messing with their hair. But she liked this kid. And his old-soul formality was adorable.

"May I call you Mr. Fitz?"

"Yes," he replied, smiling up at her.

"Good choice," she said as she slid in across from Sarah.

"More like no choice. This is the only place we can have coffee. It would feel like we were cheating on the Bentleys if we went anywhere else. They put up with us and our cheapness for years. We sat here nursing our Cokes for hours, and they never kicked us out. Betty and Joe retired, and now Jill runs it, and she's just as tolerant of teenagers as her parents were; rare breed, those Bentleys. But don't get on her bad side. Phew."

"Good to see you're immersing your son in family traditions early. He looks like a natural."

"Glad you approve of my parenting skills. So, Theo Thunberger. What do you want to know? I don't know a ton about him, as he's relatively new in town. He's from Toronto. Need I say more?"

"Hey, I used to live in Toronto."

"I rest my case. Anyway, we're not talking about you, Ms. Displaced

Torontonian. Apparently, Theo was in his final year of law school and
was working for his uncle's law firm, in the family law branch, and he
had a fling with the daughter of a client."

"Wow. His inappropriateness knows no bounds. That would explain why he's so comfortable trolling funerals promoting his obituary-
writing services. I am still appalled. I hardly slept last night."

"I would never have guessed," said Sarah, taking in the dark shadows on her friend's face. "He sure got under your skin. Are you normally so triggered by jerks? Because if you are, you must have a lot of
sleepless nights."

"It was the whole situation yesterday. My day began with a panic
attack about my future, then going out in public, then having Jim
Freaking Brownlee at our table, then meeting Theo. Not to mention
the fact that Letty went around telling people I had been fired from a
rag in Vancouver and was looking for work here in town."

"Yes, I heard some mention of that while I was getting drinks,"
Sarah said apologetically. "I wasn't sure how that rumour started. Bad
old Letty."

"Are you kidding me? You overheard someone repeat that? Oh
my God, this town is incredible. By the time we got home, Elaine
had already left a message that she had heard I was rude to Theo.
Unfreakingbelievable. And then called again so she could get the live
replay from Letty."

"Anyway, enough about that. I do some of my best thinking in the
middle of sleepless nights. And I've got an idea I want to run by you.
I'm hoping you'll think about it some before you give feedback."

"Sure. I haven't heard an idea that involves me since my ex told me
he thought I should move out. Pretty sure whatever you've come up
with is better than that."

"It's better than you thinking up plans that involve me because
those plans generally broke the law. Like stealing lawn ornaments, garden furniture, and gates because you had forgotten one or the other
of your parents' birthdays and the stores were closed. And shoplifting
chocolate bars for Mother's Day."

"Yes, well, I like to think I was a creative child. A problem solver.
Let's hear what you've dreamt up."

Aislin pulled out her notebook, some loose-leaf sheets, and two pens. She pushed the paper and one pen over to Sarah, aligning them with the edge of the table. Sarah grinned.

"Okay, here goes. I thought a lot about your comments last night about how disorganized these celebrations of life can be and how the widow or widower is often overwhelmed and has no idea how to organize or survive the event, should it actually get off the ground. And how sorry you felt for Margery's husband for that reason. There was so much empathy in your voice." Aislin inhaled deeply, looked Sarah in the eye, and exhaled as she said, "So I think you should start a funeral-planning business."

Sarah cocked her head to the left and squinted at Aislin. "You think weddings and funerals are interchangeable? That funerals are like weddings but minus the presents, bridezillas, and dresses?"

She looked out the window and watched a couple of crows squabbling lazily over a takeout container. Then turned her gaze to Jill behind the counter, her face pink from the heat of the grill. And then she looked at Fitz, who had finished his milkshake and was now helping the staff fill saltshakers, his little face puckered with concentration.

"Sure."

"Sure? That's it?"

"Yes, that's it. I mean, why not? What else have I got going on? I need to work, and Beastly Nancy Beasley owns the only wedding-planning business in the valley, and she hates me because I stole Kevin from her in grade ten. And it would be good for Fitz to see me as a business owner. Watching him over there, I think he's showing real potential as a worker bee. And it wouldn't require much overhead. Or an office. Definitely a niche market in this town. It's brilliant! I love it. But on one condition."

"Which is?"

"We do it together. We would have so much fun. And one of our services could be obituary writing. That would be your job. We could stick it to Theo."

Aislin crossed her arms and then her legs; she stared hard at Sarah, jiggling her right foot. "No, sorry. I can't stay here. This town drives me nuts. And I'm not sure that living with Letty is good for our relationship." She leaned forward and straightened her notebook and pen. "And besides, I'm not a people person."

"Where are you going to go? And what are you going to do? I don't know all the details, and I don't know the industry, but it sounds like you burnt some serious bridges, so getting another job might be tough. And as Theo said, newspapers are struggling."

"I'm looking into freelance work. I can pitch to a couple of magazines and see where it leads."

"And what are you going to live on in the meantime? What you should do is figure out how to get along with Letty because she is your one relative, get over your anxiety about everyone watching you because of who your dad was, relax a little, and work with me on this scheme of yours. I see franchise potential."

Aislin stared at Sarah. She had anticipated a litany of excuses and accordingly prepared a list of responses. She expected to launch a long slow-drip campaign. She did not expect instant acquiescence, nor did she expect Sarah to turn the tables. The seismic shift in the conversation unnerved her.

Sarah smiled as Aislin straightened and aligned everything on the table. "Your attention to detail will be invaluable for our business. No more sloppy table settings or mismatched salt and pepper sets on our watch."

"No. The business idea was for you, not me. You're always so relaxed and easygoing; you bring out the best in people, you're compassionate, and you have experience organizing events. I have none of those skills. And I'm too old to change, and I need to restart my life elsewhere."

"You're thirty! You were at a crisis point in your life, so you came back here. You came home. This is your place. And I'm here. What's not to love about that?"

"I didn't know you were here or if you had ever left. We lost contact for over a decade. Remember?"

Sarah winced. "I do remember. And I've been beating myself up about it ever since. It was entirely my fault. I let you down. I abandoned you when the bullying started. I should have stuck with you. And I am sorry from the bottom of my heart. I know that sounds weak and limp, but I have regretted my cowardliness ever since. And once I came to my senses, I didn't know how to fix it. You had walled yourself off. And then you left for university."

Sarah was treading on unstable ground. Aislin had been dreading this moment, this conversation, ever since she bumped into Sarah and Fitz at the park. She did not want to talk about it. All the hurt and hate were packaged up, gathering dust in storage.

Reconnecting with Sarah was by equal measure comforting and terrifying. She never imagined sliding so seamlessly back into the skins of their friendship. She felt whole when they were together. But, losing people she loved was a pattern. Not letting people into her heart was the solution. And Sarah and Fitz were getting dangerously close to her heart.

"As you mentioned earlier, we're not talking about me. I'm glad you like the idea. Will leave it with you to flesh out," said Aislin as she packed up her things. She put some money on the table to cover her coffee and a tip. "See you around."

Sarah grabbed her hand. "Hey, don't go. We have to get past this. We're meant to be friends. We both know that now. I'm not that shallow teenager anymore. I've grown up. Somewhat. I wouldn't go so far as to say I was mature, but I'm working on it. Please stay. Give me more info about your business idea."

Aislin pulled her hand away as she stood up. She saw Fitz, alerted by the tone of Sarah's voice, looking alarmed. He studied his mum's face, then ran to her.

"Why are you trying to run away from Mummy? Don't you want to be friends? Don't you want me and Secretariat to be friends?" Sarah buried her face in Fitz's hair.

Aislin looked up, blinking hard. Shaking her head, she sat down again. Sarah grinned and hugged her boy, whispering "Love you" into his hair. He pulled away and jumped up onto the seat beside Aislin and snuggled into her. She put her arm awkwardly across his shoulders. He wiggled in further, leaving her no recourse but to hug him.

Aislin looked at Sarah. "You do know that this is exactly what you used to do? You would cut through tension between Letty and Frank and then snuggle up beside one of them."

"Any doubt that he's my son can now be put to rest. He's so good and sweet my parents think I stole him. Every time the doorbell rings, they think it's child services coming to apprehend him."

"I'm sorry, Sarah. It's just so weird for me to be taking good advice from you. It's like living in an upside-down world," said Aislin. "But you're right. I do need to figure out how to get along with Letty. We are all there is for the other. And she needs help around the house. I was quite shocked by things when I arrived." Aislin paused and looked out the window. "I *think* she enjoys having me around, cleaning, tidying up, and cooking, but she never says so. And she's so prickly sometimes; I never know what's going to trigger her."

Sarah laughed. "She's not the only one. You two have more in common than you're willing to admit. Just roll with it. And try to wean her off Elaine. Elaine's very proprietary about her, and I'm not the only one who thinks so. However, if you intervene between Elaine and Letty, you will be required to spend more time at long, painful, poorly organized funerals because that's about the only entertainment in town for seniors. Unless, of course, we save them all from the horror. Moms has even complained that some funerals seem almost longer than the deceased's life. The trouble is you get the windbags who have stored up a hundred years of memories and will not be denied the opportunity to share. We were at one funeral, and there was almost a fight over the mic. One guest thought another had been droning on long enough, so he decided to just put an end to it. Must have been having a low-blood-sugar moment. And then there are the professional mourners."

"What?"

"Yup, it's a thing around here. And it's quite funny, in a sad kind of way. There are two groups of women who go to all the funerals. Even if they don't know the deceased, they outsing, outcry, and outpray one another. It took me a bit to realize what was going on, but now I see them almost every time. They weren't at Margery's because there isn't reliably singing or praying at a celebration of life."

"So, how many funerals have you been to since you've been back?"

"A bunch. As I said, it's the only entertainment in town besides pickleball, and not all seniors are pickleball-able. So when you dropped this idea of funeral planning in my lap, it was beyond perfect. You only suffered through one, and you came up with a solution. I've been numbly sitting through these things for months but did not see the business potential staring me right in the face."

A fissure of excitement flooded Aislin. "Are we going to do this? Can we? I don't know anything about starting or running a business.

I've only ever been an employee. And way down the food chain, so I have no idea of the machinations of a business owner."

"Me neither, but the company I worked for in Calgary was small, so we were all aware of the gritty bits about the finances. Maybe we should start with a business licence. I know that much because my brother Donny needed one for his garage. I can ask him what he had to do to set up. Although I gotta say, he wasn't terribly successful, and he filed for bankruptcy protection after a couple of years, so he may not be our best role model. I think it was something to do with filing taxes or neglecting to file taxes. But Donny has an inner spring of optimism that frequently overrides reality, and he's trying again. This time, he's narrowed his focus to just fixing motorbikes, and his primary clients are the Timber Dogs—you remember, that sketchy biker gang that's been around forever? As you can imagine, they give him all sorts of sound advice about running a business."

"I didn't know Donny had a garage. I had such a crush on him. Those long, dark eyelashes and deep blue eyes—so gorgeous. Of all your brothers, he was the one who looked out for us. I used to pretend it was because he was secretly in love with me."

"A girl can dream! Donny's the best. He and Fitz adore one another, right, Fitz?"

"Uncle Don is my best friend." Fitz sat up. "He's going to teach me how to ride a bike."

"Is he? Are you starting with training wheels?"

"Not a bicycle bike. A motorbike. A Harley, to be exact," interjected Sarah.

"What? Are you kidding? Fitz, promise me you will always wear a helmet and never ride at night. Or if you've been drinking. And be super careful at intersections. Most accidents happen in intersections and involve left-hand turns. And wear leather," said Aislin.

Sarah was grinning at her. "You forgot to include 'and don't have fun.'"

"Motorcycles are incredibly dangerous. I don't know why you're so relaxed about this," Aislin hissed.

"Probably because he's five, and there's a lot of water between now and when he's old enough to get a license. And Donny isn't the most reliable person on the planet. He drifts from one wild scheme to another. And he's also living with Moms and Pops. They mentioned the other day that they would like not to have their grown children and the children of their grown children under their roof at some point in their lives. They're threatening to get a one-bedroom condo." Fitz looked worried, so she quickly added, "But they love us, especially you, Fitz, so they put up with us."

"Are we really going to do this?"

"Yes, we are. Why wouldn't we? We have the time. We're just nuts enough. We need the money. And people could really use help during a difficult time. It doesn't require much overhead. It won't be full time. What's not to love?"

"You're so calm. I'm vibrating. Okay. We're doing it. I wonder what Letty will say. I better go and make amends for yesterday. Whatever it was that offended her needs to be sorted. And yes, I will take your oddly wise words to heart about figuring out how to get along with her. I'm counting on staying with her, at least short term. So I need to finish that conversation.

"We should both make up some lists of what we think needs to be done, what our services will be, what each of us will be responsible for in setting up and running the business. And we need a name, so make another list of potential names. And then we'll see which items on our lists we have in common. That will be interesting. I like lists. They give structure and direction."

"Yes, I can tell. I'm not one for lists or structure, but as I'm going into business with someone who is into both, I'll try to be compliant. Meanwhile, it's time to get Fitz home for lunch. When do you want to meet again?"

"Sure, why don't you come over tonight after dinner? Around eight, after Letty has gone up. We can sit out back and go over our lists."

As they were getting into their cars, Aislin called out to Sarah, "I think I'm excited!"

"What are the odds?"

Chapter 6

Letty was busy in the back garden, pruning. Gardening for Letty was either a source of peace or a vent for pent-up fury. Frank and Aislin used to judge her mood by the outcome of her pruning. On occasion, they both shuddered, thankful she had a large garden.

Aislin unloaded the dishwasher, opened a can of tomato soup, and assembled grilled cheese sandwiches as Letty came in. Grilled cheese and tomato soup were the staple "make-up" foods in the Fitzgerald household. Frank held that no one could stay mad when eating this magical combination.

"Gran, I have an idea I want to run by you, but I'd like to have lunch first. I'm starving. What were you working on in the garden?"

"What sort of idea?"

"Can we eat first? If you could set the table, the sandwiches are almost ready."

Letty nodded towards the stove where the sandwiches were sizzling in butter on the griddle and said, "Whatever you want to talk about must be big."

They ate in mutually wary silence.

"I haven't had a grilled cheese sandwich and tomato soup for years. So good," Aislin said as she cleared their bowls and plates. After plugging in the kettle, setting out the tea mugs, and wiping the stovetop clean of grease splatters, she crossed her arms and leaned against the counter.

"So, Gran, have you had time to think about whether or not I can stay here for a while? We haven't had a chance to finish that conversation. I would like to, for several reasons. But I don't want to invade your life."

"I thought this was settled."

"Oh! I didn't know it was settled. I wasn't sure what your thoughts were. That's great! Really great." She gave Letty an awkward hug. Letty pulled away.

"I don't know why you make such a fuss about things. Of course you're welcome to stay here as long as you like. You're actually quite useful."

"Gee, thanks for the compliment," slipped out. Aislin hoped the sarcasm didn't register.

"You're welcome. Is that it? I thought there was something else you wanted to discuss. But, if you've finished, I'm going back to the garden," Letty said as she rose, stiffly, from her chair.

"Just a sec. There's more. Please don't go yet. Tea is ready, we can take it outside, and I can run my idea by you and then you can get back to your gardening. And I'll help."

When they were settled around the old, white, chipped metal table and tea was poured, Aislin launched into her conversation with Sarah.

Letty's face was impassive, her thoughts unreadable. She let Aislin get it all out uninterrupted. When Aislin finished, Letty gazed over the garden, picking at a hangnail. Aislin also gazed over the garden, willing herself to ride out the silence and not read too much into it.

"As a senior who knows her time here is limited, it's hard to get excited about a business plan that sees the death of me and my contemporaries as a growth industry. It's crass and brazen."

Letty paused, removed her glasses, and polished them with a corner of her sweater, which didn't so much clean the lenses as rearrange the grime. Putting them back on and squinting at Aislin, she continued. "But, if I look at it from your perspective, I see the potential. Especially in this town. As Theo said, it's a retirement mecca.

"And the services and funerals can sometimes drag on and on, so I see the advantage of having them organized. Elaine commented last week that sometimes it seems like there's a competition for whose event is more lavish and extravagant. So, a bit like a wedding, I suppose.

"Have you considered the hazards of starting a business with your former best friend? You two have a history. Both good and bad. Have you discussed your falling out? And have you looked at why you ran away from here? Can you live in this town? Because nothing has changed; some people are interested in you and want to know all about you, and you hate that."

"Yes, we talked about our falling out. Neither of us wanted to, but it came out over coffee this morning. I think we're past it. We've both grown up a lot, and we both realize how much better our lives are with each other in it. Some friendships are just meant to be. And as for living here, Sarah pointed out that I just need to get over it. I could just give a prepared statement to Elaine, and that should take care of it!"

"Don't be so hard on her. I know she's bossy and gossipy, but she's been good to me."

"I know she has. And I promise to try to get along with her. It's just that she always seems to rub me the wrong way and make me feel as though I'm an intruder in your life. She's very protective of you. Almost possessive."

"Your issues with Elaine are all in your head. Let's talk about your business idea. What are your next steps? What are you going to call it? You need a name before you can do anything. Don't pick anything too morbid or cutesy—cutesy names turn me off."

"Sarah is coming over, after dinner. In the meantime, we're each going to put together some lists of what we think we need to do, what our services will be, and of course, potential names. I don't like cutesy either. So, we have to find something between cutesy and dark and morbid."

"Sarah could join us for dinner." Letty paused, then continued with, "And we can work on some names while we eat. Or we can wait until after dinner. It will be lovely to spend time with her after all these years. I can't remember how long it's been since she was here for a meal. I actually can't remember when I last had anyone in for a meal. We used to be so social. Remember? Always someone coming by."

Aislin looked down and folded her napkin, creasing each precise fold with the edge of her hand. It had been an emotionally tumultuous day, and it was only just past noon. Now, this: Letty inserting herself into their plan.

"And what are we going to serve? You decide. I want to finish pruning the roses. And then soak my bones in a hot bath with some Epsom salts before Sarah arrives."

The train had left the station, and Aislin had no idea how to stop it. With the tiniest flutter of malice, she decided to take Sarah's advice to just roll with it and let Sarah, the diplomat, find a way out. She also chose not to warn her. She brightened at the thought of Sarah being forced to heed her own advice.

"Let's have parmesan chicken, broccoli, and steamed rice. That's an easy recipe, and everyone likes it. I'll whip out and get the groceries now while you finish in the garden. Then I'll do a quick vacuum and dust."

Aislin sent a text to Sarah inviting her and Fitz for dinner. She thought Letty meeting Fitz might be a convenient distraction. Aislin was unsure if Letty knew Sarah's son was called Fitz. Unlikely in a town that thrived on gossip, but maybe Sarah had kept the source a secret. Or maybe Letty simply had not paid attention. Time would tell. She also suggested Sarah take a cab, as she anticipated wine would be a big part of dinner. And then added Tylenol to her grocery list.

Sarah's dad dropped them off. Fitz was lugging a big bag and looking very important. Aislin's heart hurt a tiny bit as she watched him. He had his mum's expressive face and her colouring. She wasn't sure what his father's genes had contributed.

Letty joined her at the window. "He looks just like Sarah did at that age," she whispered.

"I know. I'm not usually comfortable around kids, but he's different."

Aislin swung open the door as soon as they reached the porch. "Come on in. Here, let me take those," she said as she reached out for the bright-red tulips and wine.

Sarah gave Letty a big hug. "Thanks so much for inviting us for dinner." Then she stepped back and pulled Fitz in front of her. "Letty, I would like you to meet my son, Fitz. Fitz, this is Ms. Aislin's granny, Mrs. Fitzgerald."

All colour drained from Letty's face. She looked from Aislin to Sarah to Fitz. Then she held out her hand and said with a catch in her voice, "Hello, Fitz. I am so pleased to meet you. May I help you with your jacket?"

"Hello, Mrs. Fitzgerald," he replied, shaking her hand formally. "I'm named after you and Mr. Fitzgerald. Mr. Fitzgerald is dead, so I can't meet him. But you aren't, so I get to meet you. I can take my own jacket off."

Letty was near tears, as were Aislin and Sarah. Letty hugged Sarah again, which pushed Aislin closer to tears. Fitz studied each face and then took his mum's hand. "I've brought treats for Secretariat. May I see him?" he asked Aislin.

"Of course. He will be so happy to have treats. He lives in the kitchen so that he can be around us all the time."

Aislin nodded to Letty to take Fitz to the kitchen. She needed a moment with Sarah. "Wow, that was hard. I wasn't sure if Letty knew you named Fitz after them. I didn't know how to bring it up. I knew as soon as she met him, she would melt. He's so amazing. It's quite weird to see you as a mother."

"I wondered the same thing. Just my way of showing how much I loved and valued my time with them growing up. And yes, I get that it's weird for you to see me as a parent. It's weird for me, too, if that helps. The white-picket-fence family scenario was so not on my radar. And apparently, it wasn't meant to be! When I was with Garth, I always felt like an actor in a play. But stuff happens; you adapt and carry on, hoping you don't drift too far from your principles and moral compass in the process."

"Who are you? And what have you done with my friend Sarah?"

Sarah laughed. "Don't blow my cover. My parents still think I'm one step from the precipice of disaster, which is why they took us in. Let's go see what Letty and Fitz are up to."

Heads together, one white and one so blonde it was almost white, they were hunched over Secretariat's tank. "Kale was a good choice. I've been giving him bits from the garden, but maybe it's too bitter because he doesn't eat it. Maybe he'll like yours more."

"My book on turtles says they like kale. Lots of people think lettuce is good for turtles, but it's not. Have you fed him lettuce?"

"No! Aislin stopped me. But he does like parsley. And hamburger."

"How about I carry his tank outside so he can have some fresh air. Just keep an eye on him if you put him on the grass. He has a way of scooting off. I'll bring him back in before we have dinner," Aislin said.

While Letty and Fitz were busy bonding over Secretariat, Aislin poured herself and Sarah large glasses of wine. "Cheers to us. And our big-girl-panties venture."

"Cheers to us. And to Letty and Frank for making this possible. I don't mean to be maudlin, but seeing Fitz out there with Letty makes me miss Frank. I think he and Fitz would have been soul mates."

"I know. I'm having a tough time with all of this. I've been missing him so much since being home. Can't help thinking about the inevitability of what lies ahead. I thought I had dealt with it all, but nope, not so much."

"You're here because you need to be. You're not just fitting a visit into your busy life. This isn't a duty call. This is all happening for a reason."

"Oh, stop with the cosmic crap and set the table. What would Fitz like to drink? I'm assuming it isn't wine?"

"Water, thanks. I've managed to keep him from the sugar-water addiction cycle. Much to my parents' horror. It was like a food group when we were kids."

Conversation during dinner was primarily between Letty and Fitz. She gently asked him questions, which he thoughtfully answered while studying her face. After dinner, Sarah set Fitz up with his colouring books at one end of the table.

"Okay, let's talk names," Letty said, coming out of her trance. "I have a few suggestions. As I said to Aislin earlier, I don't like cutesy."

Sarah did not miss a beat. She just smiled and said, "Okay, good to know. Let's get going. How about we each share our ideas, mark the ones we like on each others' lists, and see what shakes out."

The only sound in the kitchen was the gentle gurgling and swooshing of the dishwasher. All heads were bowed. Letty fiddled with her rings, Sarah chewed her pen, and Aislin chewed her bottom lip. Fitz coloured intently, choosing each new crayon with careful consideration.

"Okay, how're we doing? I've chosen the ones I like, but I have to say none of them have that 'star power' I was hoping for," said Sarah.

"Same here. I've chosen three that have potential."

"I don't like any of them. None stand out. They all sound so gloomy," said Letty.

"Gee, Gran, that's a bit harsh, isn't it?"

"I agree," said Sarah. "None of these capture the essence of who we are and what we want to do."

"And just what is that?" Letty asked. "I don't know what we're going to be doing. Are we arranging funerals, or are we arranging celebrations of life? We'll compete with Otto Lawless over at The Maples if it's funerals. Now, see, that's another bland name that doesn't say anything. It could be a tree nursery or a seniors' home. We need a name that says something."

Aislin got up abruptly to get more wine. Extricating Letty from her presumption that she was part of the business would grow exponentially the longer they left it. But Sarah seemed perfectly comfortable with this development.

"I don't mind Fond Farewells," said Sarah. "And in terms of a logo, working with a double consonant provides lots of design potential."

Aislin and Letty both stared at her. "I hadn't thought about a logo," said Aislin. "Good thing one of us has some business experience."

"I don't! But I did take a graphic design course at one time and have managed to retain some tidbits."

An hour passed without a clear frontrunner. Fitz was yawning, as was Letty.

"Well, this has been fun, but not as productive as we expected. I'm going to call my dad to come and get us. Fitz, could you please pack up."

"Yes, it's late. I'm usually asleep by now," Letty said, getting up and stretching her back. "Good night, Fitz. Be sure to come by and visit anytime you like." Letty turned to Sarah. "It was lovely to see you and to meet Fitz. Such an honour to have him named after us. I am going to bed a happy old woman. Goodbye, girls."

Aislin and Sarah locked eyes. They waited until they heard Letty close her bedroom door, then high-fived each other.

"How perfect is that?" burst out of Aislin.

"Right? It's so us! And it just happened organically."

"Do you think Letty will approve? And what are your feelings about her assumption she's part of the business? The sooner we break it to her gently, the better."

"Why can't she be part of it? She knows everyone in town. Her perspective, as a senior, on our marketing will be useful, don't you think? She'll stop us cold if we get cheeky or disrespectful, which is highly probable. And, it'll be good for her to be involved in something besides her garden and being dragged around by Elaine. She's looking a lot better since you've been home, by the way."

"Really? It may be that she's eating better. Her cupboards were beyond bare when I arrived. But I don't know about having her in the business. Our relationship is a bit scratchy. Not sure how adding working with each other will improve things. But, now that you mention Elaine, she will hate this, so there's that on the plus side. What is it about that woman that rubs me the wrong way?"

"She is an acquired taste, a bit like stinky cheese is, that's for sure. Here's Pops. Let's talk tomorrow. Our next challenge is registering the company and deciding on our business structure. So much to think about. Thanks for dinner!"

Aislin was emotionally overstimulated from the evening's events, so decided to do twenty calming minutes of yoga before bed. But as soon as she rolled out her mat, a landslide of thoughts of Lara and the yoga classes they used to take together hit her. Why was Lara's decision to drop out not a red flag? She was always obsessive about never missing a class. A better friend would never have accepted the excuse that she was bored with yoga.

Aislin reached for her phone and called Lara before she could overthink things. It rang once, then a voice-mail message relayed that the number was unavailable. Blocked. What did that mean? Had Lara blocked her or had Victor taken control of Lara's phone and done it? Was she in a safe house and had to give up her phone so her location couldn't be tracked? Of all the reasons for her number to be blocked, Aislin hoped it was the latter. That Lara was in a safe house.

Guilt and shame rolled in, hand and hand. What hell had her actions precipitated? Lara's life was irrevocably changed. What was her future? Would Lara always live in fear of Victor finding her?

And here she was, comfortable, reconnecting with friends, and about to launch a business.

Sleep was an infrequent visitor that night.

In the morning, Aislin and Sarah met with the bank and a lawyer to work out their business structure details. The process was more straightforward than Aislin had imagined, which was a good thing, as Aislin was thick-witted from her sleepless night.

"What's up with you?" Sarah asked as they walked to their cars. "You don't seem yourself and you look as though you were up all night."

"I didn't get much sleep. I started worrying about the friend I told you about, the one whose life I blew up. I tried to call her last night, but my number's been blocked. I'm thinking of contacting a coworker. But I'm scared they might also have blocked me. And I don't know how I'll feel if they have."

"I think you need to try one more time. Call your coworker. You need to know how your friend is and if there's anything you can do to help her. And if you need to go to Vancouver to sort anything out, I'm happy to go with you."

Aislin looked up and held back the tears that were threatening to escape. "Thank you. You're right, I do need to know. I am going to call right now."

"Excellent. And let me know how it goes." Sarah winced as Aislin slammed her car door so hard the vehicle shook.

Aislin drank most of a bottle of water, took a deep breath, and called Jack.

"What the hell do you want?" was his greeting.

Her voice shook as she stammered out that she was calling to find out about Lara. Jack took his time replying. But his voice softened as he gave a brief overview. Victor was arrested for assault but not for assaulting Lara. He was involved in a fight that left a man with life-threatening injuries. Lara's family collected her and took her to Europe for an extended trip.

Aislin thanked him for the news and was about to ask him how he was, but he hung up before she could. This time no amount of looking up was going to stop her tears. She sat in her car and bawled. And when the tears stopped, a small smile crept along her lips. Lara was okay. Victor was in jail. It wasn't all that bad. Maybe now she could let go of her guilt. Maybe.

Chapter 7

Every day, one or the other sent a text saying, See you at the office at 10, the office being their booth at the Mugshot Café. They were generally left alone, but someone they knew would stop for a chat every so often. Over time this became less uncomfortable for Aislin. She no longer froze at the sight of a familiar face. Her shin was also taking less of a beating from Sarah as she forced herself to engage more readily with visitors.

"Well, if it isn't Curly and Moe! I heard you two were stitched back together."

"Hey, Nick! It's been years. I was wondering when I would see you," Sarah said. She gave him a quick hug and invited him to join them.

"How's the turtle whisperer?" he asked Aislin as he slid into the booth beside her. Sarah nudged her under the table.

"Secretariat is feeling much better, thanks," Aislin replied.

"I didn't ask about your turtle."

"Right." Aislin's discomfort was filling the room. Nick's easy usage of Frank's nickname for them had hit her hard. Sarah jumped in with, "So, tell us all about the adventures in Nick-land. You're married, right? Don't tell me, it will come to me. Kate Coombs! I knew I would remember. You two were inseparable in grade twelve, so no surprise. As the only currently married person at the table, what is your secret to marital bliss?"

Nick squirmed. "You know, just the usual."

"As I am a card-carrying member of the soon-to-be unmarried segment of society, I obviously do not know. I could teach a master class on how *not* to achieve long-term marital bliss."

"I heard you got married, moved to Alberta, and produced an offspring. And now you've moved back here?"

"Your sources are good. I did all of that, and said offspring is over there earning his keep by helping to fill ketchup containers."

"My sources have also informed me that Curly and Moe are starting a business. Funeral planning, if I am correct? I would never have pegged you two crazies as business owners. Or grown-ups! No offence intended."

"None taken. It was Aislin's idea. It just took one dip into reality, and she nosed out a business opportunity. We, as the Goodbye Girls, are going to take this town by storm!"

Nick laughed. "Another great name! It's so you two. Finally, something to look forward to! Which is an odd thing to say, given that your business enterprise depends on people dying. But, you know what I mean.

"So, Aislin, you didn't keep your appointment for Secretariat. I'm assuming his lethargy was temporary?"

Fitz, ever attuned to anything related to Secretariat, joined them at their booth. "Why are you talking about Secretariat?"

"Nick, I would like you to meet my son, Fitz. Fitz, this is an old friend of ours from school, Nick de Vries. Nick is a vet."

Nick looked at Sarah, then at Aislin, before offering his hand to Fitz. "I am most pleased to meet you, Fitz. That's an important name you carry, young man. Frank and Letty both played a big part in my life."

Fitz took Nick's hand and shook it solemnly. "Letty's my friend. Secretariat is the first turtle I've ever met, and he likes me. I'm teaching him to play soccer."

"Are you? That's fascinating. How are you doing that?"

"I use a tennis ball. He pushes it with his head, and I push it back. He's just learning, so he doesn't always understand when it's his turn. You have to be patient with turtles. That's what it says in my book."

"Very impressive. I don't have any experience with turtles. I want to watch you play with him sometime. It will help me in case someone else brings a turtle in for a checkup. Would that be okay, Aislin?"

Aislin had straightened everything on the table and was beginning to fidget. "Sure. Fitz and Secretariat have bonded. And Letty has bonded with both of them." She looked up, first at Sarah and then at Nick. "It's all a bit weird, but whatever."

Sarah was leaning back, with one arm around Fitz. "Do you and Kate have kids, Nick?"

"No kids. No time. Kate has her own gallery and studio now, so she's busy with shows and tours. She also teaches at the studio and community college. As for me, well, vets never have enough time. Besides my practice here, I've been running spay-neuter clinics in First Nation communities all over the island. I enjoy getting to know the people and their communities. Being accepted and earning their trust is a work in progress. I've made some five-star dumb blunders, but I'm learning, and they're incredibly forgiving, for which I am extremely grateful. Sometimes I have a hard time getting away at the end of the day because I get invited to community dinners. Next spring, I've also been invited to a potlatch, which is a huge honour. I look forward to the mobile clinics more and more each time. It breaks the monotony of looking after spoiled, underexercised, pot-bellied dogs."

Nick's phone buzzed. "Well, there's the boss. Have to run. Hey, if you're not too busy giving the dead a good send-off, I'm always looking for volunteers for my clinics. Hint, hint. I would enjoy the company on the long drives to and from the communities. We could share some laughs about those distant carefree years at school."

"I would like to go with you. I'm going to be a vet when I grow up," said Fitz.

"That's great news, Fitz. Get your mum, or Aislin, to bring you by my office so I can show you around. Maybe even put you to work, as your mum seems happy to support child labour."

Sarah pulled a face. After he left, she leaned forward. "So, what's with the extreme discomfort? You were practically redlining. I thought he was a family friend. Frank was super fond of him, wasn't he?"

Aislin stretched her neck and ran both hands through her hair. "It's a long story."

"I've got the time. Come on, spill."

"You remember how Frank looked out for Nick after his dad died."

"Yes, and I remember you were lovesick for him throughout school."

Aislin stuck her tongue out at Sarah. "Anyway, the night Frank had his heart attack, he was at the office writing about those spay-neuter clinics Nick just mentioned. And because of that, however irrational it may be, Letty has held Nick responsible. So, let's just say that Nick coming by to see Fitz teach Secretariat to play soccer is never going to happen."

"Whoa. That's a lot to process. No wonder you had a squirm-fest. And you were going to take Secretariat to see Nick, but you cancelled?"

"Yup. And that's why I was at Picnic Park crying my face off when you and Fitz came by. Talk about serendipity."

"No kidding. I'm almost speechless. So, how high do you think the happiness factor is in the Nick and Kate marriage? He dodged my question about marital bliss like a pro. Kate was always so bossy with him when they were dating. I used to feel sorry for him. You know, she's an awful lot like his mum."

"I know! And his mum is his receptionist. Another reason I bailed on the appointment. She never liked us Fitzgeralds."

"Call me crazy, but he seemed interested in you. How did it feel to see him again? He sure has grown nicely out of the gangly soccer player."

"Okay, crazy, time to get to work. Let's work on defining our services. And, I want to visit Otto Lawless and talk to him. We should give him a heads-up about our business. There may be opportunities to work together, or he may be interested in sending some business our way. Not everyone can afford a fully-fledged funeral or wants the deep dark wood, melancholy music, or stiff and stately floral arrangements."

"Do you feel any sort of twinge of conscience when you refer to death as 'some business'?"

Aislin tilted her head and twirled her pen. "I do and I don't. If we're going to be successful, we need to come to grips with just that—our business relies on people dying. But, when I feel squeamish about it, I tell myself that we are helping others when they are vulnerable and processing their loss. We're helping them by lightening their load. They're in a black hole of grief, wondering how to breathe, let alone organize a celebration of life. They may not have the mental bandwidth to think about a service or who to invite or what music to play, or how to begin to write an obituary that sums up the life of their loved one in as few words as possible because Theo Thunberger and his ilk charge the moon per word. We are going to help them navigate all of it so that, down the road, when they are further along in the many stages of their grief, they can look back and be thankful their loved one had the perfect send-off. At least, that's how I rationalize it all."

"Okay. I was close to those thoughts, but you, being the writer, have packaged it all up neatly."

"And I think we should talk to Jill about using the Mugshot Café as our caterer. If I hear Letty's discourse one more time about dry devilled eggs, my head is going to explode."

"Yes! Jill is a trained chef. She apprenticed under some bigwig but left his kitchen to start her own in Victoria, but when Joe wanted to retire, she moved back here. She might welcome the idea of stretching her culinary skills beyond staying true to Joe's standard menu of burgers and fries. Fabulous as they are."

"And what about Donny as our driver? Some older clients may need chauffeuring, and you and I will be busy. He's so charming, he's perfect."

"Donny? As in my brother Donny? As our driver? Really? He's only just gotten himself clear from his DUI, innumerable speeding tickets, and a stack of parking tickets. I don't recall ever going around a corner with him when all four wheels were actually in contact with the road."

"Everyone needs a second chance. Maybe Donny just needs to feel appreciated? And, we'll be sure to give him lots of time, so he doesn't feel the need to speed. Besides, who else is there? You said he was underemployed these days, right?"

"I love my brother, but he is flypaper for crazy. And hanging out with the Timber Dogs hasn't exactly tuned him up. Jill's dad still rides with them. I think he's the oldest member. And he's a full patch."

"Is he? Wow. I bet Jim Brownlee spent his whole career trying to bust him."

"He did and retired a bitter man. I think Jill's boyfriend also rides with them. Are you sure you want to tap into that?"

"Yup. If Jill is interested in being our caterer and is happy with our terms, that's all that matters. Her private life is private." Smiling, Aislin held the menu beside her face. "Just imagine Jim's reaction when he attends a service and sees 'Catering by the Mugshot Café'? He will implode."

"And, if we make enemies, we'll have protection."

"Exactly! How about you talk to Jill and I drive out to see Otto? Or did you want to come with me to chat with him?"

"Nope, I'm good. I'll have a quick chat with Jill, outline our business, and see if she's interested, then it's time to get Fitz home for lunch. Text me when you're back from Otto's."

Driving out to The Maples, Aislin tried to keep her focus on the beauty of the spring light filtering through the trees. Memories of the last time she had taken this drive threatened to override her resolve. She wasn't sure how much longer she could keep her delayed grief at bay. Talking to Letty was not an option, and as dialled in as Sarah was to her relationship with Frank, she didn't want to talk to her about it. Years had passed since she was last in a church, so talking to Father Sutherland was not a comfortable option either.

Aislin's commitment to the Goodbye Girls ebbed and flowed. She frequently asked herself if it was fair to Sarah to surge ahead with a partner who was on such shaky emotional ground. She pulled over before entering the grounds, rolled down the windows, and inhaled deeply. The scent of newly mown spring grass mingled with the smell of the ocean slowed her heart rate. She had not made an appointment, so she could sit there and breathe as long as needed.

She drove a bit farther. When she saw the parking lot, she stopped again. She had hoped it would be full, but no such luck. She checked for messages. No urgent call from Letty. Nothing from Sarah. After a few moments of cursing about her cavalier offer to drive out and talk to Otto, she put the car in gear and slowly entered the expansive gardens. The beds, which glowed with daffodils and cheery primula, worsened her descending dark mood. It was incongruous and wrong to have such bright floral displays in a setting that processed death.

She heard her name the moment she stepped away from her car and saw Otto emerging from behind a large, manicured shrub. Almost as though he had been watching her inch her way into the grounds.

"Aislin Fitzgerald! I've been expecting you."

"You were? Really? Sorry, I should have made an appointment. I can always come another time if you're busy," she said as she backed towards her car.

"Not busy at all. It's great to see you. Come in. I'll make some tea. We can sit in the observatory. This way," he said, ushering her along a winding gravel path. "How are you? I see Letty here and there but have never had an opportunity to speak with her. I was a bit concerned the last time I saw her, as she had lost weight. Is she well? And how are you? I've often thought of you and wondered how you were after losing Frank. I know you were tremendously close to him. He loved you so deeply."

Otto's words about her and her grandfather threw Aislin off her keel. She batted down a defensive retort and instead focused on his concern about Letty. "Letty's fine. I've moved back home so I can keep an eye on her. And yes, she had lost weight, but I think she's regaining some already." Otto's melodic voice was soothing. She paused, pushing her hands through her hair. "It's strange, you know, being here. The only time I've ever been here was for Granddad's burial. I've never come back. To visit his headstone." She shrugged and looked away. "I absolutely miss him every single day of my life."

"Frank was my best friend. And we worked closely together for decades over the obituaries. I absolutely miss him every single day, too."

Aislin did not see the torrent coming. She put her head in her hands and let the sobs pour forth. Otto discreetly slipped a box of tissues onto her lap.

"I'm so sorry. I'm so embarrassed. I didn't come here to sit and bawl like a baby. It's just when you said you missed him. And that you were worried about Letty. I've been such a selfish brat. I hurt them both, and then I abandoned Letty when she needed me most. Who does that? They devoted their lives to me, and what did I do? I ran away. I barely came home long enough for his funeral. I couldn't deal with Letty's grief. I didn't know how to fix it. So I ran like a coward back to a life I thought was more important, but it's gone now, too. I've lost my job, my friends, my whole career."

Otto waited until her sobs subsided. "It sounds as though you, my dear, are experiencing layers of grief compounded by layers of guilt. If you don't mind me saying, Aislin, you have been suffering from grief your whole life. And you have excelled at not acknowledging the complexity of your grief."

She looked up at him—relief written across her face. "You're right. I have," she replied, sniffing deeply and wiping her nose. "I grew up grieving ghosts and living with the grief of others for those ghosts. Moving away just masked it. But whenever I came for a visit, I was overwhelmed. I dreaded coming back. So I stayed away and worked as much as I could. But now I see I was just trying to stop myself from falling into the abyss of grief that always felt like it was just on the other side of sanity." She paused to pull a handful of tissues and wipe her eyes and nose. "I'm so sorry, Otto. I just barged in, blathered on about what a mess I've made of things, and used up almost an entire box of tissues."

"I know why you think you came here. Life doesn't always go according to plan. This I know for sure."

Struggling to regain composure and change the subject, after mopping her face with a wad of tissues, she asked, "How are you? I'm so sorry. I should have asked that before I had my meltdown."

Otto sat back in his worn leather chair and steepled his hands. "Actually, I'm scared. I know I'm not as sharp as I once was. And I'm tired. And I'm fed up." He paused, looking closely at her. "You've spent your whole life grieving ghosts. I've spent my entire life helping others process their grief. I never wanted this job. I've never been comfortable with the degree of emotional dependency I have to carry every day. I've never been comfortable charging what I do for a funeral. I was forced into taking over the family business and their debt.

"Do you know what I really wanted to do with my life? I wanted to be a stand-up comedian. I wanted to make people laugh. I wanted to do open mic nights. Whenever there's an open mic in Victoria, I go and sit in the back, wishing it was me on the stage. I wanted to travel and tell jokes." He stood up and threw open his arms. "And look how I've spent my life—spewing unctuous platitudes, trying to find new words of consolation. All the while planning to channel them through the showroom of overpriced caskets and urns. Do you think I enjoy doing that?"

Aislin did not even try to mask her shock. Some people just *are* their job, and Otto Lawless was one of those people. She sat perfectly still, barely able to breathe as she listened. She was in emotional overdrive and could feel herself dancing dangerously close to the edge of hysterical laughter.

"I could go for years on the circuit with all the death jokes I have amassed. Sometimes, situations are so bloody funny I have to leave the room on the pretence of needing a brochure. I purposely don't keep all the pamphlets in each bereavement room so that if I have the urgent need to step out and laugh until my stomach hurts, I have an excuse. Sometimes I have tears in my eyes when I go back to the family. They assume I'm crying with them. I feel like a real shit."

Reading her face, he stopped his rant. "I sound crazy, I know. I am just so fed up pretending to be something I'm not. The only other person who knew how I felt was Frank. I would drive into town some evenings, and the two of us used to sit in his office, drink Scotch, and tell each other jokes. He had that rich gallows humour journalists often have. God, I miss him."

Typically, if friends mentioned Frank, she was quick to redirect the conversation. She was territorial about her memories of him and did not want to hear anyone else's. But listening to Otto reminisce, and hearing the deep affection he held for Frank, was healing. She was enthralled with his stories and at ease in his company. She felt as though she had known him her whole life.

When he paused, caught by a moment of reflection, Aislin gently turned the conversation to the reason for her visit, and they discussed the goals of the Goodbye Girls until Otto finally stood up to stretch.

"I can't sit for long these days—not good for my circulation, according to my doctor."

"Oh my gosh, I am so sorry, I've stayed far too long," said Aislin, getting up. "I lost track of time." She didn't know how to leave this man who had listened to her cry out her grief, who understood her emotional state, and who had shared his own angst about his life. It was an instant, almost intimate friendship. She awkwardly offered her hand, which he took in both of his.

"Thank you for this visit, Aislin. I have enjoyed sharing my memories of Frank. He would be so proud of you. And please say hello to Letty for me. She too has a special place in my heart."

. . .

When Aislin got home, Letty was in the garden. Keyed up and unable to settle to any one thing, she wandered around the house, straightening pictures and book spines. She sometimes wished she smoked, just to have something to do with her hands. She took a hot shower, pulled on her favourite saggy sweats, and went downstairs to start dinner.

When she entered the kitchen, a sudden and systemic sense of calm and truly being at home overcame her. She had crossed a bridge—the Golden Gate of emotional bridges.

Letty came in and paused. She looked sharply at Aislin.

"Dressed for dinner, I see."

Aislin gave her a big hug, which Letty resisted at first but relaxed into briefly.

"What's going on with you? You look different," Letty demanded as she pulled away and busied herself taking off her sweater and washing her hands and some stalks of fresh parsley. She gently tapped Secretariat's tank and dropped in the greens. "Here you go, little fella," she cooed.

She turned to Aislin. "What have you been up to? You've been gone all day. Elaine heard you were visiting Otto. How did that go?"

Aislin busied herself assembling what she needed to make dinner. She tried not to slam drawers and cupboards, but the fridge did shudder when she shoved the door closed with her hip. Her newly found calm was rapidly dissipating.

"Why are you in a mood?"

"I am not in a mood. I'm just hungry and need to get supper going."

"Did you forget to have lunch? You really should eat more regularly. I don't know how people in your generation do it. You're always rushing around and just snacking. Terrible habit. We always had proper meals, even when you had soccer practices at inconvenient times."

Aislin poured wine for them both, opened a new bag of chips, and turned on the radio. Letty raised her voice.

"I haven't seen Fitz for a few days. Maybe Sarah could drop him off while you two are busy. We could sow some parsley and spinach. You know, for Secretariat. I don't think his grandparents are gardeners."

Aislin turned off the radio. "Yes, Gran, that's a good idea. Fitz would probably love to grow food for his buddy here."

"You haven't said what you were meeting Otto about."

"I'll tell you over dinner. Right now, I just want to concentrate on what I'm doing."

Letty took the hint and sat with her gardening diary, making notes, sipping her wine, and munching chips. Aislin stole a look at her. Letty's cheeks were filling out, and her thick hair looked lustrous again.

She was also neater in her habits. Aislin was unsure if Letty was simply more tuned in and making an effort now that someone else was in the house, or if Aislin's own habitual tidying up was rubbing off on her.

Letty's garden had always been immaculate and continued to be so, but that drive for order stopped at the door. Aislin couldn't remember if Letty had always left a wake of mess behind her, which would indicate that Frank had taken on the role of straightening up.

"Okay, the chops are ready. I just need to put together the salad, and we can eat. I really am starving."

Letty, uncharacteristically, did not pepper her with questions but let her eat in peace.

"So, yes, I did go visit Otto today. And we had a fascinating conversation. Beyond fascinating, actually. A bit mind-blowing. He asked after you. He said he was concerned, as he noticed you had lost weight."

"He did?" Letty ran a hand through her hair, looking down.

"What?"

"What do you mean?"

"I don't know. Just asking. He did seem quite concerned. And he told me to be sure and say hello to you. He said he wishes he had a chance to speak with you, but he's always busy officiating when he sees you."

"Otto has been a good friend for a very long time." Letty looked out at the garden and then added, "We dated before I met Frank. And then he and Frank became best friends through work. Ancient history."

"Not to me! How come I didn't know this?"

Letty set her mouth, raised her eyebrows, and stared hard at Aislin.

Aislin blushed and lowered her eyes. After a few moments, she answered her own question. "Because I never asked. I don't know anything about you or your life before you married. I'm so sorry, Gran."

"Well, you always were self-absorbed. But I think that's pretty common for your generation. Let's talk about something else."

"But now I want to know who you were before you were married."

"And I don't want to talk about it."

"You can't drop that in my lap and then say you don't want to talk about it. That's not fair. Did you know he never wanted to be a funeral director?"

"I did. He was forced to take over the family business. The poor man has been trapped his entire life. It was the same with Bonnie."

"What do you mean it was the same with her?"

Letty was warming up. "He didn't want to marry her. But she desperately wanted to marry him. She got pregnant—bit of a scandal back then, not like today. But the pregnancy didn't go full term. And her family had money. And he needed money because his father gambled heavily. Bonnie was never the right person for him. She had no sense of humour and patronized him. Theirs was the oldest funeral home between Victoria and Nanaimo. His dad was old school. She wanted to modernize the business and the services. She pushed and pushed him to expand and take on more work than was healthy. She was avaricious. Bourgeois. Common. I never liked her." Letty registered the shock on Aislin's face. "I know that sounds harsh, and I know I shouldn't speak ill of the dead."

"No worries. In my book, if she wasn't nice to Otto, then she doesn't deserve kind words." Aislin sat back in her chair, balancing it onto its back legs. "Wow, Gran, that's quite the download. And this whole time, Otto has been pining for you but hasn't said anything. This is such a classic love story!"

"Stop your nonsense, and sit properly in your chair. You haven't said why you went to see him."

"I don't think it's nonsense. There was a vibe. But I didn't realize what the vibe was until now. He seemed so comfortable telling me all about his thwarted dreams. And I was so weirdly comfortable talking to him, even though I don't remember meeting him before. He knew who I was as soon as I got out of my car. It creeped me out a bit. I guess he's kept tabs on both of us. What am I saying! In this town, that's normal."

As soon as Sarah settled in their booth the following day, Aislin asked her what she knew about Otto. Sarah didn't know much, so she texted Donny, who had worked as a gardener at The Maples for a few years.

He responded right away with some remarkably insightful observations about Otto's private life.

"Wow, way to go, Donny. Who knew he paid attention to anything that didn't have a motor?" Sarah shrugged and summarized his reply. "Donny likes him. Otto and Bonnie weren't a happy couple." Sarah looked up from her phone. "For him to notice, it had to be bad." She went back to reading aloud, "Bonnie ran everything from behind the scenes. Otto was her puppet. Otto always seemed sad. They never had kids, and Donny thinks that was why. Otto took an interest in Donny's adventures with cars and tried to help him develop some goals. Otto's dad lived with them until he died, which made things tense in the marriage. The old man was a bit of a rogue, and more than one assistant quit because of him. At one point, the dad was in a seniors' home but got kicked out, probably because he was a dirty old man. So, Otto and Bonnie had to take him in. That's about all. Why the interest in Otto's background?"

"Just curious. It turns out he was a good friend of Frank's. They used to get together at night in Frank's office, tell jokes, and drink Scotch."

"Seriously? I did not see Otto as a laugh-a-minute sort of guy. Given that he deals with grief all the time and has done his whole life."

"He's quite a sweet person," Aislin said as she gently stirred her coffee. "And he had heard about us, liked what we're doing, and offered to help us out—you know, if there's a family that can't afford a full funeral or want a celebration of life that isn't a fit for The Maples. I think he's getting ready to retire. He joked that we should buy him out. He knows Theo is trying to undercut him and isn't a fan of the guy or his uncle." She paused and looked out the window. "I am so glad I went out there. I enjoyed talking to him." Her voice trailed off. She looked up as she felt tears pinging sharply.

"You okay? What aren't you telling me?"

"He told some great stories about Frank and talked about how much he missed him." Aislin didn't want it rolled under the magnifying glass of Sarah's insatiable curiosity. She felt protective of Letty's confession.

"How did your conversation with Jill go? Is she interested in working with us?"

"Is this you changing the subject?"

"Nope, just nothing left to say about Otto."

Sarah scrutinized her friend's face but didn't push. "Yes, Jill was ecstatic about the idea. Has been looking for an opportunity to branch out with a catering business. She's so excited she started spewing forth menu ideas. She suggested we speak with one of the local wineries. We need to go on some wine tasting tours."

"That's a great idea about the wineries. We should plan to use local resources as much as possible, which would benefit us in garnering community support. Everyone we've talked to has been surprisingly encouraging. Have we covered everything on our to-do lists now? What are we missing?"

"A body?"

Chapter 8

Letty's seventy-fifth birthday was galloping down the calendar. Aislin had not been home to celebrate with her since she moved to Toronto for university. A card and a quick phone call were the only markers. One year she emailed Letty rather than sending a card but almost instantly regretted it, as it opened the door for regular communication.

She was devoid of ideas on how to celebrate her gran's birthday this year. She tried subtly asking how past birthdays had been celebrated but was delivered a withering look, which she knew was well deserved. Elaine would know, but Aislin could not stomach the idea of asking her for help.

Instead, she texted her one-stop source of information. Hey, I need to pick your brain about how to celebrate Letty's upcoming birthday.

Sarah instantly replied, Meeting at 10, in the office. The rapidity of Sarah's responses sometimes caused Aislin to wonder if she hovered over her phone, waiting for a message. She had mentioned that the transition from working to having a baby had been tough, the worst part being the empty inbox. Her solution was to sign up for a wide variety of newsletters unrelated to the sounds and smells of babies so that she could hear the satisfying ping of incoming mail. Aislin, on the other hand, relished her empty inbox.

When Aislin walked into the Mugshot Café, Sarah was leaning over the counter talking to Jill, who was busy chopping lettuce. Fitz, as usual, was absorbed helping fill napkin holders and salt and pepper shakers. Aislin felt tears trying to push their way out. The uptick in these emotional responses infuriated her. Not her style and leagues apart from her self-image as a hard-nosed reporter.

"So, we're working on some ideas for a catered open house for Letty's birthday. Do you think she would prefer to have it at her house or the community hall? We're hoping you say her house, but no pressure."

"Why don't we have it at her house?"

"What a brilliant idea. Do you think any of us would survive surprising her, or should we be more health-conscious—ours and hers—and you talk to her about the party?"

"In the interests of our collective, long-term existence, let's go for plan B. I'll chat with her when the time is right. Her birthday's in ten days. Does that give you enough time, Jill, to plan and prep? And do we need to hire servers, or can we employ the hardworking Fitz as our server?"

"As long as you don't stick him behind the bar and expect him to mix drinks, I am sure our Fitz would be just fine," said Jill. "He's been apprenticing here since you moved back to town."

"If Letty has any qualms, I think Fitz being there as the server will be the salve we need. She would be so thrilled to introduce him to her cronies as 'Fitz' and watch their reaction," said Aislin.

"And, yes, ten days is plenty of time for me. I'll email you some suggestions and prices. I'm going to waive my fee for this, by the way. Letty and Frank were always good customers, and it's an honour to be part of her birthday. Anyway, I've got to get back to work. I'll be in touch."

"I think we're looking at our first collaboration. But not as the Goodbye Girls. That would be in bad taste."

"So, who should we invite? Otto?"

Aislin squirmed. "Why Otto?"

"Because of your reaction to your visit and because he was such a good friend of Frank's? I don't think many people invite him to events where all the guests are alive. When you think about it, funeral directors must lead socially flat lives. I mean, who wants the purveyor of death at a party? Buzzkill."

Aislin thought back to their conversation. He did seem lonely and sad. "Okay. Otto's in."

"Can we ask him to be the emcee? He could fulfil his dream of becoming a stand-up comedian. I'm sure he has some good stories tucked away about Letty."

"I don't know. It's a lot to ask."

"You won't know until you do. Given the demographics of the crowd we're dealing with, we're going to have to go the old-fashioned route and call them. Which means *you* are going to have to dig around and find Letty's address book."

They tossed some names back and forth. A disturbing number of family friends had died. Sarah, as usual, knew who was alive, who had relocated to a retirement home, and who was too ill to attend.

"How do you know all this?"

"One of my many unappreciated skills. Behind this stunningly beautiful face is a database of information that would make the great Google weep with envy. My brain can retain the most innocuous pieces of gossip and create a web of hyperlinks between tidbits. I always choose the longest line when I'm shopping so I can mentally inhale all the whispered bits around me. It's a dedication to craft not many have. You're fortunate to have me as your partner, Partner."

"Remind me never to go shopping with you."

A surge of happiness filled Aislin. She marvelled at how right everything felt these days. Since her inglorious, serendipitous meeting with Sarah in the park just a few short weeks ago, her life's trajectory was heading to exciting, unknown galaxies. She grinned at Sarah, who was flipping through her phone and making notes beside each name on their list. Sarah looked up just as a cloud passed over Aislin's face.

"What?"

"Nothing," Aislin replied, fidgeting with her notebook, aligning it precisely between the edge of the table and the paper-napkin dispenser, and eyeing the salt and pepper shakers.

"You are not allowed to drift off into Anxiety Aislin without an explanation. What's going on in your head?"

"It's just, everything seems so eerily easy. I feel as though I'm being set up."

"You are not being set up. It's called being happy. It's a strange, remote emotion for those of us whose minds troll for the crap sand-wiches of life. Just don't go there. Relish the feeling. And for God's sake, stop your obsessive need for things to line up. Things sometimes don't line up. Life is messy; you know that. I know that. But we've got this super great opportunity to work together and build a business. It's not going to go smoothly. We're going to make mistakes. We're going to screw up. But we're also going to do some things very well. And the things that go very well, no doubt, will be done by Jill. You and I, we're a couple of question marks. That's just who we are. Accept it. Jill knows it, and she still wants to collaborate with us. Be grateful for the generosity of that woman's heart. And the fact that she has an entire motorcycle gang ready to rally to her defence doesn't hurt. I like to think of her connections there as our insurance. As long as it's not us they're rallying against, we're good."

"I hate it when you go all analytical on me. Fine. I hereby acknowl-edge that the universe does not have a master plan for my humiliation. And does not have any imminent plans to harsh my mellow."

"Good. Make that your mantra and recite it at least daily. I think we're done here. We have our marching orders. Mine is to tune up Fitz now that he has a real job. He's been spending a bit too much time with my brothers, so I need to talk to him about appropriate language. He swore a streak yesterday when he stubbed his toe, and Pops nearly passed to the other side."

"I was always enthralled when Donny swore. He was so creative, invoking random saints, the queen, his latest ex-girlfriend, her father, feminism, chastity, whichever car he was working on, past teachers, and sometimes the weather. And somehow, it all came out sounding coher-ent instead of manic. At least Fitz is learning from a master."

Letty put up a brief mock show of dismay about the party but quickly dropped the facade and began listing who she did not want to be in-vited. And then called Elaine and pretended to be annoyed.

Aislin did not need to fake her annoyance when Elaine asked to speak with her. Their conversation was a one-sided delivery of the guest list, when to hold it, and what to serve. Aislin thanked her for her input and assured her it was all under control, but Elaine was a force to be reckoned with.

"You know, Aislin, your grandmother has been on her own for five years now. With no one except me. She had to handle Frank's affairs, so Ed and I stepped in and provided all the support she needed because there wasn't anyone else. She and I have been best friends since high school."

"Yes, Elaine, I am well aware of how close you and Gran are. And how much you have done for her. But I am here now, so I can take some of that responsibility off your hands. You don't have to organize this party. We've got this."

"Who's we? That Quinn girl you've been running with? She's a bit unstable. Her whole family is. I don't think she's an appropriate partner for you. I never approved of her influence on you when you were kids. She had Frank wrapped around her little finger. That one's always got an agenda, mark my words."

"Thanks for sharing. Bye."

Aislin slammed the phone down and stormed into the kitchen. Letty, who had been listening, tried to scuttle out the back door when Aislin came in.

"Gran, I don't know how you've managed to be friends with that controlling, passive-aggressive, judgmental old bag." Aislin stopped, wishing she had Donny's ability to swear with colour and cohesion. "She never misses an opportunity to remind me of my failings as a granddaughter and exalt her superiority. She drives me nuts. Always has. Cold fish of a bitch. And how dare she criticize me when her own son bolted as soon as he could? Where is Tom, anyway? Don't see him fluttering around good old Mum."

Letty turned around, her cheeks pink with anger. "You can stop right now. Elaine has always been there for me. And I mean always, not just when it suited her. And not from guilt or duty. Whereas you, young lady, have not!"

Aislin blew out the front door, rattling the windowpanes in their frames. She didn't have her car keys or phone but was loath to go back in. Nor did she have her sunglasses or hoodie. She felt exposed. And observed. The curtains across the street were still settling as she passed.

She set a hair-straight-back pace, replaying her conversation with Letty, regretting her overshare about Elaine. She had always known that Elaine was untouchable. Aislin's "relationship" with Elaine was based on mutual competition for Letty's affection, as ridiculous as that was.

As her fury came off the boil, she started to take in the houses and gardens. The midafternoon light threw soft shadows through the grand old maples that lined the quiet streets. The houses were modest, with good bones. They looked lived in and loved, not tarted up and on show.

A few people were tending their front gardens or washing their cars. No one seemed to recognize her. Her jaw and fists unclenched. She even returned waves.

"Hey, Moe, you allowed out without Curly?"

Aislin stopped and stared. Nothing of what she was looking at fit together. Standing in front of her, soapy mitt in hand, was Nick. And in front of him was a hearse, covered in suds. Her mind struggled sluggishly to process the scene.

"I thought you were a vet."

Nick stood back and looked from the hearse to Aislin. "I do funerals for pets. It's a side hustle. My colleague in town does taxidermy. We collaborate."

"Really?"

"No! Just messing with you. Good to know you're still as gullible as ever."

"Very funny. So, why are you washing Otto's hearse?"

"I'm just finishing up and was about to sit down with a beer and admire my hard work. Truth be known, it's more like I need to wait for it to dry so I can see where I've missed. I'm not very thorough at washing cars. Want to join me?"

Aislin shrugged. "Sure."

Nick handed her the hose. "Spray it off while I grab the beer."

She did as she was told. While she was spraying, she looked around at the houses. She had no idea she had walked so far from Letty's or which streets she had taken. She wondered if Nick and Kate lived here, in his old home with Mrs. de Vries. She shuddered at the thought and wondered if Kate was going to join them and shuddered at that thought as well. That would be too much to bear in one day.

When Nick returned with two beers, he turned off the hose and invited her into the backyard. He brushed the yellow pollen off the garden furniture.

"I love the maples. First, they flower, then they release pollen, which triggers my allergies, then they drop their flowers, drop those sticky leaf cap things, rain down sap on everything, the sap attracts aphids, then they wrap it up by dropping hundreds of pounds of plate-sized leaves. Nonstop fun."

"Interesting. I didn't even know maple trees flowered." Her need to know was simmering, but she wasn't comfortable pushing. She was no longer a reporter.

"Okay, in answer to your question, I help Otto out now and again when he needs a driver. If he has to do a pickup at night, he calls me because I'm used to being called out at night. He's getting on, and his eyesight isn't great. I've driven with him, and it's a bit scary. His passengers have no more worries; it's those of us still on this side I worry about. He's a good guy. Not sure if you know this, but he's damn funny, and we have a lot of laughs together. And he was exceptionally close to Frank, which makes him an exceptional individual in my eyes, right there."

Aislin stared at him. Her worlds were colliding and sucking up all her oxygen. She had to concentrate on breathing.

Nick ventured further. "I get the impression he's always been soft on Letty. Elaine told Mum they used to date before Letty met Frank."

Aislin flashed up her hand. "Nope, not talking about that woman. She's the reason I am out here stumbling around like a zombie. She's a meddling, nasty, gossipy witch of a woman."

"Yup, she is all of that. But, in her defence, she does provide a service, you know. Her incessant churn of gossip keeps everyone tuned in and engaged. If it weren't for her, so many of our seniors would simply exist, isolated in their shells, with only their cats for company."

"Maybe that's true, but for me, she's grit under my contact lens."

Nick finished his beer and checked the time. "Look, I've got to finish the car, gas it up, and return it to Otto out at The Maples. Why don't you come with me? My car is at his place, so you'll have the displeasure of riding back in my old clunker."

She and Sarah used to ride around town with Sarah's brothers. Joyriding in a hearse seemed so wrong. "Are you picking up any bodies on the way?"

"And if I were? Come on. Live a little."

"Live a little? Funny choice of words coming from someone who drives around with dead bodies in the middle of the night. And what do you do if you have a call from Otto and a pet emergency at the same time? The two demands are mutually exclusive. Do you sort of adapt as you go? After all, if you have a dead body, it's not going to mind if you swing by and pick up an injured dog. Not the best impression on the pet owners if you turn up in a hearse. Kinda sends the wrong message?"

"You do dance on the dark side, don't you? I have yet to experience that conflict of requests, but now that you've mentioned it, no doubt one is on my horizon."

As Nick put away the hose and bucket, Aislin gingerly leaned in to look inside the hearse.

Nick crept up behind her. "Get in!"

She yelped, jumped, and cracked her head on the door frame. "Ouch! Not nice."

Nick laughed. "You are so not ready for your new career." He gave her a quick tour of the hearse's workings, offering her the opportunity to operate the levers and buttons. She declined and kept her hands in her pockets.

"I don't think funeral planners have anything to do with dead bodies," she said, slipping into the passenger seat.

"Sure, let's go with that." Nick selected a playlist and rolled all the windows down. "Let me know if you're cold."

His choice of music gave her the giggles. "You drive around in a hearse listening to Death Cab for Cutie? That's so weird."

He grinned at her, shrugged, and turned up the volume, tapping his fingers on the steering wheel to the music. She took the hint, stuck her arm out the window, and let her hand ride the wind. Aislin slid her eyes sideways to look at his profile. Laugh lines rippled at the edge of his eyes, but there was an aura of sadness about him, which wasn't a fit with his offhand, jokester presentation.

Otto raised his eyebrows when Aislin stepped out of the car.

"Aislin, I've only seen you once in many decades and then twice this week. You've brightened my day."

"Nice to see you too, Otto. I was going to call to invite you to a birthday party for Letty. It's on the fourteenth. I know that's short notice."

"Let me check my calendar and get back to you. I would be delighted to come. Hopefully, no one kicks the bucket suddenly and buggers things up."

"I'll put you down as a definite maybe. No gifts, please. Enjoy a glass of wine or two or some Scotch. Maybe Nick here could be your designated driver?"

"That does sound inviting. But I'll take a cab. I lean on Nick so much already. Don't want to burn the boy out." Otto paused and then asked Nick, "So, how is it you're out joyriding together? Is Kate still away on tour?"

"Yes. Anyway, I need to get back to town now. The hearse is gassed up and ready to go. I did a better job washing it this time, I think. I'm going for stripes instead of spots." They all looked at the hearse, most of it gleaming in the sun.

"Interesting that someone can get through veterinary school, do lengthy, specialized surgery, yet can't focus long enough to wash a car thoroughly," commented Otto. "I wouldn't say you were getting better; you're just more aware of your failings. A friendly piece of advice: don't quit your day job."

Aislin was just able to give a hasty wave to Otto before Nick drove off. She tried to ask about Kate's tour, but he was not forthcoming, so they rode back to Letty's in awkward silence. Aislin's shoelace hooked on a lever beneath the seat as she rushed to get out. She landed on her bum on the sidewalk. Nick leaned over and unhooked her shoelace. She pulled herself up, her face McIntosh apple red.

"That was elegant. You okay?"

"See you."

The house was dark and silent. Letty wasn't in the kitchen or the garden. There was no sign or scent of her having made a meal. It seemed an eternity since Aislin had stormed out of the house. Echoes of her argument with Letty reverberated around her head. Also banging around in her head was Nick's flip from friendly to frozen. She hadn't eaten since breakfast. She looked in the fridge, but nothing sang to her. She found some crackers and cheese, poured some wine, put it all on a tray, and took it outside. Once her blood sugar crept back up to its normal setting, she felt more capable of processing the day's unexpected highs and lows. She put Nick on the back burner. Her immediate problem was Letty and how to recover, with grace, from their fight.

Aislin could hear the shower running in the bathroom. She sighed, undecided if she should go upstairs and dig into it tonight or just let it lie fallow until the morning. She didn't have the energy or enthusiasm for another go-around just yet. She also didn't have the energy to find her phone. She poured herself another glass of wine and moved to one of the chaise lounges but stopped before settling down. Yellow pollen covered the fabric. She didn't want to think about Nick, but the sight of the pollen shot him to the forefront of her mind. She dusted off the fabric and was just settling down when Letty came out in her dressing gown.

"Your phone is in the bathroom and has been making a racket all afternoon. It's not like you to leave it behind. Where have you been?"

Aislin resisted snapping back that surely Elaine had reported on her whereabouts. "I went for a walk, bumped into Nick de Vries, who was oddly washing one of Otto's hearses, and took him up on his invitation to go with him to return the car." As Aislin was speaking, she realized how it sounded. "I've known Nick for most of my life, so it was good to catch up with him," she added lamely. "And to see Otto again."

Letty looked out into the garden. "We raised you right. I don't think you need me to point out how inappropriate it is to ride around with a married man—however ancient your friendship. But I will say that I do not condone that sort of behaviour. Not while you are under my roof."

Aislin knew it was coming, but it stung nonetheless. "Gran, I'm going to bed. Good night."

Chapter 9

She was not eager to find out why or who was lighting up her phone, but she was also too rankled to sleep. A year's worth of texts from Sarah filled the screen. The last one was CALL ME!

Sarah answered on the first ring. "Where have you been? I've been trying to reach you for ages. I've been going insane waiting. Have you heard from Jill?"

"I have no idea what's got you lit up. Yes, Jill sent a text, but I haven't read it yet. Yours sort of took over my entire phone. I was gone for like two hours. What the what?"

Sarah inhaled and exhaled all in a rush: "A full-patch member of the Timber Dogs died. Not sure at this point if it was a hit or an accident. But they want a celebration of life for him, and they want us to arrange it! And some guy called 10-Gauge will be in touch. I'm seriously weirded out."

"You're kidding, right? We can't do that! We don't know what the hell we're doing. We've never done this before. We can't start with a biker funeral. If we mess up, we're wearing cement shoes, and crabs are cleaning our bones. No. Not happening."

"Opting out is not an option. Our caterer has already agreed."

"What? She can't do that. No, there's no way one of us can agree to something without discussing it with the other two. A biker funeral? Us? Look, if the guy died in a biker war, we're all vulnerable. There are

legions of examples of collateral damage due to biker wars. I am seriously freaking out now."

"I need you not to freak out because if you freak out, I am going
to lose my bloody mind. And I can't lose my mind because I have a
dependent life form. I also can't lose my life for the same reason. Okay,
we need to calm down and think rationally. We've got Jill, and she's
going to keep us alive because she's our partner, and she lives with one
of them. Why was that not a red flag?"

"And we've got Donny. He's their go-to mechanic. And he's your
brother and uncle to Fitz. Blood is thicker than water, right?"

"Have you ever heard the full quote? The actual saying is 'The
blood of the covenant is thicker than the water of the womb.'"

"Wow, I did not know that. That actually sounds like a biker creed.
We need to meet and talk this through. But not at the Mugshot. I'm too
angry to talk to Jill. Let's meet here so Fitz can play with Secretariat.
And seeing him might reset Letty's mood. Could you come early?"

"Oh no, not another rumble between you two. See you at nine."

Aislin vibrated with nervous energy. She took a hot shower, but
there was no calming down. Sleep came in snatches that ended in
full-body spasmodic twitches. Intermittently, hysterical laughter engulfed her. It was a relief to hear the obnoxiously insistent robins. She
squeezed into her running gear and jammed on a hat. It had been a
month since she'd last laced up. She crept downstairs, careful to avoid
the creaky treads, and slipped out. It was a hard re-introduction to
running, but it was good to feel her muscles waking up. And the air
was sweet and fresh.

When Aislin got back, Letty was up and making coffee. Riding
her endorphin high, she greeted Letty cheerfully and made small talk
about her run, her running schedule when she lived in Vancouver,
and all the positive differences between the two running experiences.
Letty replied monosyllabically. Breakfast was a quiet affair.

"Sarah and Fitz are coming over at nine. Fitz wants to see you and
Secretariat." Letty's face softened. "Also, apparently, we have our first
gig as funeral planners. This all materialized yesterday while I was
out." Aislin hoped Letty would not latch onto what had gone down
between them.

"Why do you have that tone?"

"Gran, it's not what we envisioned at all, and we're not sure we want to take it on. And we're a bit concerned that Jill accepted without discussing it with us."

The front door banged open. Fitz ran straight to Letty, hugged her, and then asked Aislin if he could take the turtle outside. Aislin moved the tank and a couple of chairs onto the back lawn. She had hoped to shower first and get out of her uncomfortably tight, now damp running gear. She pulled on Letty's shapeless gardening sweater and made more coffee as Sarah paced around the kitchen, restlessly opening cupboards and peering inside.

"I wonder if they make bulletproof vests for five-year-olds? Maybe we should put BYOBPV in the announcement?"

"What does that stand for?"

"Bring Your Own Bulletproof Vest."

"Not funny. So, how annoyed should we be with Jill? Or should we just let that go because we have bigger problems?"

"Let it go. Last night, I wanted to talk to Donny, but he was missing in action. I was hoping to find out who died and how, as I think that might be important." Sarah stopped her manic pacing and pointed out the window. "Who's the dude talking to Letty? Whatever he's offering, she's buying. Look at that smile!"

"I have no idea, but I'm going to find out. Strangers can't just walk into private backyards. It's not safe, especially when Fitz is here."

As Aislin and Sarah walked out onto the porch, Letty called to them, "Girls, this gentleman is looking for you." Letty turned to the man, rested her hand on his arm, and, beaming up at him, asked, "What was your name again?"

"Alphonso Albertini, but my friends call me 10-Gauge."

The man smiled at Aislin and Sarah, who were staring vacantly at him. He raised one thick black eyebrow and walked up the steps. He focused his attention on Sarah, offering her his hand. She looked at it, then up at him.

"You're 10-Gauge? But you have such straight white teeth."

Aislin and Letty stared at her; 10-Gauge shrugged and smiled. "My father is a dentist, and my brother is an orthodontist. Between the two of them, they keep me honest. About my dental care."

Fitz ran up to him and grabbed his hand. "Come with me, Mr.

10-Gauge; I want to show you my turtle. He's not actually my turtle, but Ms. Aislin lets me play with him whenever I come over. He's really smart but sometimes a little shy."

Aislin put out her hand. "Maybe later. Right now, could you please scrub out Secretariat's water bowl? You can use the hose over there. And then pick him some new shoots of kale and parsley. And be sure to wash them before you feed him." She looked to Sarah for confirmation, but Sarah was not listening. Nor was Letty.

"Mr. Albertini, why are you here, and who gave you the right to enter our property? Uninvited," Aislin said.

"Call me 10-Gauge, please." He ran his eye over Aislin, taking in her leggings and Letty's sweater. "You weren't at the Mugshot, so Jill suggested we look for you here."

"Who is 'we'?"

"Myself and my associates. They're more polite, so they're waiting out front."

"I'll invite them in for coffee," said Letty.

"No, you won't, Gran!"

"Aislin dear, don't be rude. We have always welcomed people into this house. And that's not going to change." Letty disappeared into the kitchen.

Aislin ran down the stairs, locked the garden gate, moved Secretariat's tank to a spot visible from the porch, and then indicated that their visitor should sit at the table.

"I'm going to check on Letty. Sarah, could you please keep an eye on your son?" Sarah looked blankly at her.

Through the front door, Aislin could see Letty chatting to four large men standing by four large motorcycles. Two were smiling. Two were not. Letty looked tiny, vulnerable, and animated. The neighbours were not even trying to hide their curiosity. Letty's phone was ringing in the kitchen.

Letty walked briskly up the path. "Yes, they would like coffee, but they will take it outside. Three with cream, one black. That must be Elaine calling. I'll call her back when our guests have left."

"Gran, can I speak with you upstairs, please. Now."

Aislin pulled Letty into her bedroom, shutting the door and window. "Gran, these men are here because one of their members died, and Jill agreed we would organize the funeral, and that is terrifying. You can't invite these guys into your house. They're a gang."

"You've spent too much time on the mainland. The Timber Dogs aren't the Hell's Angels. They're local and harmless. Some of them are business owners. Some are professionals. For heaven's sake, they do toy runs for poor kids and help out at the soup kitchen on holidays! They support local charities. And 10-Gauge is charming. Now, I've offered them coffee, so they are going to get coffee." Letty paused at the door. "Stop being so dramatic and suspicious."

Aislin shook her head. "Dramatic? You've just invited a bunch of bikers in for coffee. If that doesn't invite drama, I don't know what does."

Aislin ran into her room to change. Flipping through her office clothes, she pulled out her most severe suit jacket and favourite jeans, both of which felt a bit tight. She checked her bum in the mirror and then switched to a long sweater jacket. She ran back downstairs, made sure Fitz was still in sight, and assembled the coffee tray, trying not to slam the coffee mugs. Steeling herself to be pleasant and not show fear, she went out to greet the bikers, who were smiling and chatting with one of the neighbours about the bikes.

"Good morning. Here's your coffee. Mr. Whiteside, can I bring you a coffee?"

"No, that's fine, Aislin, but thanks. I was just telling these young men how I always wanted a Harley. I had dreams of cruising through my retirement with the wind in my face, but the missus wouldn't go for it. I heard these bad boys coming well before they arrived. Couldn't believe my luck. What a great way to start the day."

Aislin hustled back to the house, feeling like she had been teleported to a parallel universe. The image of first Letty and then Mr. Whiteside being chummy with a bunch of bull-necked, heavily tattooed, leather-clad men sitting on gleaming black bikes was a visual oxymoron. On the other side of the house, Letty, 10-Gauge, and Sarah were all leaning back in their chairs, laughing; Fitz was busy with Secretariat, the sun was shining, the birds were singing.

"Does anyone need a refill? Before we get down to business?" she asked, breaking the spell.

"If we must," said 10-Gauge. Aislin was acutely aware that the smile he gave her was not the same he lavished on Sarah. Letty sighed in disappointment.

"Do you mind if I call you Alphonso? I find your other name a bit of a struggle. Alphonso, the Goodbye Girls is newly minted. Last week, actually. We appreciate Jill's recommendation, but we don't feel we have the experience required to plan a funeral for one of your, um, friends."

"And I appreciate your honesty. But you have to start somewhere. And I can mentor you," he said, smiling at Sarah, who was fluffing her curls. Turning back to Aislin, he continued, "It's not that different from any other celebration of life. You know, speeches, food, and drink. Just with more security. Which we will arrange." He finished with a shrug.

"You lost us on 'more security.' This is out of our league." She stood up into the silence and began clearing the table. "Could I speak with you both in the kitchen? Mr. Fitz, come inside, please."

"But I'm busy."

"Now!" Aislin had never spoken to him like that. His eyes filled with tears. He grabbed the turtle and ran up the stairs to his mother. Aislin closed the door. "Sarah, yesterday, you were completely freaked out, and now you're okay with this? Just because some criminally charming guy smiles at you? Really?"

"I've changed my mind. Now that I've met him, 10-Gauge seems like a genuinely nice guy. What do you think, Letty?"

"I like him. He's charming. As I said earlier, Aislin, you tend to be dramatic and suspicious."

"Well, I think I am fully justified in being both when discussing the viability of us working for a biker gang! What sort of referrals do you think will come from this? Who would hire us for their mother or father's funeral? We have to think strategically and long term." The referral excuse was lame, and she knew it. At this point, she doubted their partnership would last an hour, let alone long enough to book future jobs.

Aislin shoved her hands into her hair as she paced around the kitchen table. "Do you know how bikers die? It's not from old age. Other bikers murder them. You've heard about people being 'caught in the crossfire' in biker wars. That's exactly what I'm trying to avoid. For our collective safety."

10-Gauge knocked on the door, then leaned in. "It was lovely to meet you all, but I've got to go now. Thank you very much for the coffee and the conversation. I look forward to hearing from you soon. We want to have Twiggy's celebration next week. We've taken out a permit for Picnic Park for the fourteenth."

"There you go. We can't take this on, as we have Letty's birthday party that day."

"My party isn't important; the date can be changed," said Letty. Aislin sighed.

Reaching out to shake his hand and smiling widely, Sarah said, "Thank you for considering us. I look forward to working with you. I mean, *we* look forward to working with you."

"I'll be in touch."

Aislin busied herself, bringing in coffee cups from the front and back porches. Sarah and Letty tried to help, but she batted them away. The house filled with the ascending roar of the bikes as they fired up.

"Mr. Fitz, could you please take Secretariat back outside? I'll be out in a moment to bring in his tank." When the door closed behind him, Aislin leaned against the counter. "What just happened?"

Sarah answered. "We have our first gig?" Then she flung her arms in the air. "What are the odds!"

Letty smiled at Sarah's attempt to lighten the mood. "Shall we celebrate? I don't know about you, but I feel like a little something. We must have some liqueurs somewhere. It's been quite an exciting morning."

"Gran! Really? Isn't it a bit early?" Aislin shook her head and sighed, knowing she was outnumbered. "I guess it's a done deal. We're in, but I am neither happy nor comfortable. For the record." She crossed her arms. "And, I suggest we all prepare our last wishes before we get going. And further to that thought, who will do our funerals if we all die in the crossfire?"

Letty poured liqueurs for each of them, which they drank in silence, Sarah and Letty grinning, Aislin frowning. Sarah started jigging around the kitchen. She grabbed Aislin and dragged her in. Then Letty joined. Sarah began bellowing the only lyrics she knew from "Twist and Shout." Soon, the women were belting out the same three lines of the Beatles tune. And then Elaine barged in.

"What is going on? I've been worried sick about you, Letty; I have left numerous messages. I heard a biker gang was here. And here you are all dancing and singing? And drinking? It's not even noon! Letty, you know you're supposed to avoid excitement. It's not good for your blood pressure."

And then Jim Brownlee barged in. "Anyone hurt?"

"What're you doing here?" Aislin asked.

"Heard the bikers paid you a visit."

"And where did you hear that?" Aislin asked, looking at Elaine.

"Jesse Whiteside called. She said five bikers roared up the street. Scared the hell out of her. She saw one guy sneak into your backyard. Vincent hustled out to stop the rest of them from pouring after the first guy."

"Oh, interesting. When I took some coffee out to them, I heard Vincent saying how he wished he had a bike, but Jesse wouldn't let him."

Letty interrupted. "That's ridiculous. We're fine. We had a very nice meeting with their leader, 10-Gauge. Charming young man. And so good looking."

"They were here for a meeting?" Elaine and Jim said in unison.

Aislin almost jumped in to tell them it was none of their business but decided to leave it to Letty. She sat down with the remainder of her liqueur.

"Aislin, Sarah, and I have formed a funeral-planning company, and it so happens that 10-Gauge and his friends have lost a member of their club and they would like us to arrange a celebration of life in Picnic Park next week. We were celebrating our first job."

"I don't even know where to begin. You can't do that," spat Jim. "Bikers are killers. You're going into business with a bunch of criminals. What would Frank think?"

Aislin held her breath. Letty narrowed her eyes. "Don't you dare bring Frank into this. And don't you dare presume to tell me what I can or cannot do. This is none of your business."

"But, Letty, dear, this sort of excitement and . . ." Elaine swept her eyes around the kitchen resting briefly on Sarah, "disorder is not good for you. You know that." Running her gaze over Aislin, she added, "You used to be so careful."

"I wasn't careful. I was bored. I had nothing to do but work in the garden. I couldn't even bother to eat. Living it up was going to funerals. I was just putting in time until I was the star of the show and could join Frank. And Larry and Cathy."

Aislin's spine stiffened at the mention of her parents. Sarah, Jim, and even Fitz were still as rocks.

"And here I thought I was doing you a favour by inviting you to go along with me. I thought you enjoyed getting out. I am extremely disappointed and hurt."

"Elaine, I don't mean to sound ungrateful. I appreciate all you and Ed have done for me since Frank died. But it's time for me to expand my horizons, as they say, while I can. I need to live again before I die."

"I just don't know what to say. I don't know what's gotten into you. You were never like this before *she* moved back home."

Jim butted in. "You call this living, Letty? You're going down a dangerous path if you do business with a biker gang. A bunch of loser criminals is what they are. You have no idea what you're getting into." He paused to find the right words and looked out the window. "What the hell is that kid doing with a turtle? I've told you, Aislin, that those things are dangerous. They're disease carriers. You need to get rid of it."

"Jim, that's quite enough. Stop your premonitions of doom. The turtle is fine. Fitz washes his hands diligently. Now, we have business to discuss. Thank you both for your concerns, but I'm fine. We are all fine," said Letty, nodding her head at Aislin and Sarah. "And Elaine, I feel invigorated with Aislin here and Sarah and Fitz coming and going. Getting to know Fitz is wonderful. He's a lovely little boy."

Letty ushered Jim and Elaine down the hall and out the door, both trying to get in the last word.

Sarah shook her head at Aislin. "Don't say anything. Just leave it to Letty. She's got this."

"That old biddy. She's always had it in for me. And for you. I was so close to telling her where to shove her passive-aggressive comments."

"No kidding. But what's cool is that Letty stood up to her and has decided to live life large. With us!"

When Letty returned, she busied herself putting the coffee mugs in the dishwasher. No one spoke. Fitz cautiously opened the door and asked if he could come in to use the bathroom. Sarah looked to Aislin for permission.

"Of course. But wash your hands before and after you use the toilet because if you don't, you might die."

Fitz looked horrified. "I always wash my hands."

"It's okay, Fitzie. Ms. Aislin was making a joke. Come on, let's get you to the bathroom." Sarah grinned and shook her head.

Letty sat at the table and poured more liqueur for them all.

"Anyone know how to plan a funeral?" asked Sarah, returning with Fitz.

"Not a clue," replied Aislin. Looking at Letty, she said, "Was hoping, with your vast experience in attending them, you would be our advisor."

"I've only been to funerals for people who died of natural causes. Nice people. Not murdered bikers."

"Really? You're suddenly aware that we have a problem here? Where was your concern when Mr. 10-Gauge was dripping charm all over you two? I still can't believe we're going to work with a guy called 10-Gauge!"

The kitchen door opened, and Otto peered in. "Hello. I knocked, but no one heard me, and the front door was open, so I let myself in."

Letty sat up straighter and ran a hand over her hair. "Otto, this is a surprise! But it's been a morning of surprises, so what's one more? How odd that you should be here right this moment, as we are discussing something you might be able to help with."

"It's not a coincidence. I did a pickup early this morning, and your names came up."

The three women leaned in. "What did you pick up?" asked Sarah.

Otto looked at each of them. They stared back. "Here's a hint: it wasn't a cold, but it was cold." No one spoke. "And I had an escort of bikers."

"Oh crap! You picked up the dead biker. Wow. Is he outside? How did he die?"

"Yes, I picked up the deceased known as Twiggy, and no, I did not bring him here. How he passed is information I am not at liberty to divulge. I'm here because you three are in a vulnerable situation. Babes in the woods."

"Exactly what I was worried about," said Aislin, slapping the table. "Otto, we are way out of our league. Heck, we don't even have a league. Have you ever done a biker funeral? I am sorry to ask, as I know you're busy, but we would be super grateful if you could throw any pearls our way."

Otto laced his fingers and, looking down at them, said, "I suddenly have lots of time, as I just sold The Maples. I am finally free of everything."

A stillness settled. Sarah's eyes were whipping between Letty and Otto while her grin built momentum. Aislin abruptly asked her to help Fitz, who was struggling to clean Secretariat's tank. Sarah hesitated but complied after reading Aislin's expression, and the two walked outside to the tank-cleaning operation.

"Was there a vibe happening? Or was it just me?"

"Yes, there was a vibe, and it has been living underground for decades."

"Have you been holding out on me?"

"I guess. It's something I discovered after I visited Otto. Letty and Otto used to date. And then Bonnie came along and orchestrated Otto's future, so to speak. And Frank and Letty got married. But the vibe has always been there. And this is a super awkward conversation because I don't think Frank ever knew, and it makes me uncomfortable."

"Holy snapping arseholes. That's a love saga fit for a Harlequin romance. Do you think they'll run off together?"

Aislin shrugged. "Not on Elaine's watch!"

"I get the feeling that man is a smouldering volcano looking for a crack in the rock. Anyway, if he does agree to help us, they will be spending time together. We will be aiding and abetting their unrequited love. Cool."

"I prefer 'weird.' Everything about this day is weird and surreal in a super creepy way. I honestly do not know how we will get through the next week. We are so screwed."

"Don't be so fatalistic. We've got Otto now. He's our knight. And he has a vested interest in keeping us all alive so he and his one true love can finally be together."

Aislin sprayed Sarah's legs with the hose. "Stop talking nonsense." And when Fitz looked up, she sprayed his legs, too.

He eyed her with suspicion. "Ms. Aislin, why are you so mean today?"

"I'm sorry, Mr. Fitz. I shouldn't have yelled at you earlier. I was feeling anxious. And just wanted to keep you near. Can you forgive me?"

"Yes."

"Can I have a hug?"

"Yes. Just not a long one."

Chapter 10

Aislin said goodbye to Sarah and Fitz, then crept upstairs, resisting the urge to eavesdrop on Letty and Otto. She checked her messages and found three from Nick, which she double deleted without reading, and one from Jill to her and Sarah, inviting them to a meeting to discuss the food for Twiggy's service. Aislin did not respond.

She got comfortable on her bed and turned on her laptop. It was time to dig into Twiggy's death. It didn't take long. Philip James Masterson, otherwise known as Twiggy, was a full-patch member of the Timber Dogs. His body was found in the bush off a remote logging road. A vet and a conservation officer discovered the body following a lead on an injured Roosevelt elk bull. The vet was Nick de Vries.

Aislin tried unsuccessfully to resuscitate the messages from Nick.

She returned to her research. There wasn't much information specifically about Twiggy, other than that he was known to the police. However, she found a few articles sketching out the relationship between the three gangs on the island. It looked as though they each stayed on their home turf.

The RCMP spokesperson said they didn't have any leads. Aislin felt a minuscule drop in her level of anxiety. The situation didn't seem as dire. Maybe Twiggy's death was not related to his biker activities. Mistaken identity? But if that was the case, why had 10-Gauge mentioned security?

She searched for articles on biker funerals. Available information

covered how many bikers the funeral drew and whether there was violence. Her search deviated to images of hearses flanked by hundreds of
bikers. Then she drifted into a series of photos showing battle-scarred
men holding semi-automatic machine guns, scanning the crowd of
mourners. But those images were from the United States and some
European countries, as far as she could tell.

Gang activity was boiling over on the mainland. Shootings were
increasingly frequent and brazen. She toyed with the idea of contacting the reporter who had built her career covering gangs. They had
met at award ceremonies, but she doubted the woman would remember her. She looked up her contact info and composed an email draft.

Anxiety took root. With so many questions and worries buzzing
around her mind, Aislin could not follow one thought thread through
to a conclusion. She opened a spreadsheet and began creating to-do
lists, which calmed her. She opened a second spreadsheet for questions. Then she shared both with Sarah and asked her to use her experience as an event planner to fine-tune the to-dos and create a timeline.
And to tap into Donny for his input on her questions about the Timber
Dogs and how much of their activity was illegal.

Time was tight, but the journalist in her relished the challenge of
working to a tight deadline. She had never missed a deadline in her
life. She closed her laptop and lay back with her arms stretched out
across the bed. Adrenaline was throbbing through her system. She
welcomed it back into her life and wondered if this was how addicts
felt when they used again after a period of abstinence.

Hearing the front door close, she leapt to the window and hid behind the curtains. Otto moved as though he was walking on land for
the first time after a long sea voyage.

Aislin moved over to the bathroom window to watch Letty in the
garden. Her face was a study of emotion as she deadheaded rhododendrons. It was the way she moved that explained Otto's unsteady gait.
The hesitation that preceded movement was gone. Aislin was amused
to see her lift her bucket with ease, straighten her back, and slip with
agility between the tangled branches.

Aislin had never been drawn to gardening but needed something
to keep her hands busy. People waxed poetic about the calming effects
of working with plants.

"Gran, can I help?"

Letty started. "What's that?"

"Just asking if you wanted some help."

"Where did this sudden interest in gardening come from? We used to threaten you with no supper to get you into the garden. But, yes, I would appreciate the help. These bushes are so big now it's hard for me to get the top ones."

Letty showed Aislin how to hold the stem and break off the spent rhododendron blooms without harming next year's buds. Aislin had not thought to bring gloves, so her fingers quickly grew a thick coating of dirty, sticky sap. She hated the stickiness.

"If you can't manage the deadheading, why are you so careful not to break off next year's buds? It seems like you're aiding and abetting your doom."

"What a question! Why would I deny myself the indulgence of all this colour after a long, wet winter? Most people think of spring bulbs as the harbingers of better days, but not me. I like to watch the big buds swell. And I like the solid comfort of the trunks and branches. Bulbs are a bit ephemeral for me."

"If you say so. But it seems to me you need to watch what you wish for." Taking advantage of the unscripted opening, she followed up with, "Speaking of wishes, how was your conversation with Otto?"

Letty picked up her bucket and moved to the next bush, keeping her back to Aislin. Aislin followed her.

"Did you have a good chat with Otto?"

Nothing.

"He's looking healthy. And happy. Not that I know him well enough to make that judgment, but there was a lightness to him. Did you know he was selling The Maples? I wonder who bought it."

"The same people who bought the paper. The Thunbergers."

"What? Are you kidding me? What do they know about the funeral business? It's kind of a big jump from writing obituaries to embalming bodies. I can't believe it!" Aislin slid out from the shrub she was deadheading.

"I don't know why you're letting yourself get so worked up about it. It's got nothing to do with you."

"But it does! That smug little twerp is going to be our competition.

I wish 10-Gauge had gone to them and not us. That would have been perfect." Aislin pushed her hands into her hair, but the residue on her fingers stuck to her hair. "Shit. Ow. Can this day get any worse? How do I get this stuff out of my hair and off my fingers?"

Letty turned and appraised her. Aislin was red in the face, and her hair was full of little sticky leaf caps. "You're a sight. That's why I wear gloves when I do this job."

"Well, thanks for telling me that now. You couldn't have mentioned it when I offered to help?"

"Hi! Do you mind if I come in?" Nick was already closing the gate behind him. "Hello, Letty. You're looking well, and your garden is more beautiful than I remember. And everything is a lot bigger." Letty glared at him, so he turned to Aislin, taking in her wild hair and dirty face and hands. "I've been trying to reach you all day. I've had an interesting twenty-four hours. And, oddly, it affects you."

Aislin was acutely uncomfortable. Her worlds were colliding. Again. Her head throbbed from the pressure of her accelerated heart rate. She glanced at Letty, trying to assess her reaction to seeing Nick again after all these years of harbouring her belief that Frank would still be alive if it weren't for him. She also flashed back to her awkward conversation with Letty the previous day about how inappropriate it was for Aislin to be driving around town with Nick. And then her mind flitted to the awkwardness of their parting. She did not have any space left in her head to assess why she was also so uncomfortable about her appearance at this moment.

"I saw the article about you and some conservation officer finding a dead body. And yup, the Goodbye Girls are doing the guy's funeral or celebration of life or whatever. Not sure what there is to celebrate for a biker dude who was murdered and dumped in the bush. Not sure how my life became such a mess so fast."

Letty walked over to Aislin and, standing very close, said, "We did not raise you to speak like that about the passing of someone. Whatever the circumstances of that young man's death, he was someone's child. There are people who, right this minute, are mourning him. So, young lady, as I said just the other day, it's not all about you." She stepped towards Nick, who shrank into his clothes. "It's nice to see you, Nick. How's Kate?" Not waiting for an answer, she turned and walked up the stairs to the porch, raising her eyebrows at Aislin as she passed. The kitchen door closed with emphasis.

"How about those Canucks?"

Aislin shook her head but smiled despite herself. "I don't even know where or how to begin to unscrew this mess." She sat on the grass and tried to pick the sticky smudge off her fingers. "I am increasingly regretting coming back home. I thought my life in Vancouver was bad, but it was a walk in the park compared to this chaos."

Nick sat down across from her, awkwardly folding his long legs. "Why did you move back?"

She looked up briefly, just long enough to see the concern in his blue-grey eyes. She shook her head and dropped her gaze. "Not going there." She sighed and turned to look at Letty's rhododendrons. "Hard to believe I've been here less than a month. And to think I came home to regroup because I thought nothing ever happened here—that this town was in some sort of slipstream of tranquillity and calmness-slash-boredom. I thought I was running to my safe space. And what do I get? A business with a somewhat unhinged former-but-current best friend and my grandmother who alternately supports me and despises me, both of whom are questionable judges of character, and our first gig is the funeral for a murdered biker! I mean, what's not to love about my new life?"

"Well, now that you put it like that, I don't know why you're whining. But seriously, Aislin, we need to talk about this biker gig. A lot is going on behind the scenes that you may not be aware of, and I'm worried about you and Sarah bumbling into something that you can't charm your way out of."

"Finally, someone gets it! Letty and Sarah don't seem at all concerned about the potential for violence. Not sure what rock they've been living under that they've not heard about gang violence increasing on the lower mainland and the very real likelihood that it will spread to the island. If the cops over there, who are experts, can't get a handle on it, what the heck are the doodges over here going to do?"

"Look, I don't want to tell you what to do or how to run your business. But I know some of the guys who ride with the Timber Dogs. They're decent guys. But Twiggy? He was trouble. And not because he was involved in criminal activities but because he was a womanizing little bastard. Women were crazy for him. He was constantly on the make and usually with married women. From what I've heard, that's the reason behind his demise."

Aislin sat up. "Oh, that's not so bad then! If he wasn't killed by another gang, just some pissed-off husband, then there won't be a gang war! And there won't be bullets flying in Picnic Park during his funeral. So, we're not all going to be collateral damage. I feel so much better! What a relief!"

Nick blinked at her. "Interesting way to distil what I just said. Not the conclusion I would have drawn. When a biker dies, no matter the cause, bikers from all over attend his funeral. And from what I've heard, there's going to be a big turnout for Twiggy. The 'boys' haven't had a reason to ride together for a long time, and this is just the event to bring them all together. This is going to be enormous. The hotels are all booked, as are the campgrounds. And the ferries. The RCMP is bringing in extra resources. Cops are coming over from the mainland. Stuff's going down, and it's going down fast. That's why I wanted to talk to you."

Aislin shook her head. "No, just no. This isn't happening. We can't do this. I can't do this. Damn Jill for getting us involved. How do we get out of this mess? I don't even know if we *can* get out of it. Alive, that is. Does anyone say no to a guy called 10-Gauge? He must have earned that name."

"I've been thinking about this ever since the body was identified. First, you and Sarah need to call a meeting with 10-Gauge. Have it at the Mugshot, not here. The fewer times those boys ride up this street, the fewer heart attacks there'll be. Let me know when it is, and I'll be in a booth nearby. Sit facing me. I'll be doing paperwork. I often go there to get away from everyone.

"It's going to be challenging, but you need to take the whip hand in the meeting. 10-Gauge will try to manipulate you. He already has Sarah sewn up, from what I hear. You need to call the shots. And minimize what you agree to arrange or provide. Ideally, you keep it to food and flowers. But realistically, you're going to have to organize seating. And there will be a hierarchy to the seating plan. And parking will be a logistical nightmare, so you will need to work with the city on that.

They're well aware of what's coming." Nick paused. "Are you following me?"

"What do bikers eat?"

He studied her face. "You're hungry, right? Have you eaten lately? You're very pale, and your hands are shaking. Classic symptoms of hypoglycaemia."

"I am? I had a cookie earlier. And some coffee. And some Bailey's. I don't even know what time it is. This day feels as though it's gone on for a week. But I am following; it's just a lot to take in. And my heart is hammering so hard I can hardly hear you."

"Is that your normal diet? Coffee, cookies, and Bailey's? Impressive. I'm sorry if I've overwhelmed you, but I was on the road all night, so I've had time to think about your predicament." He checked his phone. "I've got to get back to the clinic. Please keep me posted on what Sarah thinks about my strategy. You going to be okay?"

Aislin looked blankly at him. "I think you're right. I do need to eat. My brain isn't functioning." She stood up and shook her legs to clear the pins and needles. "Why are you so kind? Why do you care what happens?"

"You and I grew up together; we both had missing parents, albeit for very different reasons. Frank was my self-appointed surrogate father. I owe him. And Sarah—well, she's still a bit of a wild card, as are her brothers, but we all go way back. And this is the most exciting thing that has happened in my life since I stole Otto's hearse when I was fifteen and took the guys to the beach where we proceeded to drink our faces off and pass out."

"Really? How come I didn't hear about that?"

"Because Frank and Otto sorted it out with their buddies on the force. It was handled in-house. That's how I came to be the gardener at The Maples, at the paper, and here. I was paying my dues."

"I always wondered why you spent every weekend working. After all these years! You badass."

"And when you said this town was boring, you were dead right. Some days I'm ready to gnaw off my right arm just for some excitement."

"That's a bit extreme, isn't it? Would you have opened your clinic somewhere else if it weren't for your mum? Where would you have gone?"

"Those are questions for another time. I've got to go," said Nick, brushing the grass off his pant legs. "Keep me in the loop. But you have to give me a bit of a heads-up so I can clear appointments, if necessary, to be at the Mugshot."

Aislin watched him leave, expecting him to turn and wave, but he didn't. She wandered around the garden, then picked up the discarded buckets of spent blooms, dumped them in the compost pile, then put away Letty's tools. The garden shed smelled of gasoline, grass, and earth, as it always had. Nick used to mow their lawn every Saturday afternoon. After he left, she would go into the shed and inhale deeply, trying to pick up the smell of him. She closed the door gently and leaned against it.

Chapter 11

"Don't even go there," said Letty from the porch. "You cannot entertain ideas about Nick de Vries. He's married."

The sharpness shattered her reverie. Aislin pushed herself off the door. "I don't know what you're talking about. It's been an insane day, and I'm exhausted. And starving." She pushed past Letty and stood with her hands on her hips, staring blankly at the stove, willing it to produce a hot, creamy, carb-loaded casserole. She had formerly avoided carbohydrates, but since coming home, meal planning with Letty had caused a shift. She became aware again that her jeans were feeling snug. She stood straighter, tightening her abdominal muscles, which didn't respond with quite the alacrity she expected.

Loudly opening and then closing cupboards kept any further conversation at bay. She found the ingredients for a tuna noodle casserole, comfort food from her childhood. Suddenly, thoughts of slurping warm, gooey noodles and chunks of tuna consumed her.

Letty settled at the table and began calling out the recipe ingredients and measurements as Aislin buzzed around, opening cans, boiling water, and crunching up potato chips. Once the casserole was in the oven, Aislin assembled a plate of cheese and crackers and poured wine for them both. Not making eye contact, they sipped and chewed.

Aislin finally looked up to find Letty scrutinizing her. "What's that look for?" she asked.

"You know exactly what that look is for. Nick is off-limits."

"Gran, you've got an overly active imagination. I am grateful to Nick for his assistance in this mess that, I might add, you and Sarah got us into. You should also be grateful. He offered to help us because of his debt to Frank. That's all that's going on. Enough about me—let's talk about you. Why don't you tell me all about your conversation with Otto?"

"There's nothing to tell. He sold his business and is starting life anew." A flash of something swept across Letty's face.

"Good for him. About time he had some fun. God, I can't imagine what it's like to spend your life holding the hands of the bereaved. And you're stuck doing it because your father ran up debt." Aislin caught herself before she went too far onto thin ice. "And how is he starting anew?"

Not looking at Aislin, Letty said, "Well, actually, I wanted to speak with you about that. The Thunbergers took immediate occupancy of his home, so he moved his furniture into storage and is now living in his RV. He needs a spot to park it, and I suggested he park it in the driveway. It will just fit."

Aislin's eyebrows shot up. "Seriously? Otto is moving into our driveway? He's going to basically live with us?" She sat back. "I have no idea what to think about that. This is kind of huge, Gran. It's a lot to process! And it's a bit weird, isn't it? And apart from how I feel, this will light Elaine right up. She will have an opinion. And she will share it. With you and everyone else. Are you and Otto ready for your friends to feast on your bones?"

"Yes, we talked about that. But we laughed about it too. People will think what they think, and we can't stop them."

Aislin bit back suggesting Letty take her own advice. Her muscles whined when she stood up to clear the table. She ached all over. The repercussions from her first run in months kicked in. She moved with effort to load the dishwasher. Letty did not offer to help. Aislin glanced over her shoulder at her grandmother, who was looking blankly at her garden, her mind clearly not on the unfinished deadheading project.

Aislin stacked the dirty pots beside the sink, too tired to continue. "I'm going to bed with a book. Is there still a copy of *Alice in Wonderland* in the living room? I feel as though I've fallen down a rabbit hole."

. . .

The next morning, Aislin set up the meeting with Sarah and 10-Gauge, then texted Nick the time. She didn't invite Letty, and she asked Sarah to leave Fitz at home. She had to keep reminding herself that she was a partner, not a sole proprietor. Apart from brief relationships, she had lived her adult life as a unit of one with no need to accommodate or consult. It was a hard habit to break.

She didn't tell Sarah about Nick's involvement. She had a vague concern about Sarah's grasp of reality and stronger concerns about her obvious attraction to 10-Gauge.

Bright-blue sweater, black jeans, and ankle boots were her final selection after mining her entire wardrobe. She styled her hair with more care than she had since she had returned to town. The results underwhelmed her, so she added a bit of blush and some mascara and brushed her lips with a light-pink lipstick. She looked more like her city self now—confident and competent.

Wanting to avoid unsolicited observations about her appearance, Aislin waited until Letty was in the back garden before zipping out the front door. She was ahead of schedule, so she drove to Picnic Park to assess it regarding access, toilets, parking, and proximity to neighbours. If City Hall had already issued a permit, it was not her problem if the neighbours complained, and she was pretty sure they would. If they were smart, they would lock their doors and leave town for the day—an appealing thought.

The park maintenance crew was out in force, trimming up trees, edging walkways, installing extra garbage cans and portable toilets. Traffic barriers were stacked and ready to be placed.

Despite the whine of machinery and a small army of workers, there were some die-hard park users. And then she realized they weren't locals out for a walk; they were undercover cops. She watched the workers and noticed some were more efficient and focused; others were not. One gave her a hard once-over as he strolled past with a rake. She assumed they had recorded her license plate and taken her photo.

The parking lot at the Mugshot had few cars beside Sarah's and Nick's and was bereft of motorbikes. Aislin scanned the area to see if she could spot other agents. Her anxiety was climbing. Nick was in a booth when she walked in, and Sarah was leaning against it, chatting.

She scrutinized the two other patrons, but they were chowing down on their breakfasts and looked harmless.

"What's going on?" It came out harsher than she intended, so both Sarah and Nick studied her face.

"What's going on with you is more to the point," said Sarah, hugging Aislin. "You look fabulous."

Unwelcome heat flooded her face. "Back at you!" Sarah had also spent some time on her appearance. Aislin fervently hoped it was to appear professional and not for the benefit of 10-Gauge.

Nick leaned back in the booth, grinning at them both while taking in Aislin's palpable tension. His eyes flickered to the parking lot as five bikes rumbled in, and his grin disappeared. He casually pulled out his laptop and set his phone on the table. "Nice to see you both, but I'm here to get some office work done, so if you don't mind, I'll catch up with you later."

Aislin slid into their booth so she was facing Nick and patted the seat beside her. "We will sit together on this side. Our clients can sit across from us. I think we need to control the conversation and not get dragged into providing all sorts of extra services."

"Hello again, Aislin and Sarah," said Otto, pausing briefly before taking a seat at the counter.

"Hi, Otto, wow, it's so great to see you again. I guess now that you've retired, you can hang out and do whatever you like. I didn't know you came here," said Sarah, her voice light and happy.

"Good morning, Otto," said Aislin, looking at Nick for confirmation this was planned. He gave an almost imperceptible nod.

Aislin watched as 10-Gauge took off his helmet and shook his hair out. His conceit on full display. Sarah was openly admiring him.

"He's pretty damn gorgeous," she whispered to Aislin. "And he's coming our way! How do I look?"

Aislin shook her head but gave Sarah a quick side hug. "This isn't a date! Remember our strategy."

"Hi, 10-Gauge. We're over here," Sarah called, waving. Aislin's stomach knotted.

"Good morning, ladies, you're both looking lovely today," said 10-Gauge, his eyes roaming slowly over them, nodding in approval of

what he saw. Aislin knew he assumed she had dressed with care for his benefit and wanted to reach over and slap the smug assumption right off his face.

"Thank you for taking the time to meet with us," she began. She cleared her throat as she reached out to align the condiments. Catching herself, she folded her hands on the table. "We called this meeting to nail down the details of who is responsible for which aspect of this end-of-life celebration for your colleague, whom I understand goes by the name of Twiggy." She paused, then said, "Sorry, went by Twiggy." Her mistake rattled her, and she involuntarily looked to Nick for reassurance; he nodded, then dropped his eyes to his screen. She glanced over at Otto, who was sipping coffee and ostensibly reading the paper. But his head was slightly tilted in their direction. A rush of warmth and gratitude to these two men flooded her.

"Food, booze, and flowers," offered Jill. "Coffee all round? Anyone for decaf?" she asked, looking at Aislin.

"Won't you join us, Jill?" Aislin asked, scooching over to make room. "As you are providing the catering, you'll need approximate numbers."

Jill nodded, called out the order to the cook, and then sat with Aislin and Sarah, wiping her hands on her apron. "So, Alphie, what's the deal? How many are you expecting, and don't give me any bullshit. My reputation is at stake. I don't like being embarrassed by running out of food, and I equally don't like wasting food. So, how far out has the call gone?"

"Jill. How are you? How's your father?"

"He's well. Said to tell you he doesn't like his daughter being embarrassed. And that you'll know what he means."

10-Gauge laughed. "The old bugger. Joe hasn't lost his touch for subtlety." He slowly rolled up the sleeves of his denim shirt, then rested his tattooed forearms on the table. "Twiggy was an apprentice. Media got it wrong when they said he was a full patch. Twiggy was on his way to full patch. He was keen, trustworthy, and committed. Unfortunately, past habits got in the way, and he's no longer with us."

Aislin and Sarah looked blank. Jill was nodding. "I heard. He had an unfortunate propensity for married women. I also heard he had more than one family."

He laughed again. "Speaking of families, his birth family is also planning, shall we say, a more traditional funeral. At The Maples."

Aislin pushed her leg into Sarah's, hoping she wouldn't voice the connection. Sarah nudged back and kept quiet. Aislin sensed a shift in her business partner's cognition of the situation.

"Are they? Interesting. And what day is that planned for?"

"Same as ours."

"Let me get this straight. The Dogs weren't invited or welcomed, so you're planning a parallel ceremony?"

"We are."

"Interesting. Burial or cremation?"

"Cremation."

"Which of you gets the ashes? I doubt you're splitting them."

10-Gauge just smiled. Jill opened a food-stained, tattered notebook. "Numbers?"

"Upwards of three hundred bikes."

"Are you kidding me?" Aislin's dam of stress burst. "Three hundred? At Picnic Park? And the City issued a permit? I doubt that many attend Canada Day celebrations there. That's way too big." She looked to Jill for support. "Can you churn out food for three hundred bikers?" Then to 10-Gauge, "Does that number include their wives?"

"Wives? Yes, most of our ol' ladies and a few mamas will attend. Hard to call how many. So, plan for, say, four hundred."

Coffee arrived, and everyone was silent as they dressed their drinks. After pouring an avalanche of sugar into his coffee, 10-Gauge placed the container in line with the other condiments, then pushed it askew and gave Aislin a slow smile.

Aislin smiled back at him, wrapping her hands tightly around her coffee cup, willing herself to focus on the conversation. "Is his whole family attending the other service?"

"His birth family, yes, as far as I know. He has a couple of ex-girlfriends he had kids with. They'll come to ours. We used to tease Twiggy about his one-man effort to support population growth. Don't get it myself—having kids, that is—but he loved them."

"Just how many ex-girlfriends can we expect? And children? Is this a suitable event for children?" asked Aislin.

"What do you mean by suitable?"

"It's just that . . ." Aislin faltered, glancing across at Nick as if he could bail her out. The café was suddenly silent.

10-Gauge leaned back and studied the three women across from him.

"I think what Aislin is concerned about is the safety of small children with four hundred bikes milling about," Sarah offered.

"We protect each other, and that includes our kids."

"Got it," Sarah said, nodding rapidly. She glanced at Aislin for permission to take the lead. "We need a rough idea of what you're planning, 10-Gauge. Do you see people speaking at a podium on a stage or something more casual? Do you want seating? For how many? I don't think Picnic Park can accommodate seating for four hundred. Or are there a select few who will be seated? And if so, what about the rest of your group? And what about music?" Sarah's wedding planner experience was kicking in.

"Here's how the day's going to go: All the bikes will assemble in Bowser, and then we will ride down the island as a group. Make a show, you know? We expect to arrive at the park around one p.m. We want a platform, a podium, and wireless mics. And seating on the platform for about twenty. The rest of the boys will stay with their bikes on the road. The boys will fire up and leave for the campground when the speeches are over. But there will be nonbikers there who knew Twiggy. So, Jill, you only have to provide food and booze for eighty to one hundred." He paused. "Can you manage that?"

"Shouldn't be an issue. Finger food, canapés, and sandwiches. No hot food. A couple of kegs or bottled beer? Wine? Pop for the kids and nondrinkers. Tea and coffee. Do you want a cake?"

Sarah squirmed and interrupted. "If you decide on bottles of beer and wine, we could have labels made up with a picture of Twiggy. What were his favourite colours? I think that would be so nice. Just not sure if there's enough time."

"That's my girl. Such a pleasure to work with someone who comes up with ideas and solutions." He swung his eyes to Aislin. Her face coloured. "We're partners in a brewery in Nanaimo, so they'll take care of the labels. Don't want wine. Yes to pop, tea, and coffee. No to the cake."

"We need to talk about security," Aislin said.

10-Gauge ignored her and spoke to Sarah and Jill. "We're having bullets engraved with Twiggy's name. Mementos, you know?"

Sarah pushed her thigh against Aislin. "So, you're handing out bullets. That's different!"

"We're having keychains made. We had thought of having a few grams of his ashes compacted into the bullets, but there wasn't time. We also considered sending him off in fireworks, but the planning committee thought the noise would be too much for the neighbours. We didn't want to flood the hospital with a bunch of oldies keeling over with heart attacks. The bikes alone are going to have them di-alling 911. We've got some volunteers going door to door with flyers explaining the event."

"You have a planning committee? And volunteers? As in people who voluntarily do stuff? I wasn't aware lower-order bikers were given choices," said Aislin.

"Your assumptions are showing. Again."

They all sat in silence for a few minutes. Aislin was drowning in her humiliation.

"Anyway, as I was going to say"—10-Gauge paused, looking at Aislin—"Twiggy is only just going in the oven tonight, according to the guy at the cooker. A bunch of newbies running the place now. The twerp I spoke to said there wasn't time to get the ashes into bullets. He tried to convince us to move our date to the following week and have it at his place. He talked a streak about doing a themed funeral." 10-Gauge glanced in Otto's direction as he spoke.

Aislin nudged the sugar shaker into alignment with her pen. Of course he knew who Otto was. He was a savvy bastard. But he nailed it when he called Theo a twerp. How dare the twerp try and steal this event?

She needed to push the reset button on her relationship with 10-Gauge. Frank had always preached that you bring your best to the table once you commit to something. Or step away. It was too late to step away, and she was not about to willingly give this event up to Theo. She forced a smile at 10-Gauge. "I wholeheartedly agree. Theo Thunberger is a twerp. And heartless. But let's focus on creating a timely, respect-ful, and appropriate send-off for Twiggy. Should we talk with your planning committee to see what's been done so far?"

"You're talking to the head of the planning committee. Not good enough for you?"

Fixing this relationship was akin to turning an ocean liner. She fought her impulse to apologize. "At the risk of seeming to make another assumption, we do need to discuss security. I was just at Picnic Park. I spotted several undercover cops posing as park maintenance workers. And dog walkers. I've heard that the gang violence experts from the lower mainland will be here. If they're concerned, then we're concerned. Are our concerns valid?" The media alert signal buzzed on her phone. Habituated by her years as a reporter, she clicked on the alert. Then looked at their client. "A missing-person alert has gone out for the prime suspect in Twiggy's murder."

10-Gauge did not respond, but his right eyelid twitched. Nick looked up from his laptop. Sarah went rigid. Jill vigorously stirred her near-empty coffee cup. It was she who pointed out the elephant in the room.

"You don't look surprised, Alphie. Worried but not surprised. We need to go back to Aislin's question about security. What sort of assurances can you give us that everyone will be on their best behaviour?"

"Assurances? You know how things go, Jill. This is a friendly ride. It's not a show of colours. Twiggy was popular. The boys want to pay their respects. But things can happen when a bunch of clubs get together. And that's all I'm going to say." He looked at his phone. "I'll be in touch."

Sarah was the only one who called out a goodbye. Jill clenched her jaw, tapping her fingers, then moved quickly to each of the remaining customers, who promptly paid up and left. She then spoke with her staff, who also departed. She locked the door, flipped the sign from open to closed, and pulled down all the blinds.

"Just give me a few minutes; I'm going to make us some sandwiches."

Sarah looked at Nick, then at Otto, then turned to Aislin. "It wasn't a coincidence they're here, is it? You arranged to have them here. Without telling me. What's that about? I thought we were partners."

Aislin was unprepared for the question. She looked to Nick for help and then Otto.

"Nick invited me, not Aislin," said Otto.

"And I invited myself," said Nick.

"Still need an explanation, Aislin," said Sarah.

"Okay, fine. I was—am—concerned about your apparent attraction to 10-Gauge. It scares me. And from the business perspective, it's not professional to fish off the company pier."

Nick and Otto both winced.

"What the hell does that mean?"

"It means it's not cool to be lusting after a client. And, it's not safe to be lusting after the head of a biker gang. What about Fitz?"

"Are you serious? Are you questioning my parenting skills? Wow. Still the same old judgmental Aislin. You sure haven't changed."

Aislin's hands were manically rearranging the condiments, spreading them out in a line and then regrouping them equidistantly apart. She watched her hands as if they belonged to someone else.

Jill plonked a large platter of sandwiches on the table. "Aislin, apologize to Sarah. And leave my condiments the hell alone. Nick, sit over here, and Otto, you're over here, too."

Jill's tone shocked everyone. Aislin pulled her hands away. Her humiliation was complete. She fleetingly considered crawling under the table and bolting.

"Waiting," said Sarah.

"Okay! Fine! You're right. I should have told you that Nick and I had arranged for him to be here. I acted unilaterally, and that was wrong. We're partners. I won't do it again."

"And?"

"And what?"

"Say the words, Aislin. Say you're sorry."

Aislin made fists with her hands and curled her toes in her shoes. "I'm sorry."

"I need more than that. I need you to enunciate what you're apologizing about."

"Geez, Sarah. Really?"

"Really."

"Sarah, I am sorry I didn't involve you in the planning for this meeting, and I'm sorry I questioned your parenting skills."

"In the future, could you both bring your adult selves to the table? This isn't high school. This isn't a lark," said Jill, banging plates in front of each of them. "Now, we're going to eat my delicious food, and we're all going to get along."

Someone knocked on the door of the café, and Jill bellowed, "We're closed. Come back tomorrow."

"It's me, Donny Quinn. I was supposed to be here for a meeting Sarah was having."

Aislin swung her eyes to Sarah, who was suddenly very engaged in choosing a sandwich. "So, you invited Donny without telling me?"

"Grow the hell up!" Jill slapped the table so hard the spoons jigged, then unlocked the door. "Donny Quinn! Come on in and join the fun. Sit between your sister and Aislin. They're not playing nicely today. I'm going to assume Sarah invited you because of your connection to the Dogs. I'm not sure how much you know about what's been going on on our side, so I'll give you a recap. And then you're going to tell us what you've heard."

Chapter 12

When Jill finished her summary, with a few additions from Aislin, Sarah, and Nick, Donny sat back and ran grease-stained hands through his hair. "Holy Mary, Joseph, and baby Jesus, that's fucktangular alright. How did you two get yourselves into this mess?"

Aislin and Sarah looked at Jill, who promptly put her hand up. "My bad. Actually, it was my dad's bad, but I'll own it. You know how he is about looking out for me. So when I told him about going into the funeral-planning business with these two, he put our name forward to the Dogs when news of Twiggy's demise hit. He billed it as a quiet little send-off, a bloody far cry from three hundred bikes from different clubs descending on Picnic Park. And here we are."

"A couple of the boys have their bikes in my shop, so they've been gassing with one another while I tinker. Sometimes I listen, sometimes I don't. Lately, I've been listening." Donny paused, enjoying their rapt attention. "Twiggy messed with the wife of the wrong guy." Donny drew his hand across his neck. "The husband was no Prince Bloody Charming. He'd been inside for three years for manslaughter. And while her husband was preoccupied on the inside, his wife was preoccupied on the outside. Her tastes were wide and varied. The day he got out she was with Twiggy. Makes you wonder if it was a setup. Twiggy's women, and there were a lot of them, always seemed to be married to a badass. But he was serious about this one, more than she was about him. He was making a pest of himself. She was tired of him and realized it was in the interests of her long-term health to pick up the matrimonial thread of her marriage."

His audience was hanging on every word. "I think something's gone down regarding the husband."

"He's missing," said Aislin. "I got a media alert while we were meeting with 10-Gauge, and when I told him, he took off."

"Okay, so now things are going to get interesting."

"*Going* to get interesting?" asked Aislin, twitching from the effort of sitting on her hands.

"What does that mean, Donny?" Nick asked. "Did the husband belong to a club?"

"Not that I know of, but he was involved in drugs. The Dogs have an immediate, tangible problem. They are under surveillance, so they have to mind their manners. And, from what I hear, they have a rather large, ahem, object they need to move."

Otto, who had been quietly observing the range of facial expressions and gauging the comprehension levels of his tablemates, steepled his hands, then spoke. "I no longer run the cooker, as your associate termed it, but have offered my services until they hire a technician or train one of their own. I will be processing Twiggy tomorrow." He paused and looked at them each again. And continued. "So, it is conceivable that the large object could be dealt with."

Donny nodded, Nick shook his head, and Jill played with her rings. Aislin and Sarah's eyebrows were in danger of joining forces with their hairlines.

"How?" asked Donny.

"Years ago, a movie was filmed at The Maples, and some props were left behind, one of which is a coffin with a false bottom."

"Otto, no. You don't want to do this," warned Nick. "You've led an exemplary life. And now you want to throw in with the Dogs? You are finally free to do whatever you want with your life, and you want to damage your reputation and risk that freedom?"

"Nick, thank you for your concern, but I have led a very dull life. I was married to a very dull woman whom I did not love. I have a very dull job. And now, I finally am free to do whatever the hell I want. And I want some excitement. I want to feel fear. I want to feel adrenaline pumping so hard I can't breathe. I want an endorphin high!"

Donny clapped his hands then slapped Otto on the back. "Holy Mother Mary and sweet skateboarding baby Jesus! You rock."

Otto blushed and looked at Aislin. "How do you think Letty will react?" Everyone leaned in, Sarah grinning.

"I'm not sure how *I'm* reacting. To any of this." She was still working through the fact that they were calmly discussing what to do with an extra body. Now Otto had put her on the spot. "I don't know, Otto. Do you think it's appropriate to talk about Letty? Here? Now?"

"How is Letty involved?" asked Donny, turning to Otto. "Are you making a move on her? That's bloody awesome. Never too old, eh?" He gave Otto another hearty slap on the back, then lost his toothy grin. "Time's a hard mistress, folks, so we need to get some serious planning done pronto."

Otto and Donny were soul mates when it came to creative problem-solving. For every challenge Donny presented, Otto found a workaround. Nick worked to find flaws. Aislin, Sarah, and Jill listened and took notes. After an intense hour of point-counterpoint, they were all spent.

Donny, who had slipped into the role of leader of the pack, sat back and smiled. "Well, ladies and not-so-gentle men, I think we have a plan. Yes?"

Everyone nodded. Jill went to the kitchen and returned with a bottle of Scotch and six shot glasses. "I think we need this, and I don't want any goody two shoes blathering about what time it is," she said, looking at Aislin. "It's noon somewhere in the world, and that's good enough for me."

"You're a brilliant woman, Jill, and a mind reader to boot," said Donny. After Jill had filled the glasses, Donny ceremoniously stood, arm raised, and said, "I would like us all to stand, please, so I can give a toast to our future endeavours. To hell: May the stay there be as fun as the way there."

They all drank solemnly, checked their phones, found their keys, and drifted out to the parking lot.

Aislin touched Sarah's arm. "Are we good?"

"Ya, we're good. I get why you're worried. I was a bit swoony over 10-Gauge, and he seemed to dial in on me. And I fell for it. It's been ages since an attractive guy noticed me. How sad is that?"

"He's a manipulator. And it would suit his purpose to drive a wedge between us. And, truth be known, I was jealous. Or envious. Or maybe possessive. Not sure which. But we are on a trajectory I could never have imagined. Who knows if things will unfold according to our master plan? I hate to admit it, but I am kind of excited. I've never done anything remotely close to what we're planning." Aislin paused, then asked, "Are you okay with it?"

"I am, actually. This may be our only gig as the Goodbye Girls, but what a gig! I just don't want to end up behind bars. Orange is not my colour."

"Mine either. I'm better in blues and greens. If things do go horribly wrong, I hope we end up inside together."

Worst-case scenarios were having a high-speed chase through the alleys of Aislin's mind as she drove home. Otto's car was in the driveway. She sat in hers, stared at the house, and considered what might be going on behind those walls. There was no faint hope that Letty and Otto were just going to age out of life as friends. A sexual current was very much a real thing, and she was struggling to analyze her feelings. It was more than just loyalty to Frank. Was it envy? Was she an ageist? Whatever the source of her discomfort, she was going to have to find a way to mask or manage it. Letty would be hypersensitive and pounce on any little comment or facial expression.

"Big-girl panties time," she muttered as she walked up the steps. As she reached the top, Otto barged out, looking completely rattled.

"What's going on?"

"Your grandmother. Just flew at me like a crow," he said, hurrying down the steps. "Never seen anything like it. It was like a scene from *The Birds.*"

The final, frayed thread of her composure snapped. Laughter roared out of her. Wave after wave. It felt good. Otto looked back as he fumbled with his keys. His expression of concern mixed with horror set off fresh waves. He pulled away from the curb without so much as a wave. Aislin sat down heavily on the top step and looked out at the street. It seemed so calm and normal.

"What's so funny? I don't see anything funny about this plan of yours. How could you go along with such a ludicrous idea?" Letty barged onto the porch, her blood still up.

"Well, Gran, the seeds of this plan were sown the minute 10-Gauge walked into the garden. If you recall, you and Sarah were smitten, and I was not. And so here we are today with a biker gang as a client and an extra body that needs moving. This is how normal people get caught up in gang life. This mess is not my fault."

"I still think you could have stopped Otto from being roped in. He's too old for this sort of thing."

"Are you kidding me? It was his idea! Nick tried to talk him out of it. Otto wants to live life large. He's been bored for decades. So, Gran, if you're going to have a relationship with him, you better be prepared to fasten your seatbelt. And wear a balaclava."

"Now you're being ridiculous. And what makes you think I'm going to have a relationship with him?"

"Oh, come on. It's all over his face and yours. Well, it was all over his face until you flew at him like a crow—his words, by the way. He may have changed his mind. He's never seen the Letty he has adored from afar unleashed."

Letty wriggled. "I wasn't that bad. I was just shocked that he was involved in this ridiculous plan. I may have raised my voice a little." She paused, then asked quietly, "Do you think I should call him? He was going to move his RV in today before all this nonsense took over."

"Oh my God. Of course, you should call him. I know it's been a while for you, but dating rules haven't changed much."

Letty played with her wedding ring. "How do you feel about, you know, Otto and me?"

"Honestly? At first, I was shocked, but if it feels right for you, go for it. Why wouldn't you? Otto said today that he was bored. You're bored too. There's more to life than dragging around with Elaine discussing the quality of the devilled eggs at funerals. I was quite worried about you when I first came home. The house was dirty, you weren't eating well and had lost weight. Look at you now. You're all fired up and mad as a wet cat. Which is normal." Aislin dropped her voice at the end, fully expecting Letty to take umbrage at the dirty-house comment or reference to her temper.

Letty gave her a swift sideways look. "I suppose you have a point." She got up. "I'm going to make us some tea." As she reached for the door, she fired back, "My house was not dirty."

Aislin picked at the peeling paint of the top step. The porch and steps had always been a dull, dark, light-sucking green. She turned and looked at the tired grey clapboard siding and envisioned it in steel blue, the windows crisply white and the porch a rich burgundy. When the funeral was over, she thought she might enjoy some outside painting should she still be alive.

Chapter 13

Otto picked her up in the hearse the next day at the appointed time. Aislin spent an excessive amount of time deciding what to wear. She uncharacteristically drew Letty into her tumult of indecision. She had nothing that even remotely met the dress code for visiting a biker club-house in a hearse to pick up a body.

"I think camouflage is appropriate," said Letty, helpfully.

"Sorry, Gran, but I have never needed to buy camo-themed clothing."

"Well, that's unfortunate," said Letty.

"Oddly thought you might see that as a positive. What about this?" Aislin asked.

Letty looked at her critically and shook her head. "Not a white blouse. Don't you have any baggy T-shirts? Are all of your pants that tight? I don't know how you can sit down in those things without being cut in half."

"That's the style, Gran. They're called 'skinny jeans.' And they have Lycra in them. So that we can sit down." Aislin twisted around, trying to see her bum in the mirror. Her grandmother's allusion to her weight gain mortified her.

"You've put on weight," Letty continued, oblivious. "But you look better. You were too skinny when you came home. But now your skin is shiny, and your hair is less lank. You should stop dyeing it. You're already blonde. Why do you want it white blonde? And thank God you've stopped wearing all that eye makeup. You looked like a hungry albino raccoon."

They finally agreed on a blue-and-white striped T-shirt and blue jeans. Aislin also wore a jacket with lots of pockets, as she had decided against taking her purse.

When Otto arrived, Letty went out to speak with him. Aislin had unwisely sought courage in caffeine, so she used the bathroom again before she joined them. Letty looked anxious and unhappy, while Otto looked excited.

"Let's ride!" he said, patting the top of the hearse.

Aislin and Letty both laughed nervously. "Bye, Gran. Don't worry. We'll be fine. I'll call you when we're at The Maples."

The clubhouse was in a decaying strip mall at the edge of town. It was here that small businesses, unable to afford the high rents in the town centre, congregated and thrived. It was once home to a dry cleaner, a tailor, a tiny bookstore, a used clothing store, a bakery, a butcher, a mom-and-pop corner store, and a mechanic in its glory days. But the advent of big-box stores slowly sucked the oxygen from the small, independent shops. All but a few storefronts now were empty.

Aislin recalled riding to the mall with Sarah to poke through Eclectic Funk, their favourite secondhand clothing store, on the hunt for something unique. They fancied themselves cutting-edge fashionistas. Sarah's taste in clothing was always more dazzling than Aislin's.

She and Otto shared stories of their memories of the mall as they drove. Neither had been there for at least a decade. Otto pulled over just before its entrance.

"Are you sure you're okay with this? I expect they will have heavy protection on display. And, from the moment we approach, we will be on all sorts of cameras: some theirs, and some the RCMP. But if we go inside, that's the end of the RCMP's surveillance. So, as Donny said, only speak when spoken to, and if they ask a question, keep your answer short. A simple yes or no would be best. I expect they will direct questions to me, as they are a patriarchal bunch. Try not to let that get up your nose. This is not the time for social justice."

"Noted. I will just acquiesce to you, should anyone ask me a question. I mean, really? Women are still seen and not heard? Freaking unbelievable. That 10-Gauge is a chauvinist prick."

"Did you hear anything I just said?"

"Sorry. Yes. I shall be a model of compliance and silence."

Otto smiled. "No, you won't. You're Letty's granddaughter. Compliance is not in your genes. But just try not to get us killed, okay?"

There was no mistaking which building was the headquarters of the Timber Dogs. They had taken over the corner that formerly housed a mechanic's shop and side lot, now encased by a high, black, galvanized steel fence.

Two imposing men approached wearing black T-shirts emblazoned with "Snitches Are a Dying Breed" in Gothic lettering. *Lump One and Lump Two*, thought Aislin. They indicated to turn off the engine and step out of the hearse. Otto gave Aislin a reassuring pat.

"We'll take your phones. And then we're going to check you both and the car," said Lump One, the larger of the two.

Aislin was about to object, but Otto gave an almost imperceptible shake of his head. He spread his legs and arms wide as though he were ready to embrace the world. He was wearing a tracksuit, which had seemed like a fashion misstep to Aislin, but now she recognized the wisdom. She writhed with fury and the effort to keep quiet as Lump One moved his hands over her. He held her eye as he slipped his hand into her waistband and slowly felt along its length. She involuntarily tightened her abs, which earned a leer. Lump Two did not take nearly as long to frisk Otto.

The gate to the lot slid open silently. A third, unspeaking man drove the hearse through. Aislin snatched a look before it closed. The lot was full of bikes and one large transport truck.

With his massive shaved head, Lump Two indicated that they should follow him. He stopped at the door and nodded to Lump One, who produced two black blindfolds. Thunderclouds of a panic attack were marshalling at the edge of Aislin's mind. She looked to Otto for reassurance, but he stared straight ahead.

The blindfold was roughly tied around her head, catching some of her hair in the knot. They were pushed back into what felt like a sofa. Aislin reached out and touched Otto, but he pulled away. She felt alone, vulnerable, and scared. She had trouble regulating her breath. She had to go to the bathroom.

She crossed and uncrossed her legs. She leaned forward, then sat up straight and shifted from buttock to buttock. She was in constant motion.

"What are you doing?"

Aislin froze. She was so engrossed in quelling the need to use the bathroom she forgot someone might be watching. And she did not want to admit she needed to use the bathroom.

"Me? Are you speaking to me? I have a cramp in my leg. I really need to get up and walk it off. Are we going to be here much longer? And this blindfold is too tight. I see stars. And I feel like I might hyperventilate. I think I need fresh air."

"I'll get you some water."

"No! No water, thanks. I just need to move around. When I'm super stressed, I can't sit still, and quite frankly, I am super stressed right now, what with not being able to see and being terrified I am going to be killed and my body dumped in a bush. My poor grandmother would be heartbroken. At least I think she would be heartbroken, but we have an odd relationship. It's been like that for years. You see, she raised me after my parents died suddenly, and I don't think she ever got over my dad, her son, dying. I don't even really remember my parents, but the whole damn town loved them. Almost idolized them. Sometimes I was resentful of that idolization, as it made it hard for people to just see me like a regular kid and not the progeny of a super couple. And don't get me started on how people hovered."

"More worried about how to get you to stop."

"No need to be rude. We're here to help you guys, and you're treating us like enemies."

"Stop talking!"

"I don't know which one of you goons just said that, but I'm going to discuss this with 10-Gauge. This was definitely not in our contract. No way did we have a clause that said, 'And the client will blindfold the vendor and subject them to physical and verbal abuse.'"

"Hey, old guy, can you make her shut up?"

Otto sighed deeply. "Unlikely."

Aislin heard the door open and some low muttering. She was roughly dragged from the sofa and pushed outside. As soon as her arm was released, she untied the blindfold and threw it on the ground. Otto was then shown out and his blindfold removed. Lump One returned their phones. The hearse was parked at the curb, engine running.

When they had cleared the mall, Aislin rolled down her window and leaned out to let the warm breeze blow across her skin.

"You okay? That was quite a lot of personal information you shared with those gentlemen."

"Barely, but I really do need to find a bathroom."

"The only public washroom between here and The Maples is at Picnic Park, and for obvious reasons, we want to avoid going there. But Nick's place isn't far off our route, so see if he's home. It's lunchtime, so we may be in luck. And his neighbours are used to seeing the hearse in his driveway."

"I don't know. What if his mother is there? Or worse, Kate. She never liked me."

"Do you always overthink everything?"

"It's a habit that pops up when I'm stressed. And I am stressed. But not as stressed as when we were blindfolded. That was awful. I thought my head was going to explode. And my bladder. I didn't think I would make it but was too scared to ask to use their bathroom. And with the damn blindfold, I wouldn't be able to check its cleanliness. And would one of the Lumps have gone with me? And watched?" Aislin was aware she was talking too much. She texted Nick. "All clear. His mum's at the clinic, and he didn't mention Kate's whereabouts."

Nick was waiting for them. He showed Aislin to the bathroom and then joined Otto in the hearse. When Aislin returned and Nick got out, he gave her shoulder a brief squeeze. Aislin hesitated. She urgently needed a full-on hug. It had been a very long time since a man had hugged her. The rare, quick hugs with Letty were okay, but she wanted a big, warm hug right this minute.

"You have feelings for him, don't you?" Otto said when they were underway again.

"No, no, nothing like that. We just go way back."

"Keep telling yourself that."

"Why has the traffic slowed?"

"Damn! There's roadwork ahead. And I can't detour around it. We didn't plan for a pitstop, so we're off route."

Otto slammed his hand on the steering wheel. They had come to a complete halt. Pedestrians were passing them and staring.

"Do people always stare, or am I just paranoid they know something?"

"Yes, they always stare. They're wondering if there's a body on board and if they know the person. Can you lean out and see how long the lineup is ahead?"

Just as Aislin leaned out, she spotted Jim Brownlee on the sidewalk across from them, gawping at her. He had Herman with him, and the dog was lunging at the hearse and barking.

"Oh shoot, there's Jim Brownlee. I can't stand that guy. He's so nosey and bossy."

"What's wrong with his dog?"

"That's Herman. He found my turtle." Aislin looked at Otto. "Oh shoot. He's a tracking dog!"

She scrambled out and ran over to where Jim was struggling with Herman. The dog desperately wanted to get to the hearse.

"Hi, Jim, so nice to see you. Herman, remember me? You found Secretariat." She stood between the dog and its object of attention and tried to distract him by rubbing his ears. "Let's go stand in the shade of that maple over there."

Jim pulled Herman back and gave him the "leave" command, then turned to Aislin. Herman stopped barking and lunging and lay down, facing the hearse and panting heavily.

"Never stand under a maple at this time of the year. They drop sap, and it gets on your clothes and in your hair and attracts aphids. Next thing you know, you're covered in the damn things. Don't you know anything? And what are you doing driving around in a hearse? Anyone we know in the back?"

"Ha. I always learn things when we chat. Anyway, I wanted to thank you for your information regarding the safe handling of turtles. Letty and I are very diligent about washing our hands after touching Secretariat."

"A turtle is a stupid pet. They're dangerous. Are you trying to kill your grandmother? And yourself? And that Quinn kid and his mother? Disgusting creatures." Aislin wasn't sure if he meant Sarah and Fitz or turtles. Either way, his statement was not going to go unpunished.

"Gosh, it is hot out. This heatwave is something else. Isn't the pavement too much for Herman's feet? Every summer, when I was a reporter, we ran articles about pet health in a heatwave and how walking your dog on pavement is a no-no. Just like locking them in a car with the windows up."

Jim's expression changed. His bulbous, watery blue eyes narrowed. "Herman always walks on the grass verge. I never let him on the hot pavement."

"Yet there he lies! And he's quite worked up. Do you carry water for him? Hydration is crucial."

Jim jerked Herman's leash and pulled him onto the grass. The traffic was beginning to move again.

"Lovely chatting. Bye, Herman, hope you have some nice cool water waiting for you at home."

Aislin caught up with the hearse. She felt like panting. She looked back at Jim, who was on his phone, watching them drive away.

"Well, that was awful. That guy needs to get a life. Thank God we're moving again."

The traffic lightened as soon as they left town, and their spirits lifted as they cruised along the shady, maple-lined streets. Aislin was chewing over everything she wished she had said to Jim.

"Do you hear sirens?" asked Otto.

Aislin rolled down her window. "Yup, and it sounds as though they are coming from behind us."

Two RCMP cruisers raced up to them, and as Otto pulled over, one parked in front, blocking them in.

"Let me handle this. Please," he said. He opened his window as the officer approached.

"License and registration, please. And then I need both of you to step out of the vehicle."

"Of course. How are you, Constable Murray? I saw you at your uncle's funeral a few weeks back. How's your aunt doing? She looked quite frail. Do you see much of her? She must need help out at the farm." Otto's voice was low and soothing. His professional funeral director's voice.

Aislin stumbled onto the sidewalk. The pulsating police lights were blinding and disorienting.

"Open the cargo door," ordered Murray.

"Of course." Humming quietly, Otto did as instructed. "This heat is extreme. I fear for the health of our seniors."

The casket slid out on its runners. Aislin gasped. The deep dark mahogany lid bore the Timber Dogs' logo and "RIP, little buddy." A black leather vest, which she assumed was Twiggy's, was artfully draped beneath the artwork. It was a beautiful tribute.

Aislin suddenly felt profoundly sad. Letty's admonishment about her attitude came back to her. Twiggy was a son, a father, and a lover. And he was dead. Hot tears were stinging her eyes, so she looked up at the network of branches above, hoping Letty's trick would not fail.

When the constables opened the casket, the vest slid off. She moved to pick it up, but a warning hand stopped her. The vest lay crumpled where it landed. Murray stepped on it as he moved around the casket, probing its lining with his fingers.

They spoke in low monotones into their radios as they worked. Murray put the toe of his boot on the vest, dragged it to him, then kneeled on it to look at the undercarriage of the hearse.

Aislin moved to protest, but Otto elbowed her and shook his head before she could.

"Will you be long?"

"Long as we need."

After finger-combing the hearse, the constables told Otto he could go. Glaring at them, Aislin picked up Twiggy's vest, shook it vigorously, and patted it into place on the coffin lid. When she finished fussing with the vest, Otto put the hearse in gear and drove off slowly.

"They were so rude! Using Twiggy's vest as a kneeling pad! Really? I feel like yelling at them. I bet Jim Freaking Brownlee called them. He was on his phone the minute I walked away." She squirmed around in her seat to look back.

Otto flicked the window auto-lock on the console. "They want to get under your skin. I wouldn't give them the satisfaction—just garden-variety intimidation tactics. We'll likely see more before this is over. They're frustrated. They know something is going on right under their noses, but they don't want to confront the Timber Dogs until they have something solid to move on. We're low-hanging fruit. I was getting a bit worried there, I must say. They obviously haven't seen the movie filmed at The Maples. I can't even recall the name. Apparently not a blockbuster, which is a good thing."

Otto slowed as they entered the grounds of The Maples. "Expect Theo to randomly pop up. He has a knack for that, and I'm not sure it's unintentional. He's an odd one, that Theo. I haven't quite put my finger on why he repulses me. But, having said that, and knowing that you feel much the same way, when he does turn up, it's your job to distract him while I unload and get things cooking, so to speak."

"Oh sure, give me the tough job! How am I supposed to distract him?"

Otto smiled. "With your feminine charms, of course."

"Right. I can't stand breathing the same air as that pompous prick."

Otto swung the hearse into the loading bay, reversing smoothly to the double doors. Before exiting, he patted Aislin's shoulder. "This part is the trickiest of this whole crazy convoluted plan. I'm counting on you. Good luck."

Before disappearing through another set of double doors with the casket, Otto threw Aislin a quick wave. A deep silence settled in his wake. It was unnerving. Noise was normal. Silence was not.

Chapter 14

Aislin had no idea what to do with herself. She was hot, hungry, and stressed. She had actively and effectively avoided thinking about the logistics of what Otto was doing behind those closed doors. Snatches of scenes from *Cries in the Night* flooded her mind. She and Sarah had watched the movie every Halloween, scaring themselves skinny each time. She shook her head, trying to shake off the images.

One side of the long corridor was lined with a series of shiny steel doors. Besides the one Otto disappeared through, there were four more. She checked the ceiling for cameras but didn't see any. She wished Sarah was with her. Sarah wouldn't hesitate to investigate.

Clearing her throat, she wandered over to the closest door and tried the handle, praying it wouldn't open. Her prayer was answered. The next one was unlocked, so she pushed it open.

"Ooops, sorry to interrupt."

"No worries, come on in, if you like. You're Aislin Fitzgerald, aren't you?" asked the woman seated at the long table. She was applying garish pink nail polish to the hand of a wax-coloured corpse. "I'm Beverly; I do Letty's hair. I heard you were in town and were starting a funeral-planning business with Sarah Quinn. What a great idea. So many bereaved have no idea where to begin. Have a seat. If you like this colour, I'll do your nails next. This is my last one today. Maybe forever if the new owners make too many more changes."

"Um, no thanks." Aislin quietly sat down and tucked her hands beneath her thighs. "I mean, it's not that I don't like it."

"Suit yourself. I don't mind. The daughter chose it. Not what I would choose. Not for her skin tone. I would have gone with something more subtle. People don't understand colour. They want their relatives to look bright and shiny. Even if they weren't bright and shiny when they were alive. I'm always happiest when the family chooses a dignified palette.

"Hungry? I brought a big lunch because I thought I would be working on that dead biker, but his family doesn't want him fixed up before he goes into the retort. Funny bunch. Did you read about the murder? I don't like working on murder victims. I get caught up in their last thoughts before they die, and it affects my work. And some of them require a lot of work, let me tell you!"

Beverly slid her stool away from the bench, washed her hands, and plunked a large shopping bag on her desk. She identified the contents of each container as she unpacked.

"Potato salad, carrot sticks, hummus, crackers, grapes, and Hawkins Cheezies. It's spring, so I thought I would try to shift some of this weight before beach season, you know what I mean? I always bring an unopened bag of Cheezies and try my damndest not to open it. I feel victorious if I resist, but then I go and open them anyway just to celebrate, you know? And once the bag is open, well, that's it. A Hawkins Cheezie has never gone stale in my house!

"Sometimes Otto joins me and brings toasted tea scones. He's the nicest man. I've worked for him for decades—would do anything for him. Wasn't crazy about his wife or his father, mind you. Did you know them?"

Before Aislin could reply, Beverly resumed her chatter.

"If you ask me, you could darken your hair a bit. The white blonde doesn't suit your colouring. You look as though you're naturally a honey blonde. I don't know why you would cover that up. Now me, with my colouring, I could never do any sort of blonde, you know what I mean?" She laughed, plumping her dark poodle curls. "I also run the best and only hair salon in town. So I know what I'm talking about. Working on corpses is a side gig. I took a course on embalming but didn't like all the chemicals. This was a few years ago, mind you, and the industry has changed. But too late for me. I'm happy doing up the dead ones so they go to their next gig looking good, you know what I mean? There's a lot of job satisfaction in that."

Aislin nodded. The aroma of the garlicky hummus was making her stomach grumble, and she was so hungry she was having trouble following the dips and turns of Beverly's conversation.

"Here you go," she said, passing Aislin a plate loaded with an assortment of goodies from her lunch bag. "I worry about Otto. I don't think he's eating enough. And now that he's moved into his RV, well, who knows what's going to happen.

"When your parents died, it was just so tragic. They were such lovely people. People still talk about them, you know what I mean? I always felt so sorry for you. Near broke my heart. But Letty, well, she never talks about them or you. She clams right up tight whenever I try to bring them up. I'm a little scared of her if you don't mind me saying. She's a good tipper, though. I'll say that."

"This is not a party pad!" Aislin and Beverly jumped.

"When I heard you talking, Beverly, I assumed you were talking to Otto, who's here somewhere. I don't know where in the world you got the idea that it was acceptable to entertain guests while you're supposed to be working. And it's past lunch. I seriously think we need to introduce a time clock. Otto may have overlooked lax work ethics, but we do not."

"Mr. Theo, I only wanted to finish up this ticket before I had lunch. I don't like to eat when I'm in the middle of a job. It upsets my stomach."

"Your digestive issues are not my concern. In the future, stick to the schedule. And stop calling me Mr. Theo. I've asked you repeatedly to call me Mr. Thunberger."

Theo turned to Aislin. "And just why are you here? Looking for a job?"

Reminding herself of Otto's words, Aislin replied, "Theo! Just the guy I was hoping to see." Clenching her hands, she continued. "I wanted to apologize for my behaviour when we met. I would appreciate talking to you about any opportunities at *The Standard* that may be a fit for a journo with my experience. Do you have an office where we could talk?" She handed her plate to the speechless Beverly, grimaced at her, and opened the door.

Theo looked her over, then said, "Of course I have an office. My uncle just bought this place. I am the director of operations. Follow me." He led her outside. As they crossed the parking lot, Aislin looked back and saw a plume of dark-grey smoke rising straight up into the bright-blue sky. Her stomach scrinched.

Theo ushered her into what was formerly Otto's office. The door now bore "Theo Thunberger, Director of Operations" in ostentatious gold lettering.

The room was transformed. The former aura of welcoming comfort was now one of sterile efficiency. The furniture was angular and spare, the walls an oppressive beige. The paintings were cheap Norman Rockwell reproductions that seemed incongruous and insensitive. Aislin tried to imagine what had gone through the minds of Twiggy's parents as they sat there, trying to reconcile the reality of their son's life with a Norman Rockwell depiction of familial bliss.

Theo settled himself into his ample leather chair and indicated Aislin to sit. Splaying his soft hands on the desktop, he began with, "You were fired from your last job, right? And I assume you're finding it hard to get anyone to hire you."

"Well, you know what they say about people who make assumptions! For the record, I was not fired. I resigned from my position due to personal issues that I am not prepared to discuss." He was winding her up, and she was letting him. "I am a versatile reporter. I have covered everything from municipal affairs to strata title disputes to resource development. I particularly enjoyed reporting on resource development projects."

"There's not much going on around here in terms of resource development, apart from the odd dispute between some lazy, filthy tree huggers and hardworking loggers trying to keep their families fed."

Aislin did not take the bait.

Theo leaned forward and hissed, "I know why you're here."

"You do?"

"I know all about your new business venture. You can't fool me with this fake interest in working at the paper. I'm onto you."

The strain of remaining civil made her sweat. Wiping her damp palms on her jeans, she said, "Okay. What are your thoughts about why I am here?"

"You're here to sniff around and see what you can learn that will help your business."

"You're partially right. I don't want to work at *The Standard*. But I'm not here to find out how to steal clients. That's a ridiculous assumption. You offer something completely different from the services we offer. I was hoping we could develop a relationship based on reciprocity. We send people your way, and you send some our way. Nothing more devious than that."

Theo opened the door. "I don't think we have anything further to discuss."

Aislin had no idea how long Otto needed at his end. The smoke was a good sign that things were at least underway. But she figured he couldn't process a body in the short time they had been here.

She followed Theo down the hall and out the door. "I'm actually here because I'm wondering if you would like to go on a date?"

He stopped so abruptly she nearly ran into him. "A date?"

"You know, to dinner or something? Unless, of course, you're in a committed relationship. In which case, forget I asked," she said, praying he was engaged or gay.

"You want to go on a date. With me."

"I guess. I mean, yes. For dinner."

"Why?"

"Um, because I think you're interesting? We're kind of in the same line of work. And you're new to town, and I'm newly back to town, and everyone I know from way back when is in a relationship. Or I think they're in a relationship. Still, whenever you ask about their partner, they take evasive action and never answer the damn question, so you're left wondering about the state of their relationship. I mean, they've known each other for decades, so maybe they've just drifted apart." Theo's expression stopped her from going further.

"Well, that was more information than I needed. Yes, I suppose we could go out. Where do you want to go?"

Aislin panicked. She hadn't been out for dinner in her hometown for years. "Jack's." It was the only restaurant she knew apart from the Mugshot, and there was no way in hell she was going on a date there.

"You want to have dinner at Jack's? It's a hole in the wall."

"No, it isn't. It's been part of this town since the dawn of time. I love their food. The menu is the same as it has always been."

"No. I am not eating at Jack's. We can go to a restaurant in Victoria. I have a few favourite haunts where I'm well known. They have good food and interesting wine lists. None of this local bilge water. It would be good to get out of here for at least an evening. I love how my Porsche handles the twists of the highway. As long as we don't get stuck in crawling tourist traffic. So a weeknight is best. Leave it with me. I'll take care of the details."

"Victoria! That's a long way. And a long drive home, and it'll be dark by then. I'm just not sure." She was suddenly dizzy and unsteady. She bent over and put her hands on her knees. "I, um, just need a moment. I think I need a glass of water. Do you mind?" she said without looking up.

"What's wrong with you?"

"It's a long story. I just need some water."

"Get her some water, stat," bellowed Beverly, barrelling up the path. She put her arm around Aislin's shoulders and guided her to a shady bench. "Now, you just put your head between your knees and breathe normal like. I'll stay with you. Mr. Theo had no idea what he was saying. He doesn't know the story of your parents." She rubbed Aislin's back gently.

"Good thing I came along when I did." Then she lowered her voice and whispered, "Otto says he needs another twenty minutes." And then added, "I overheard you invite him on a date. Are you really interested in that twit? You're way too good for the likes of him."

Aislin shook her head and gasped. "Can't bear to breathe the same air."

"I get it; it's a stalling technique. Well, you sure shocked me. And him, I think."

"Shocked myself."

Theo was run-walking towards them, trying not to sploosh water on his khaki pants. "You can go now, Beverly. You're still on the clock. I'll speak to you later about why you were wandering around out here. The gardens are for the enjoyment of the bereaved, not staff. Go. Go."

He sat so close his thigh rubbed hers. He placed a hand on Aislin's back and patted it. Heavily and awkwardly.

She sat up, shifted her body, pushed her hair back, and turned her face to the sun.

"What just happened? Do you have epileptic fits or some weird disorder?"

She shook her head. "No, I am not epileptic, and I do not have any disorders other than I sometimes randomly hyperventilate." There was no way she was going to elaborate. But she needed to occupy him.

"I just need to sit here for a bit, if you don't mind. I would feel better if someone sat with me. I could always ask Beverly if you're too busy."

"No, definitely not! I'll stay." He placed his arm along the back of the bench, behind Aislin. She couldn't lean back without touching him, so she remained bolt upright.

"Thanks, Theo. Why don't you tell me all about yourself and your family while I rest?"

He blathered on about himself, his uncle, and his father. Didn't mention a mother. Or siblings. His dull diatribe brought her heart rate straight back down. She hoped Otto would arrive soon and save her. The smoke plume had disappeared.

She interrupted his monologue. "So, Theo, what do you know about cremation? Have you processed a body? Is that the right term? 'Process'? How long does it take? And how long does it take the ashes to cool before you can box them up?"

The abrupt change of topic threw him. He sighed his annoyance. "Why do you want to know? I thought you wanted to hear about my family."

"I did. I do. But I have a short attention span. Now I'm curious about cremations. You're new to this business, so what's the learning curve like? You're so lucky to have Otto as a mentor. I mean, no one knows the funeral business like him." She threw that in because she recalled how he had rudely implied Otto's cognitive powers were slipping.

"I have learned a great deal on my own. I have the sort of mind that absorbs details, which is why I was good at law. Otto has been somewhat helpful. With the hands-on stuff. But his record keeping has really done a nosedive. For decades, he was meticulous. And then, all of a sudden, these last few days, his accuracy is just gone. We can't figure out who has been run through the retort, so we have no idea who is in which urn. It's a colossal mess. He started using nicknames! I mean, really? So unprofessional. I tried to get him to explain it all the other day, but he said he needed to sort it out on his own. We have two important funerals this week, so he better get on it. I just hope he's kept track of who's planted where. Can you imagine the hell if those records are also a mess? Uncle Bob is not impressed. We'll keep him on the payroll a bit longer, but we're not prepared to support him in his retirement. Obviously, he's gone gaga. Good thing we bought the business before he ran it into the ground." Aislin checked his face to see if it was an intentional pun.

While Theo was busy listing Otto's failings, the man himself emerged from the crematorium. Jumping up, she said, "Gotta go."

"Wait a sec. What's your number? And what day's good for dinner? My calendar's pretty full, but I can make room. For you."

"Good to know. I'll be in touch. Gotta run. Otto's leaving." She jogged down the path to the parking lot. Otto opened the door for her and handed her a cardboard box. She was shocked at its insignificance.

Otto moved around to his side of the car with surprising agility for a man his age. He tossed Twiggy's vest into the back seat. As they sped out, Aislin checked on Theo in her side mirror. He was stomping down to the crematorium. No doubt to ream Beverly out for her latest infraction.

"So, everything went well?"

Otto struggled with his seat belt as they raced off, the car weaving wildly. "As well as can be expected when one is illegally processing the body of a suspect in a murder case," he said, steering back into his lane. "And filling in the forms with incomplete information. And then switching those cremains with another murder victim. And then stealing the latter." He tipped his head towards the box on Aislin's lap.

"So this is Twiggy? I'm holding all that remains of a whole person. In a box. On my lap. A person I have never met. It feels kinda weirdly intimate. And it's not very heavy. I mean, considering it's a whole person."

"It's not actually a whole person. Cremains are the bones. Tissues, organs, skin, etcetera are burnt off." Aislin put her hands over her ears.

"Too much information!"

"Sorry. Hazard of spending one's life in a profession no one ever wants to think about or learn about. When I have a captive audience and a box of cremains, I tend to seize the opportunity." He looked at her. "Are you still okay being part of this?" he asked.

"Well, I had to swallow my bile and pretend I wanted to go on a date with the vile Theo. For that, I will always have regrets. He actually believed me! And he wanted to go to Victoria for dinner, which gave me an anxiety attack. But Beverly saved me. She's awesome. And then he patted me on the back. He actually touched me—made my skin crawl. Wish I could have my skin surgically removed, cleansed, and replaced." She paused. "And yes, I know none of that compares to the risk you've just taken."

Otto waved his hand dismissively. "I am quite enjoying myself. I feel alive. And it feels good. I want to feel like this for the rest of my life, however long that may be."

Something in his tone pricked Aislin's heart. She glanced at him as he drove. His face looked drawn. She didn't know him well enough to know if that was normal.

She was suddenly profoundly exhausted. And she still needed to eat. "Was a lunch break part of our itinerary? I'm so hungry I can't remember what we're supposed to do next. Beverly had just handed me some food when Theo burst in and started in on her. Why is she still there if it's just a side gig and she has her own business?"

"Beverly has been a joy to work with from the very first day she arrived. Her commitment to her craft is a gift. She truly cares about people's appearance, dead or alive. She has been integral to the business. And to my sanity. As questionable as that may be at this moment. But she understood that I needed to sell. I am deeply sorry the only interested party was the Thunbergers."

"How much does she know about what we're up to?"

"She knew something was amiss as soon as I started being rather casual, if you will, about record keeping. I needed to show a sharp decline in my mental prowess for today's entry not to set off alarm bells. She didn't ask for details but did ask how she could help. So, I asked her to keep an eye on you. We both knew it was detrimental to her long-term employment at The Maples. But she's ready to go. The Thunbergers, especially your pal, are a nasty bunch."

"Not my pal. I couldn't stand him the minute I met him. He was trolling for obituary-writing opportunities at funerals. He's a mincing, prancing Nazi."

Otto laughed. "You are so like your grandfather. That was one of his expressions." He pulled into the Mugshot Café parking lot, which was uncharacteristically empty. "Bring Twiggy, will you?"

Aislin stopped herself from refusing. She was near tears from Otto's comment about her being like Frank. She couldn't remember anyone ever drawing a comparison.

She carried the box at arm's length, but it was too heavy, so she had to hug it against her chest. Jill opened the door for them. "You two have had a busy morning, according to the grapevine. I have lunch all ready for you. Sit at the counter so you can regale me while I dish up."

Jill served loaded Reubens on rye, with borscht and beer. Recalling Letty's comments about weight gain, Aislin hesitated a beat, but the aroma won her over. She tried not to slurp the rich, tangy soup. Beside her, Otto was moaning ever so slightly as he bit into his Reuben.

"I'll hit you with questions after you've eaten. But while you're eating, I'll fill you in on what's been buzzing around. Apparently, Jim Brownlee was behind your being pulled over. He's a nosey son of a bitch, that one. The cops know something's going on but can't put their fingers on just what that is. 10-Gauge was called in for questioning. They've also questioned Donny Quinn, so they're digging deep. And closing in. I'm assuming they're watching the Mugshot. Which means they're looking closely at each of us. So don't be surprised if they come knocking. But we're all pretty squeaky clean. Pillars of society, you might say. However, that won't stop them from paying each of us a visit. So, watch yourselves and be prepared."

Otto sat back, satiated, wiping his fingers and face. "Jill, you do make a mean Reuben. Better than your dad's. It feels good to feel full. If I may be so honest, the only thing I miss about my late wife is her cooking."

Aislin raised her eyebrows at her sandwich. She hoped Otto wasn't expecting expansive culinary skills from Letty. Letty had always been a rudimentary cook. Memorable meals were created by Frank, who was a robust and adventurous but infrequent cook.

Jill wrapped both hands around the box and pulled it across the counter. She closed her eyes, hung her head, and hugged the box. Aislin and Otto watched and waited. After a few moments of stillness, Jill drew herself up, patted the box, and whispered, "Still love you."

She came out of herself. "Twiggy and I were a thing at one time. He was a character. He had a way of filling your heart. But he loved women, all women, too much, so he never could commit for long. His parents disowned him early on. They're stuffy professionals who wanted their wild child to grow up and fall into step with their expectations. It wasn't ever going to happen. So, he found his family with the Dogs. And the instant families that sprung up from almost every woman he was with. I have no idea how many children he has scattered up and down the island. The ceremony could be quite interesting from that aspect alone!" She laughed. And sighed. "My heart hurts when I think of him. A light has gone out for so many people who loved him."

"So that's why there are duelling ceremonies. Because his family couldn't accept him being a biker. That's just so sad," said Aislin. "But wouldn't they want to know the people who were important to him?"

Otto, who had seen every configuration of dysfunctional family over the decades, remained silent.

"In a perfect world, in a Hollywood version of a perfect world, yes, there would be a great big, wet hugfest," replied Jill. "Twiggy was emotionally damaged by their rejection. He blamed his father and his sister more than his mother. His father was an unforgiving, cruel bastard; his sister a mini-me of her father. I'm not sure if his parents even know they have a bunch of grandchildren. At the park, I saw one little guy who was the spitting image of Twiggy, and he was showing off to some little girls and making them laugh."

Jill stretched and twisted her torso left to right. An audible series of cracks followed. "That feels better. Back to business. I'm expecting 10-Gauge any minute. He's going to take Twiggy to the clubhouse for an in-house send-off. They're working on making his bike, which he never took care of, presentable. 10-Gauge will trailer it on the ride. Which means he will be in front—the leader of the pack. That'll nourish his overfed ego."

"So you don't like the guy either. I thought it was just me, as everyone else in my life swooned at first sight." Aislin covered a yawn. "Can we go home now? It's been an exceptionally long, emotionally exhausting day. So far, I've been searched and blindfolded by a bunch of thugs, sucked up to Jim Freaking Brownlee, was pulled over by the RCMP, hung out in a crematorium with a woman doing up a dead person, and to top it all off, I got up close and personal with Theo Freaking Thunberger, which made me hyperventilate." She rested her forehead on the counter.

Otto patted her shoulder. "You've been a delightful partner in crime. I couldn't have pulled this off without you."

"If you want your day to end on a lower note, hang around until 10-Gauge turns up. Otherwise, skedaddle home and take a hot bath," suggested Jill. "I can take care of this next leg of the plan on my own."

They were a few blocks away when 10-Gauge and his sidekicks blew past them without a glance.

Chapter 15

Arriving at Letty's brought more shock waves. Squeezed into the driveway was Otto's enormous RV. The beige and brown exterior wore a patina of green mould. Its enormity dwarfed not just the garage but also the house.

Standing in front of the RV were Nick and Letty. Aislin twitched as she resisted the impulse to pull down the visor and check her appearance. But if she looked as wrung out and ragged as she felt, it was best not to know.

"The Behemoth will look less imposing once it's been power washed. I may have to ask Nick for assistance. I tried to do it last week, but I was standing too close, and the force of the water blew me onto my ass," Otto said by way of apology. "It's a good sign that they're talking, isn't it? I know Letty has harboured ill feelings towards Nick for years."

"She's built those ill feelings into a potential towering inferno. I just hope this face-to-face doesn't set it alight." Aislin was unsure of the best approach. Letty looked steamed. She decided on a charm offensive.

"Gran! Nick! Phase One done and dusted."

Letty swung her attention to Aislin and Otto as they walked up the path. "You've been gone all day on this crazy scheme, fraternizing with criminals, breaking the law, and who knows what else. And I haven't heard a single word. I've been worried sick. One of you could have called to let me know you were still alive!"

Letty stormed up the steps and slammed the door. Nick studied his feet. Otto studied his RV.

"She's always the maddest when she's relieved. She'll calm down in a bit. I guess we should have called. I turned my phone off before we got to the Dogs' clubhouse and forgot to turn it back on. There was just so much going on. Kinda bounced from one crazy scene to the next, right, Otto?"

"It's been an exhilarating, albeit occasionally harrowing day. Most fun I've had in decades. I felt so alive." Otto rubbed his hands together. "I have some beer in the fridge. I'll get that. While one of you gets Letty," he said over his shoulder as he disappeared into the RV. He popped his head back out. "And thanks, Nick, for driving the Behemoth over and parking it. I don't know if I could have managed to get it into this spot without inflicting some serious damage."

"You're welcome, Coward," called Nick. He turned to Aislin, smiling, and said, "I guess that leaves you to go warm her up."

"Thanks! I barely have the energy to get up the stairs, let alone sweet talk Letty down from her platform of righteous indignation." She scowled at the Behemoth. "It's kinda ugly and huge, isn't it? I am still grappling with what all of this means. It's a sideshow to the main event, right?" she said, pointing at the RV. "I feel as though I've been sucked into the vortex of Crazy Town. I'm doing and saying things I never, ever would have even considered in my former life."

Nick leaned over and gave her an elbow poke in her ribs. "Come on, admit it, at some level, you're enjoying this new, deeply doubly weird life you're living. You look a lot healthier. And happier. It's called living life large. And it's what we're meant to do."

Aislin blushed. And shrugged in agreement. She mentally tabbed his comment about her appearance for examination at a later date. Right now, she needed to deal with Letty.

"Wish me luck. And if I'm gone for more than an hour, send backup."

Closing the door gently behind her, she leaned on it and relaxed briefly into the cool, soothing, familiar darkness of the hall. Even the sound of Letty banging around in the kitchen was comforting.

"Gran, I'm so very sorry about not calling you and worrying you so much. It's been quite a day."

Letty halted her assault on the kitchen china and leaned on the counter, arms crossed. "I've been worried since the moment you left. I imagined all sorts of horrors. How could you be so heartless?"

"Heartless is a bit strong, don't you think? I mean, I've been kind of stressed all day, too!"

"You don't need to take that tone with me, young lady." Letty slammed her hand onto the counter. "You never consider other people. Never have, probably never will. No wonder you're single."

"Excuse me? What has my relationship status got to do with anything? You're also single, by the way."

Otto cautiously opened the door. "May I borrow a bottle opener? I don't seem to have one in the RV."

Letty flung open the utensil drawer, rattling its contents, picked out the bottle opener, and raised her arm to hurl it at him. But Otto was quick and had her wrapped in a big hug before the corkscrew was airborne.

"It's okay, darling. We're all okay. Everything's going to be okay." He waggled his head at Aislin, indicating she, too, should join the hug. Aislin hesitated, but her overdue need for a comforting hug won over. Otto adjusted his arms so the two combatants could hug within his hug.

When Nick walked in, he saw a tangle of arms, heads, and legs rocking back and forth. He paused for a moment, smiling, then reversed back out. Aislin watched him from beneath Otto's armpit, where her head was uncomfortably jammed. Otto's deodorant had not been entirely effective.

She got the distinct feeling the other two were enjoying the closeness more than she was. She held her breath as she tried to extricate herself from Otto's armpit and Letty's arms.

Letty untangled herself first. "Enough of that," she said, patting her hair back into place. "Shall we have drinks in the garden so you two can fill us in on what you've been through? Aislin, go fetch Nick."

A rush of happiness flooded her weary body. Nick was sitting on the front steps looking at his phone. "Hey, join us in the garden for drinks for the debrief. Letty's orders."

He shook his phone at her. "Something's come up. Would have enjoyed the debrief, but duty calls."

"Bummer. Another lethargic turtle? I like to think I'm your only turtle-owning client."

Nick grinned. "I hate to break it to you, but you aren't my only turtle-owning client because you didn't keep your appointment; ergo, you're not a client. Remember?" His face deflated as his smile faded. "It's a personal, not professional, matter." He stood up, stretched, and sighed. "I've avoided it as long as humanly possible. You know what they say, you can run, but you're just going to die tired."

Her need to know was tempered by her past experiences with Nick when he flipped moods. "Hey, if there's anything I can do, let me know. Even if you just need an ear. You've been such amazing support for me during all of this; I would be honoured to return the favour." She put her arms out to hug him, but Letty's sudden appearance at the door left her awkwardly standing with her hands out. Nick quickly slapped them, then held his up for high fives. Neither made eye contact.

"Thanks, Letty, for the invitation, but I've been summoned." He took the steps down two at a time, just as he had when he used to come to do yard work. Aislin had always marvelled at his agility. He never tripped. She tried it once, but it did not end well.

"Yes, well, that's disappointing. He's turned out alright, despite his mother. We're waiting for you in the back. What should we have for dinner? You're probably too exhausted to cook. Let's order from Jack's. My treat."

Aislin wanted to call to Letty's retreating back, "Who are you, and what have you done with my grandmother?" Instead, she followed her through to the back porch. Otto reclined in a comfy chair with a beer, and Letty was just settling into the other with a glass of wine. That left a hard-backed teak chair behind theirs for Aislin.

"Anything in particular you would like, Otto? We have a standard order, but we're open to adapting."

Otto gave his preferences, Letty gave her credit card number, and Aislin gratefully retreated to the kitchen to place the order. She then headed upstairs for a much-needed shower before the food arrived.

As Aislin was drying off, she heard a banging on the front door. She called to Letty through the window that the food had arrived.

Steam had engulfed the tiny bathroom, so she flicked on the fan. She rubbed a clear circle on the mirror and studied her reflection. Did she look better, as people mentioned? Her face was fuller. A few months ago, that observation would have propelled her into an enhanced fitness regime and a diet of rice crackers. She pulled on her sweats and scrunched her wet hair into a clip. She grinned at her newly found confidence to dress for comfort, not appearance. *Otto, if you're going to hitch your giant RV to the Fitzgerald women, you're going to have to accept the good, the bad, and the ugly.* When she turned off the fan, she heard the voices of Sarah and Donny, not the delivery driver.

"You shouldn't have gone to all that effort," said Donny, taking in her appearance when she rushed in. "Despite the grunge look you've adopted, you're glowing, but woe my broken heart, I don't think it is I who have you lit up like a firefly."

Sarah smacked her brother and hugged Aislin. "God, it's good to see you. I've been so worried all day. Would a call or text saying 'The eagle has landed' have been too much to ask?"

Aislin shot a look at Letty, expecting her to reignite.

"Don't go there. Just don't. For the record, I am very sorry to have not been in touch. My extreme bad. What's up? When I heard the knocking, I thought it was Jack's delivery driver."

"We would love to stay for dinner; thanks so much for inviting us," said Donny, giving Letty a sideways hug, which was rebuffed.

"Donny, behave," said Sarah, thwacking his temple with a finger. She turned to Aislin. "We've got trouble."

Her brother waved a hand dismissively. "Don't be so dramatic, dear sister. We're not in dire straits. The bereaved Mrs. Weronika Czekoj, wife of the late Aleksy Czekoj, who offed her former amour Twiggy, has been going around telling everyone her husband is dead."

"What the hell? Who spilled? My God, this is going to land us all in jail," Aislin wailed.

"Don't be hysterical," Letty snapped. "This Weronika woman must be stopped."

Aislin paused in her pacing and asked, "Define stopped?"

"What exactly does the widow Weronika know? And who is her source?" interjected Otto calmly.

"It seems our lascivious widow sought solace for her loss in the arms of one of 10-Gauge's associates, and he may have overshared in a moment of passion. I believe it was one of the two who stood guard over you while you were enjoying the hospitality of the Timber Dogs at their clubhouse."

The doorbell rang, and Aislin pushed Donny aside in her rush to get to the door. "We ordered lots of food, so put out plates for everyone," she called behind her. There was a churn of noise in the kitchen as everyone shuffled left and right in an effort to stay out of Letty's path as she banged through cupboards and drawers.

"Otto, go get two bottles of wine from the dining room," Letty barked. "Sarah, set the table. Donny, sit over there, be quiet, and stay out of my way."

Donny scuttled to the appointed chair and sat with his hands clasped on the table, watching the action. Sarah, who knew her way around the kitchen, had the table set in a flash. She gave Letty a quick hug and sat down beside her brother.

Otto poured the wine while keeping an eye on Letty, who was assembling the plates. Aislin set the food and serving spoons on the counter. Grandmother and granddaughter managed to stay out of each other's shipping lane, despite the crowded kitchen.

When everyone had served themselves and were settled at the table, Otto cleared his throat. "Today, at last, I have fulfilled my life-long wish: I lived up to my last name 'Lawless.' As a child, in my fantasy life, I was a daredevil, a rule breaker, a ne'er-do-well. In reality, I was a rule follower, an ethical business owner, and a paycheque producer. Today, I broke rules! I was in a biker clubhouse. I was pulled over by the RCMP for the first time in my life, and I'm seventy-nine years old! I was license-revoking professionally unethical, and it was the most fun I have ever had."

Donny clapped the table, making everyone jump. "Hear, hear! Otto, my man, you are an inspiration to all us young, law-abiding dullards. Hope fills my breast."

Sarah turned to her brother. "What are you going on about? You've never been law-abiding. Ever."

"Shush now, sister, and let the good man speak. He has more on his chest he needs to share."

Otto smiled tenderly at Donny. "Your perception is admirable. I do have more to say. I want to thank my coconspirators for allowing me to live my dream. And I especially thank Aislin for riding shotgun, for enduring our experiences at the clubhouse with good grace, for distracting Jim Brownlee, and for keeping the loathsome Theo Thunberger occupied while I was busy in the crematorium. Cheers to you, Aislin."

Heat flooded her face. She grinned and raised her glass. "Thanks, Otto."

"But you can't stand Theo! How on earth did you distract him?" Sarah asked.

Aislin's grin deepened. "I invited him on a date!"

"No way."

"Yes way! I did. I invited Theo Freaking Thunberger on a date. I didn't plan to, but I needed to keep his attention and I just blurted it out. I think I shocked both of us. And he said yes!"

Aislin told her story, haltingly at first and fiddling with the alignment of glasses and cutlery, but as she warmed to the experience of being the centre of attention, her hands calmed down and became part of the telling. When she had finished, her audience, including Letty, clapped and cheered. As they did, she looked around the kitchen she grew up in, at the begrudging pride underwritten with concern on her grandmother's face, at the mile-wide smile on her best friend's face, at Otto's reflective expression, at Donny's goofy toothy grin, and felt a rare sense of calmness suffuse her system. These were her people. And they loved her as she was. Flaws and all.

One face was missing. She hoped whatever Nick was dealing with was not soul-crushing.

Sarah caught the shift in her expression and went straight to the core. "Where's Nick, by the way? Shouldn't he be here with us? He has a major role in all of this."

All eyes returned to Aislin. "He had a personal matter to deal with," she replied as her hands resumed their incessant ordering of items.

"I think that wife of his has developed a taste for something not on the menu," said Donny cryptically.

"What on earth does that mean?" Sarah asked before Aislin could. "But, before you answer, tell us who your source is so we can judge the validity of your intel."

"I heard it while I was having a haircut with the lovely Beverly. She was not the purveyor of the information but conveniently stopped talking just long enough for me to overhear two gasbags discussing the marriage of the town's esteemed vet and his marginally talented artist wife."

"And?" Sarah urged, looking at Aislin, who was studying her hands.

"Well, seeing how you're asking, I will lower my standards and stoop to sharing street gossip. Kate, it seems, has begun to spend an inordinate amount of time personally mentoring a particular student." Donny paused for effect.

Aislin was not eager for the dish Donny was about to serve. She felt it was disloyal to Nick to be discussing his marriage. She glanced at Otto to see if he felt the same way, but he was busy gauging Letty, whose eyes were riveted on Donny.

"But this is not your garden-variety mentoring relationship. The student deserving of Kate's unrelenting attention is a Ms. Caitlin Reed."

For a few moments, the only sound in the kitchen was the bump bump bump from Secretariat as he moved around his tank. Then Letty pushed her chair back and stood up. She collected the plates and scraped the leftovers into the bin. Aislin looked at Otto. Was this news about Kate new to him? Had Nick confided in him? Otto's face was inscrutable.

"Um, we still have a problem we should talk about," said Aislin, anxious to move the conversation away from Nick. "What are we going to do about this Weronika?"

"Donny, how concerned should we be? What does she know?" Otto asked.

"She doesn't *know* anything. She is a woman who enjoys being the eye of a storm. Thrives on drama. The living, breathing definition of a diva."

"We can't let her whip up the rumour mill. We are all implicated in this coverup, to one degree or another. Up until now, it was just crazy fun. Now it's getting a bit scary," Sarah said.

In an unusually sombre tone, Donny continued. "Yes, we are co-conspirators, and as such, we are breaking any number of laws, but we've come this far, and it's not feasible to step aside. Not without dire consequences, and I am not speaking just of the legal morass that would come our way. We must not forget our so-called partners. They don't smile benignly at turncoats. Retaliation may not be immediate, but it will be harsh."

Otto spoke into the vacuum created by Donny's assessment of their situation. "We can't undo what we've done; therefore, we have no choice but to carry on with the plan. Damn the torpedoes, as they say. Are we all in agreement?" He looked at Letty, who pursed her lips and held his eyes but eventually nodded. Otto turned to Aislin, who looked at Letty, then nodded. Aislin then looked at Sarah, who paused slightly, then nodded. The room was silent.

Donny's laugh broke the film of silence. "You all look like a bunch of demented bobbleheads! Now, let's get on with the business of getting on. The question on the table is how do we manage the lustful avenging Weronika? I think we need to pour balm on her emotions, which are high at this point and a bit erratic, and encourage her to attend Twiggy's funeral at The Maples. We just need to remind her how much he loved her. Play to her ego. She's going to want to be there because there's more potential for creating drama with his family. And, seeing how the ashes being interred during that farce of a funeral are actually those of her late beloved, she will unwittingly be attending his send-off to the other side as well."

"So we're buying time," stated Otto.

"Exactly! We are a fluid, resourceful bunch. We will come up with something. If and when needed. I'm going to see 10-Gauge tonight. I think he's the perfect guy to manage our libidinous Weronika." Donny looked squarely at his sister, who was suddenly busy examining her fingernails.

"I agree. I like Donny's plan. Who knows? Maybe she'll set her sights on Theo!" said Aislin, her mischievous side leaking out.

"And I say we need to call an end to this discussion and this day," said Letty. She stomped to the sink and turned on both taps full blast.

Sarah and Donny took the hint. Aislin called her goodbyes without getting up. She felt rooted to her seat, suddenly too exhausted to stand up. She watched Letty punishing the cutlery. Her back was straight and stiff. Never a good sign. Aislin reminded herself that Letty had been remarkably accepting of the chaos that had interrupted her formerly quiet life as an elderly widow living alone. But Aislin suspected Letty begrudgingly enjoyed the vitality of that chaos. Elaine and her control issues had receded from Letty's life. Aislin indulged in a brief musing on how Elaine would view the current goings-on.

She pushed herself up with effort. "I'm off to bed. If I can make it up the stairs." She tapped Letty on her back. Her grandmother took her time drying her hands before turning. Aislin wrapped her in a big hug, which Letty eventually relaxed into and returned. "I love you, Gran, and I'm sorry I worried you today, and I'm sorry for this chaos, but it will all work out," she whispered in her ear before kissing her cheek. Otto watched, a small smile on his lips.

"Good night, Otto. Thanks for a wild day." Aislin patted him on the shoulder as she squeezed out the kitchen door.

Chapter 16

The following two days were filled with meetings, phone calls, site visits, and putting out minor fires as they finalized the details for Twiggy's celebration of life. Aislin took on her new role as an event planner with her typical piercing focus and determination to excel. Sarah was a calm and efficient mentor. They frequently congratulated themselves on their brilliance.

There was little communication from 10-Gauge. They sent a daily list of action items completed. Apart from texting a few questions, he left them to do their job. There was no more noise from Weronika. Aislin wanted to ask Donny or Jill if they had heard anything. Sarah's advice was to forget about it, but Aislin couldn't shake her anxiety. At night, her mind served up endless scenarios of Weronika crashing Twiggy's event.

The other slipstream of anxiety keeping sleep at bay was Aislin's concern about Nick. She obsessively checked for texts and scanned for his car when running errands. She wanted to ask Otto but held back.

"You look tired," Sarah said over coffee at the Mugshot the day before the big event. "What's keeping you awake at night? Ghosts of dead bikers? Untimely appearances by unwanted widows? The waxing moon?"

Aislin shrugged. "My last solid sleep is barely a memory. I fall asleep as soon as I go to bed, but about an hour later, I suddenly wake up and then my overly active imagination takes control and keeps my brain hopping for the next four hours and then right before the damn robins start shrieking, I fall into a deep sleep."

Sarah squinted at her. "Have you heard from Nick at all?"

Aislin shook her head, marvelling at Sarah's ability to take her last statement and go right to the heart of her anxiety. "Nope."

"It is a bit weird, isn't it, for him to drop off the face of the earth now of all times?"

"It is. Not that it matters. I mean, we don't need him for anything." She fiddled with her coffee spoon.

"Have you reached out to him?"

"Nope."

"It's a concept when one is concerned about a friend, you know. Showing you care is a much valued and regrettably rare human emotion."

"I don't want to appear nosey."

"Nosiness and concern are two very different things. Maybe he's waiting to hear from you. You should text him and ask. He's probably wondering why he hasn't heard from you. Go on, do it."

"You think so?"

Sarah rolled her eyes dramatically and sighed. "Would I ever give you bad advice?"

"Well, yes, actually, you have a history of giving me bad advice, especially where Nick is concerned. You were the one who advised me to try and kiss him at that horrible dance in grade nine. That went well. Kate saw me and pulled my hair. And then told all her snarky gal pals. I was humiliated."

"One bad idea and you write me off? Sheesh. That's fickle. You know you're dying to hear from him, so just put yourself and me out of our collective misery."

Aislin pulled a face. "Fine." She sent a one-line text, then slammed her phone down and stared at it. Then flipped it over face-down. Then put it in her purse. And then rearranged the condiments so that they were in a line of ascending height. "So, what else do we have to do before tomorrow? Can you believe we're almost at the end of this nutso gig? I hope our next client, should there be one, is a pillar of society."

"I think you should make a move on Nick. He's vulnerable. And he's obviously besotted with you. And you with him. What have you got to lose?"

Aislin shook her head. "You're nuts. There's quite a bit to lose. A really good friend, for starters. My self-esteem, which is still on the mend. My fragile sense of belonging. That enough for you?"

"You are so dramatic. Come on. Live a little. And decent guys are few and far between in this town. Nick is a standout."

"You're comfortable overlooking the fact that he's married, happily or otherwise? And, I may add, you were the injured party in your marriage when your husband played around."

"Wow, way to go for the jugular." Sarah's knuckles were white as she gripped her coffee mug. "Different players, different scenarios. Completely different."

"Really? Did not know that the ties that bind are valued on a case-by-case situation. You're either married, or you're not."

"And what do you know about marriage? Or long-term relationships?"

"Stop it, you two!" Jill was suddenly at their booth. "I can hear you bickering over the deep fryer, as can everyone else. So, either keep your private business private or live with the consequences of this entire town discussing what you were just discussing. Play nice or play somewhere else."

Aislin collected her phone, notebook, and pen. "I think we've covered everything we need to cover." She stalked out, back straight, shaking from shock at her tinder-dry temper. And dismayed at the fragility of her relationship with Sarah. Hot tears pierced her tired eyes as she fumbled with her key fob.

"Aislin, come on, don't leave mad. We're more than this. We have to learn how to work through disagreements and rough spots," Sarah called, hurrying to stop her before she got in her car. She touched Aislin on the shoulder, but Aislin pulled away and slid into her seat, slamming the door before driving away without a glance at Sarah.

Unseen by both women was Nick, who had just stepped out of his vet van. "Hey, Curly, what was that all about?"

Sarah spun around, fury on her face. "You! It was about you, you jackass." Sarah got in her car, rolled down the window, and yelled, "Sort your bloody life out so my partner and I can get on with ours."

Nick crossed his arms and leaned against his van. Jill came out with his order. "Those two were mad as wet cats. What the hell was that about?"

Jill patted him on the shoulder. "You, my dear."

Nick put up his hands in defensive mode. "Me? What could I possibly have done to mess up Curly and Moe? I've been on the island's north end for the past two days running my spay-neuter clinic. There's no coverage up there, and I've been driving since midnight so haven't looked at my phone."

"It's more what you did not do that's the problem. If you ask me, and I am sure you were just about to, so I'll save you the effort, you should talk to Aislin. That girl is carrying a torch for you. Always has. Everyone but you saw it. But you married someone else. And Aislin left town. And now she's back. And you're sending mixed messages. Classic storyline."

Nick kicked a small rock across the parking lot. "Why is this happening now? There's so bloody much going on. My life is a shitshow. The town is upside down with bikers, dead and alive. I don't need this on top of everything else!"

Nick got in the van, slammed the door, then got out again. "I'm sorry, Jill, I shouldn't have yelled at you. You're the messenger, a good friend, and the creator of the best food in town. I know you care about those two. And me."

"Thank you, but no apology is necessary. We go way back. Curly and Moe will work it out. And I hope you and Kate work out whatever is going on. Speaking as someone who has tried and failed spectacularly at being married, I can offer advice from hindsight. Whatever the issue, try to act like adults as you sort it out. Then you can get on with getting on with the minimum of long-term emotional damage."

Nick started to speak but stopped. He shook his head. "Almost downloaded all my angst on you because you're such a rock. Thanks for the advice."

Hands on hips, Jill watched him drive away. When she turned on her heel, she saw her customers clustered at the windows. She gave them the finger and indicated they should be back in their seats before she reentered the coffee shop.

Chapter 17

As Aislin drove home, gale force winds gathered strength deep within her. She jammed the car into park, slammed the door behind her, not bothering to lock it, then stormed into the house.

As Otto watched her from the window of the Behemoth, his phone vibrated. He glanced at it, saw Nick's number but let it go through to voice mail. He slipped out, locked the door, and hurried down the street.

The house shook as Aislin walloped the front door closed, jarring Letty upstairs in her room. Letty carefully crept across the floor, avoiding the creaky spots, and quietly closed her door.

Aislin burst into the kitchen, looking for her grandmother, looking for a fight. She scanned the garden. Letty usually left a trail of tools and debris, but it was devoid of all signs of occupation. Letty's car was in its usual spot, yet there was no sign or sound of her in the house.

She poured a glass of cold water and sat at the table. A few days ago, in this same room, she had felt surrounded by love and a sense of belonging. Now, as she looked around, she felt nothing.

Aislin put her glass in the dishwasher, wiped the counter, folded and hung the dishcloth over the stove handle, pushed her chair into the table, took a final look around the room, then went upstairs to pack.

As she was loading suitcases into her car, Otto returned from his walk with a newspaper under his arm. He stood and watched her, not offering to help. When she returned with the second load of suitcases, he was sitting in a lawn chair by the Behemoth, reading the newspaper with a cup of coffee. There was still no sign of Letty.

She pushed and shoved and swore as she forced her luggage into the car. Red-faced from the exertion, she finally closed the doors by leaning on them until the latch took hold. She stood back and pushed her hair from her sticky forehead.

"So, I'm going. Goodbye and good luck with all of this," Aislin said, waving her hand at the Behemoth and the house.

"Thank you. Are you planning on saying goodbye to your grandmother?"

"She's not around. You can say goodbye for me."

"No, I won't do that," replied Otto, his eyes still on his paper. "But, if you tell me where you're going, I will let her know where to forward your mail."

Wrestling with her luggage had drained her anger and all the energy fuelled by that anger. She sat down on the lawn and stared at her car.

Otto continued to read his newspaper. He glanced at the house and saw Letty peeking out the window of her room. He winked at her.

"I'm going to refresh my coffee. Would you like a cup?"

"Sure, why not. Sorry, Otto, I mean, thanks, that would be great."

He returned from the RV, handed her a full mug, and patted her shoulder before settling again in his chair with his newspaper on his lap. They sipped in silence. The sun slid behind a massive low cloud pregnant with rain. The temperature dropped, and Aislin became uncomfortably cold, but all her sweaters were in one of the many suitcases jammed into her car.

The rain started not gently but torrentially. Large and expressive. Otto hurriedly folded his chair and paper and moved inside the Behemoth, calling Aislin to join him. She did not hesitate.

"Wow, that's some rain!"

"Yes, they forecast a shower, not a monsoon. Now it's turned to hail!"

"Would you like me to refresh that for you? I think we could do with something warm inside while we wait for this storm to pass."

Aislin watched him move around the tiny kitchen. She could never live in such a confined space. Every summer, there was an outbreak of these monsters, typically driven by someone elderly and typically holding steadfast in the passing lane, too stubborn or terrified to change lanes.

She looked up as he handed her a fresh mug of coffee. His big soft face, so full of concern, warmed her. She flashed back to the day she visited him and how she had poured her heart out. He was an eminently compassionate and decent man. A different species from the men she had known as an adult.

With his back to her at the sink, he asked what had triggered her sudden decision to leave.

She didn't answer right away. She was uncomfortable and embarrassed by her flash-flood temper and the triviality of her emotions.

"Oh, you know. Something came up in a conversation."

Otto chuckled. "That's a very good nonanswer. No, I don't know, which is why I'm asking. Last I heard, you and Sarah were meeting this morning to go over the to-do list for tomorrow. So, what item on that list led to you packing your bags?"

Aislin squirmed. Her hands needed to be busy, but the table was empty. She just had her mug, and it was sloshing coffee as she twirled it. She looked around desperately. Otto placed cutlery and napkins on the table and wiped up the splatter of coffee drops.

With his back to her, he began to make sandwiches. "Go on," he prompted.

"Fine. It started with Sarah goading me into contacting Nick. He's disappeared, and I was worried. Last time we spoke, he was going home to deal with something 'personal' and then dead air. It's normal to be worried. That's what friends should do. They should worry." Her heart squeezed as she thought of Lara and how Aislin had not worried, had not read the signs right under her nose.

Otto remained silent. She continued slowly, reliving the scene. "And then we got into talking about his marriage, her ex, and my continued state of singlehood. She got all judgy." The pace of her hands slowed. "And then Jill got in our faces about being so loud everyone could hear us. And I got mad and left."

Otto took his time cutting the sandwiches and tidying the tiny counter. Aislin watched and waited for him to say something comforting. That Sarah was wrong to judge and that she, Aislin, was fully justified in her anger. But he was grinning when he joined her at the table.

"Well, I can clearly see why you would want to leave town! I mean, what other option was there?"

He waved his hand, silencing her retort. He picked up a sandwich, studied its contents, took a large bite, and chewed slowly, nodding. Three more bites and the sandwich was history. "Oh, I needed that. Sometimes I go too long between meals, and I feel a bit faint. Beverly, bless her, always kept a full assortment of snacks in her desk, which she pushed at me throughout the day to keep me fuelled. After a Scotch, I used to go in there in the evenings to see what I could rustle up. Not sure why I never bought my own. I think it was the joy of doing something illicit, however minor. I do miss her.

"So, back to you. You and your best friend, your soul mate, your business partner, had a difficult conversation that led you to pack your bags and leave. Without saying goodbye to your grandmother. Or taking your turtle. Am I on track here?"

She stared at him. She was so invested in nurturing her anger she had forgotten all about Secretariat. She had impetuously packed up and moved numerous times, and he was always with her. He was her one constant companion. She would have driven off without him if it had not begun to hail. A tide of shame rolled over her.

"I guess I really am the shallow, selfish, self-absorbed twit everyone says I am."

Otto smiled and shook his head. "No, my dear, you're not. But you do have your grandmother's mercurial temperament. Which is why the two of you spar so frequently."

He opened the door and looked up at the house to see if Letty was still watching, but she wasn't. The hailstorm had ended, leaving their world covered in a bumpy white blanket. A neighbour could be heard sweeping their steps. "Would you like a hand getting your suitcases back upstairs?"

"Otto, you're the best. Just to the porch would be fantastic. I can get them the rest of the way. Before Letty gets home from wherever she is."

Aislin chose a soothing playlist to listen to while restoring order to her room. Calmness through order. When her jackets and blouses were hung according to colour and everything else was precisely folded into drawers, she went downstairs to visit Secretariat. She put him on the floor as she cleaned his tank and changed his water. Then she sat down next to him and watched him explore. It seemed a long time since Fitz had been over. The craziness of the past few days had consumed them all. She found her phone and texted Sarah, inviting her and Fitz over, saying Secretariat missed his buddy. Sarah replied immediately that they were on their way.

While she waited, Aislin reflected on Otto's words about her mercurial temper. Each time she spontaneously combusted, she sabotaged work and personal relationships. She couldn't count the number of times she had shortened a visit with Letty following a spat. Today she had come very close to repeating history. Thankfully Letty had not been home when she blew in looking for a fight. Had she been, Aislin was pretty sure she would be sitting in a ferry lineup with no idea of where to go or what to do rather than waiting for Sarah and Fitz.

Aislin wondered where Letty was, as there had been no communication from Elaine for days, and Letty's car was here. As far as she knew, her grandmother didn't go for walks, and if she was out for a walk, why wouldn't she have invited Otto to join her? The doorbell stopped her from going any further with that line of thought.

Aislin greeted Sarah and Fitz with a big group hug on the porch. Otto was watching, smiling.

"I'm sorry, Sarah, for being such a hot-headed idiot. Apparently, I have my grandmother's mercurial temper. But I am going to work at keeping a lid on being so reactive."

Sarah went in for another hug. "I'm the one who should be sorry," she said through Aislin's hair as she held her tight. "Apparently, I inherited my mother's bossy nature. I need to mind my own business."

"Stop hugging," said Fitz disgustedly, sitting down to pull off his boots. "Where's Letty?"

"I am right here," said Letty, coming down the stairs, smiling at Fitz. "I've missed you. We have lots to catch up on in the garden. It's too cold to take Secretariat out, but I want to show you how much the kale has grown. The leaves are all splattered with mud from that heavy rain and hail, so we will have to wash them carefully before we give them to Secretariat." She avoided looking at Aislin as she marshalled Fitz back into his boots and out the door.

"Well, that's weird," muttered Aislin to herself. "Anyway, we have bigger issues to discuss. Such as the weather. They're forecasting rain again for tomorrow. We'd had nothing but sunshine for weeks. Was it too much to ask that it last through tomorrow night?"

They discussed tents and how to work around the weather challenge. They finally decided on a tent to cover the food tables and provide shelter for people to munch and mingle, a raised platform large enough for the emcee and seating for special guests, and a tent to cover it.

Sarah immediately began calling local vendors, of which there were few. She found one in Victoria who was thankfully able to deliver on such short notice. She sat back with a sigh. "Hope for the best and plan for the worst is all we can do. And if rain is the worst thing that happens, we're getting off easy. I can't wait until this time tomorrow when it's behind us. How are we going to celebrate?"

"*If* Jill is still speaking to us when it's all done and dusted, I think we should reconvene at the Mugshot, eat leftovers, drink our faces off, and congratulate ourselves on hosting-slash-surviving a biker funeral as our first gig as funeral planners. Not to mention the small line item of illegally cremating a person of interest and switching ashes."

"What are you going to wear?" asked Sarah.

"Whatever still fits. I've put on some weight in the last month, and my office clothes are a bit tight. I wonder if I can rent a tent to wear."

"Get out. You look so much healthier than you did when I first saw you. You were skeletal skinny, hiding inside super baggy clothes, and all covered in that messy Alice Cooper eye makeup. I barely recognized you."

Aislin grinned. "That bad, huh? What are you going to wear?"

"A very stylish bulletproof vest. Just not sure how to accessorize."

Letty and Fitz came in from checking the progress of the vegetable garden. Fitz went immediately to Secretariat's tank and lifted him out. Letty put out milk and cookies.

"Be sure to wash your hands before you eat," all three women said in unison, then laughed.

"That Jim Brownlee is going to cause us trouble tomorrow. Mark my words," said Letty. "He is an old, old friend, but he's a nosey, self-righteous, vindictive old fart."

"Gran! You never swear!" And then Aislin hissed, "And in front of Fitz!"

Letty glanced guiltily at Sarah, who shrugged. "He lives with Donny. He's heard far worse."

"Jim drinks too much, and when he drinks, he gets ornery. I feel sorry for Delores, as she has her hands full trying to keep him from offending everyone they know. He'll be drunk by the time the ceremony starts, so keep an eye on him."

Aislin groaned. "One more thing to worry about. One more sleepless night. It's the full moon tomorrow night, by the way, for those of us governed by its tyranny."

They went over their lists, discussed weather-management plans, and their mutual frustration over the lack of input from 10-Gauge. They kept their conjecture about how many things could go terribly wrong to a minimum.

After saying goodbye to Sarah and Fitz, Aislin asked Letty where she had been all morning, but her grandmother turned on the ancient kitchen radio. It was a long-standing house rule that when the radio was on, all talk ceased. Radio rules.

Aislin went up to her room to rummage through her clothing. As soon as the kitchen door closed behind her, the radio was turned off. Letty was avoiding conversation. Aislin was chagrined to think that Letty might have been hiding from her. And embarrassed that her grandmother had witnessed her temper tantrum. While she assembled potential outfits, Aislin puzzled over why she was comfortable with Otto having a front-row seat but cringed to think that Letty knew what had transpired.

Nothing in her closet inspired joy. She was gripped by a nervous energy that needed an outlet. She ran back downstairs.

"Gran, I'm going for a run. It's too early to start dinner and I need some fresh air," she called as she laced up her shoes.

The storm had passed, but the temperature was still below what it had been in the past few days. Aislin warmed up with a brisk walk and then broke into a gentle jog. She didn't run with music. The rhythm of her steps and her breath were all she needed. When she ran, her anxieties broke free from their tethers. Her world calmed down as her heart rate rose.

She rarely chose a route in advance but made decisions as intersections appeared. Her random choices on this run took her to the path that circled Picnic Park. She hesitated briefly but decided to do the loop and then work her way home.

The park looked stunningly serene. And empty. Nary an undercover agent posing as a homeless person or a park maintenance worker to be seen. No bikers. No noise. She felt a qualm of guilt knowing that tomorrow this space could be teeming with trouble. And mud. The calm before the storm.

After showering, she went downstairs to start dinner. Tranquillity and the pleasant sensation of tired muscles infused her. She poured two glasses of wine, put one on the table with a bowl of chips for Letty. She was trying to quit her new habit of eating chips while cooking dinner. If she could resist reaching for the first one, she was okay. But if she succumbed, she was doomed to munch her way through the whole bowl.

The kitchen filled with the rich aroma of onions, ground beef, garlic, and chili powder. Aislin flashed back to her first night home, which seemed like years ago but was in reality just over a month. She and Letty creeping around each other trying to avoid triggering topics. The shocking state of the kitchen, Letty's weight loss, her own desperation. The slow-dawning realization that home was her best port in the storm that had driven her out of Vancouver.

Her flight from the city featured less and less in her mind. She missed Lara. And not for the first time, she was shaken by the fragility of friendships. Was it a generational thing or just her? Letty and Elaine had been friends for decades, although of late, Elaine was missing in action. Aislin enjoyed just the tiniest smile of malicious victory as she took off her apron.

"Gran, dinner's ready!" she called out. No answer. Aislin bounced up the stairs and tapped on Letty's door. No answer. Her car was sitting exactly as it had been all day. Aislin slipped her shoes on and went out to the Behemoth. At that point, she began to have an out-of-body experience. She watched her hand reach out to knock on the metal door. She saw herself lean over to peer through the window next to it. She saw herself looking at Letty and Otto all tangled up on the sofa. She saw them turning towards the window and looking back at her. She saw her own shock reflected in their faces.

She spun and scrambled back to the house. Grabbing the bag of chips and her wine, she flew upstairs, slamming the door behind her. She texted Sarah.

Sarah called immediately but her words were lost in the snorts of laughter. "Sorry, can't stop laughing. You stumbled onto your gran and her lover getting it on! God, I hope I meet someone I want to get it on with when I'm seventy-five. That's just the best. I can picture your face."

Sarah continued to snort and snuffle wetly. She stopped long enough to blow her nose. "Sorry. Under control now. Come on. You must have known this was on the horizon. The sexual tension between those two was intense. Why are you so horrified? They are both well over the age of consent."

"Because it's my grandmother. I never thought of her as, you know . . . being like that."

"Oh for God's sake. Say the words. Say, 'I never thought of my grandmother having sex.'"

"Nooooooooo, too gross. I can't think of it, let alone say it, because then I get visuals, and they aren't pretty."

"Oh my God, you are an ageist! I am shocked. Well, not really. You always were more of a puritan than yours truly. Moms and Pops get it on all the time. The house almost rocks off its foundation some nights."

"Really?" For all the years Aislin had known Sarah, Sarah's mum had worn different versions of a flowered dress with a little white collar. Very chaste and prim. But her dad, now that she thought about it, had a different energy. His work shirts always seemed to have one button too many undone. The dark, curly chest hairs were quite visible.

"Yup. It's always been like that. Why do you think there are eight of us Quinn kids? Not through immaculate conception, that's for sure."

"Still? They're still going at it? What do you say to Fitz?"

"Yup. Still. I told him that Moms and Pops were having sex. What else am I supposed to tell him? And if I tried to couch it in some sort of euphemism, dear brother Donny would knock that out of the kid's head. Easier to be straight up."

The inner workings of Sarah's robust family had always fascinated Aislin. It was so alien to her home life. Which is why the sight of her grandmother hotly kissing Otto had delivered a full-body shock.

"Okay, Ms. Worldly, what do I say when I see them? We all looked so mortified. And then I ran away." Aislin giggled at the memory of Letty's expression. "I guess it is pretty funny."

"I don't know. Just go with the flow. Ask them if they're hungry." Sarah snorted through her laughter. "Sorry. Not helpful."

"No, not helpful. As if there isn't enough drama going on. I think I'll just act as though that whole horrible scene never happened."

"Well, good luck with that. And call me anytime. I'm loving this new development."

While she was talking to Sarah, Letty and Otto had come inside. As she came downstairs, she could hear their low tones in the kitchen. She crept to the door and listened.

"Aislin has made a big pot of chili. Perfect for a cool day like this," she heard Letty say.

"I hope she will eventually accept us. I would hate to become a bone of contention between you two."

"I think she will. Eventually. She is very fond of you. We haven't really talked about it." Letty paused, and Aislin could hear her vigorously stirring the chili. "She has such a quick temper I'm never sure what is going to set her off."

Otto left that statement alone. Aislin grinned. Otto was indeed a wise man.

"When she turned up at The Maples a few weeks ago, all broken and confused by her grief, we had a very good talk. That girl has had a hard time of it. She's spent years hiding her layers of grief and wearing that grief like armour. I think perhaps it's her ticket to staying emotionally unavailable."

"Well, her closest companion is a turtle! That speaks volumes."

"I think being home with you and reconnecting with Sarah is exactly what she needs. This is her safety net. She just has to recognize it as such."

"This business she and Sarah have started has potential. Maybe it will be the anchor she needs. I must say, having her and all her drama is just what I needed to feel alive again. And you. I needed you."

Aislin tiptoed carefully down the hall and out the front door, wiping her eyes and gulping the cool evening air. She sat on the top step, staring blankly into space. Otto was dead right. How did he know her so well? Or was she so transparent that everyone saw her as he did? Sarah obviously did. What about Nick? Did he see it, too? So what if he did.

Sighing, Aislin pushed herself up from the porch. She was cold and hungry. And resigned to suffering through the imminent, unavoidable, awkward conversation, followed by an awkward dinner and topped off with a long, sleepless night.

Chapter 18

Rain falling heavily on the roof provided the soundtrack for Aislin's fragmented sleep. It tormented her by increasing and decreasing in strength. Each time the flow ceased, she tensed, hoping the storm had moved on. In the vacuum of sound, she relaxed, giving in to her need for sleep, only to startle awake as a new round of rain pounded the roof.

Was cancelling due to weather a possibility? With that thought came the image of hundreds of bikers, wet and angry, denied their ritual of sending off one of their own. She had a feeling that bikers were not the fair-weather type. Then she thought of Twiggy's vest, drenched, draped over his bike, being towed by 10-Gauge. Such a sad, miserable image. But before she wallowed too far in that puddle of despair, Weronika came to mind. And sprung a new waterspout of anxiety.

A few days ago, Aislin and Sarah had done an online search. There were plenty of interviews with Weronika about her missing husband. In each interview, she said she knew her husband had been murdered. She did not come right out and say it, but she implied she knew by whom. Aislin noticed a shift in Weronika's comments in the more recent articles. Her focus changed from hysterical fear for her husband's well-being to self-pity. Weronika was enjoying her fifteen seconds of fame.

And when Aislin needed a break from that source of anxiety, her thoughts landed on Twiggy's extended family. It was Donny's job to invite the biker's girlfriends and their children to the podium. He had tried to wriggle out of the assignment. He claimed to not know which of Twiggy's girlfriends were married, which ones were short liaisons, or which ones he had had legitimate long-term relationships with. And what constituted long term? More than a week? Was he supposed to invite them all? And who was going to keep them and all their kids from fighting? Sarah had finger-thwacked her brother.

Just before dawn, Aislin descended into a deep, deep sleep. And a nightmare. It was a dark, wet night. She was being chased through a forest by a man in black. She zigzagged crazily through the trees. Her eyes watered from the sting of branches slapping her cold skin. She gulped for air, her throat burning. Her heart pounding so hard it felt like it was trying to escape from her body. Her pursuer so close she could feel his breath on her neck. He grabbed her arm, and she fell heavily onto the forest floor thick with leaves. He shook her violently. She tried to scream for help, but no sound came out. She fought hard—kicking and punching. And then he tried to drown her.

"Aislin! Stop that noise. Ow! Wake up!"

Aislin opened her eyes and saw Letty leaning over her. She looked groggily around her room. Then felt her face. "Why is my face wet?"

"Because I threw cold water on you. You were thrashing around and screaming loud enough to wake the whole neighbourhood. I couldn't wake you up. You hit me. So I threw water on you."

"I hit you? You threw water on me?" Aislin sat up slowly and swung her legs over the edge of the bed. "I had a horrible dream. Some guy was chasing me, and then he caught me, and I couldn't scream."

"Oh, you could scream alright. Nothing wrong with your lungs."

"I'm so sorry, Gran. Did I hurt you?"

"No, but I was afraid you were going to hurt yourself the way you were carrying on."

"I was awake most of the night and then finally fell into a deep sleep. What time is it?"

"That's the other thing. You slept in. The itinerary has you leaving here in half an hour to meet Sarah at Picnic Park."

"No, it's not ten already, is it? Holy shit, I'm late. I don't even know what I'm going to wear. And I have to shower. But honestly, I am so discombobulated right now I don't even know where the bathroom is."

"It's across the hall," said Letty with a questioning look. "You shower, and I'll bring you some coffee. Really, Aislin, of all the days to sleep in."

The hot water somewhat restored Aislin's equilibrium. But the shadow of the ice-cold terror and leaden helplessness haunted her. She flicked on the fan and opened a window to speed the process of clearing the mirror so she could dry her hair. While mindlessly running the blow dryer, she tried to focus on what lay ahead. Which, on this soaking cold, grey morning, felt as though she was trying to pull herself out of one nightmare so she could enter another.

When Aislin emerged, Letty not only had coffee and toast waiting for her but had laid out two outfits on the bed. Her choices were professional yet elegant. For practical reasons, Aislin chose the slim-leg black dress pants and peacock-blue silk blouse over the wide-leg, dove-grey wool pants and blush-pink cashmere turtleneck. Gumboots and rain pants would have done just as well and might even have earned her brownie points with the biker crowd.

The coffee and toast revived her. The nightmare slowly receded. She dressed quickly, applied minimal, waterproof makeup, then raced downstairs. Otto and Letty were at the table, grey heads together going over Otto's talking points. Aislin hesitated a nanosecond before moving to stand behind them, a hand on each shoulder.

"So, this is it—the big day. Otto, has Letty laid out your clothes as well? She made excellent choices for me. What does an emcee at a biker funeral wear? Do you have leather chaps or an emblazoned leather vest?"

"Sadly, I do not. Letty, what do you suggest? Jimmy Carter cardigan and tie or sports jacket and open-neck shirt?"

Letty beamed at him indulgently. Aislin couldn't recall her ever looking at Frank that way. But Sarah was right. It was churlish of her to resent her grandmother's happiness. And they were pretty cute together. And so hopelessly in love.

"Sports jacket and open-neck shirt," said Letty. "You don't want to look too square."

"My muse has spoken."

Letty and Otto smiled into each other's eyes. Aislin couldn't suppress a grin herself. She hoped Otto would pull himself together and turn up on time at the park with his speaking notes. "Okay then, I'm off. See you both soon? Things kick off at noon. Fingers, eyes, nose, and toes crossed that we get through this alive, and none of us end up in jail."

Aislin texted Sarah that she was running late. She tried to stay within a reasonable approximation of the posted speed limit, but her anxiety gave her a lead foot. Nick was standing in his driveway as she shot past. He raised a hand to flag her down. She tooted her horn but kept going. She was proud of herself for resisting the urge to stop.

She pulled over abruptly, scrolled through her playlists to find the soundtrack to *The Adventures of Priscilla, Queen of the Desert*, selected "I Will Survive," turned up the volume, rolled down all the windows, and burned out. Her driving horrified a couple picking their way around puddles on the sidewalk. Their disgust gave Aislin the giggles. She raced through the wet streets, rocking and bopping to the music.

As she approached Picnic Park, she increased the volume. She spotted Sarah instructing the tent setup crew. They all turned and stared. She parked beside a delivery truck but didn't get out right away, just sat there, letting the music pump her up.

Sarah dance-stepped over to the car, singing along loudly to the final lines, did a shimmy shake, then struck a pose with one hand on her hip, the other pointing skyward.

Aislin hopped out of her car and stood back-to-back with her, mirroring the pose. As preteens, they had spent countless hours working on their choreography for this song and constructing outlandish outfits. Letty never complained to them about the number of times they played the song or the volume. Aislin overheard her telling Frank she sometimes danced around the kitchen with the whisk as her microphone. An image that, at the time, had grossed Aislin out but now she wished she had witnessed.

"Well, you're in a fine frame of mind. I wasn't sure which Aislin would show up today and am heartily relieved it's the 'I Got This' Aislin. And you do realize that our behaviour is wholly inappropriate given we are managing a celebration of life?"

"Oh, right. Sorry. I needed something to boost me up. My day began with Letty throwing cold water on me." Sarah raised her eyebrows. "Don't ask. Anyway, feeling a bit manic. I'm in a 'go ahead, make my day' mood. We are going to get through this crap sandwich of a day, and then we are going to laugh our faces off. So, where do you want me, and what do you want me to do?"

"Oh, I *love* this Aislin. Okay, as you can see, the lads have the tents up and are working on tables and chairs. I am just waiting for 10-Gauge to call. Last I heard, they were behind schedule due to the rain. He said to make up time they weren't making any stops but riding straight down the island and that they were about an hour out. So, that gives us just enough time to make sure Jill's crew has everything they need for the food tent, test the mic, and sober up Donny."

"Wait! What? Donny's drunk? But we need him. He's our guy for the seating."

"Let's just say he started his day with coffee and vodka and is now onto beer and vodka. He's racing—eyeballs spinning in their sockets. But not yet throwing up, so that's a blessing. But the day is young. So we—you and I—need to start sussing out who might be one of Twiggy's women. Criteria? Every woman with kids. Why else would you drag your kids to something like this? Your thoughts?"

"Donny had coffee and vodka for breakfast? That's hardcore. What triggered him?"

Sarah didn't answer. She shifted her feet and turned to watch the men setting up the sound system.

"Come on, spill. I know the signs, Sarah."

"Turns out he's recently become involved with one of Twiggy's 'widows,' Jaylene. He went to offer her his condolences, and the tragedy of her situation—a young woman with three kids all under five, no job and no prospects, and brokenhearted over Twiggy—appealed to his gallant side. So, he started dropping by to help! Of all things. Lord knows he couldn't help with the cooking or cleaning, so he helped with the only tool in his toolbox he knows how to use! But she broke it off with him last night."

"No! Really? Oh my God. Poor Donny!"

"Poor Donny be damned. He's a daft bastard. The woman was heartbroken, and Donny took advantage of her fragile state. And now he's in a self-induced, self-indulgent fragile state. I could do with some coffee and vodka myself."

"Why not? Got any?"

"Fortunately, no. There's Jill's van. Let's check in with her."

As they picked their way through the wet grass, Jill emerged, slamming the door with such vigour the van shook. Her helper crept out the passenger side.

"Uh oh. That's not a good sign," Sarah muttered. Aislin immediately veered off in the direction of the sound technician, but Sarah grabbed her arm. "You are not deserting me. We need to find out what has Jill lit up like a Christmas tree." Sarah's voice held a threatening edge.

"Hey, Jill, great to see you. Wow, whatever you have in the van smells delicious. Any chance you need some food testers?" Sarah called in a saccharine-sweet voice.

"Do you think I don't test the food before loading? Where's the bloody food tent?"

"Right beside you. Nice and convenient. Yesterday's rainstorm was unfortunate, but at least it's not raining now."

Jill gave Sarah a skin-blistering glare and began barking orders at her helper, who was unloading the chafing dishes. The girl slipped on the wet grass.

"If you drop anything, Amanda, I'll skin you, then fire you!"

Aislin wanted to give Amanda a big hug. She tried to catch her eye to give her a sympathetic smile, but Amanda kept her eyes down.

"Are you allowed to threaten to kill your employees?" Aislin asked in a whisper.

"She's family, so apparently she's exempt from employment rights. On second thought, let's not find out what's up Jill's nose. Let's talk to the sound guys. They look nice," whispered Sarah. "Next time she turns her back, we're out of here."

Chapter 19

The park was filling. People carefully picked their way through the wet grass to congregate near the stage. The age range of the guests was midtwenties to late thirties, primarily men and casually dressed. Aislin spotted two older women who looked quite out of place. They looked like Queen Elizabeth impersonators who had arrived at the wrong gig. Aislin wondered if these were the two "professional mourners" Letty had mentioned.

Otto appeared from nowhere. He hefted a large tote onto the back of the stage, then introduced himself to the sound technician, saying something that made the man laugh. They ran a few tests of the mic, and when both were satisfied, Otto waved Aislin and Sarah over.

"Everything's in order up here. Quite a crowd already. More than I expected. How are things going on the ground?"

Sarah and Aislin exchanged looks. "Just a couple of hiccups, but we're working through them," replied Sarah.

"Anything I can help with? I have some time before I kick things off. Is that Donny over there? Is he alright? He doesn't look well."

"Oh, he's alright. Just sick in the head and sick in the stomach," said Sarah. The menace in her voice did not go unnoticed.

"Is this one of the hiccups?" asked Otto. "Donny looks like he has a few under his belt. We're relying on him to identify who should sit on the stage. None of us know Twiggy's various liaisons. Everyone is grieving. We don't want to embarrass ourselves. I better go have a word with the lad."

"That man is a saint. If he weren't already spoken for, I would make a play for him," said Sarah. "I wonder what he has in that tote."

Aislin smiled fondly at Otto's retreating figure. "He is. He's magical."

Sarah's phone buzzed. "It's 10-Gauge. They're here, just waiting for our cue to ride in." She forwarded the text to Otto.

Otto gave Donny, who looked near tears, a bottle of water, spoke into his ear, and patted his back. Donny straightened up, guzzled the water, and followed Otto to the stage. Otto checked his phone, nodded to Sarah, picked up the mic, and began.

"Ladies and gentlemen, my name is Otto Lawless, and I will be the emcee for this celebration of life for Twiggy, also known as Philip James Masterson by some. The weather, unfortunately, did not receive the memo requesting continued sunshine and warmth. We could not set up chairs for everyone due to the potential harm to the grass. We do, however, have chairs behind me for members of Twiggy's family. Please come and have a seat."

No one moved. Everyone eyed everyone else, the atmosphere thick with suspicion and tension. A woman in her midthirties stepped forward. Her young son hid his curly head in the skirt of her raincoat. She picked him up and carried him, squirming, to the stage and chose a seat in the back row. The child continued to squirm and struggle, pulling at her hand. Otto spoke to her, wrote in his notebook, then, pulling the tote forward, reached in and lifted out a pink plush elephant, which he offered to the boy. Now on his mum's lap, he shook his head violently. Otto squatted beside them, rummaged through the tote, and pulled out a wooden truck. The curly head nodded.

"And he never had kids. How did he know to do that? It didn't occur to me to bring a toy box for the kids, and I'm a mother," Sarah whispered. Aislin was near tears.

As Otto stood up stiffly, an RCMP cruiser abruptly pulled up. Two officers swaggered towards the stage. Aislin recognized them as the two who had pulled her and Otto over a few days earlier. She scanned the crowd. A little apart stood Jim Brownlee, hands on hips, grinning at her. Delores was not with him, nor was his dog.

The two officers stepped onto the stage. They spoke quietly to Otto. He nodded, pointed to Aislin, placed his notebook on a chair, and followed them off the stage.

"I am going with these gentlemen to their office. I'll be back as soon as I've answered their questions. Donny can pick up where I left off," said Otto to Aislin, his eyes twinkling. He wore a face-splitting grin as the cruiser drove off.

A wailing child broke the hush that had fallen with the officers' arrival. Then everyone started talking. They moved as one to the food tent. Jill stepped in front of her bank of chafing dishes, crossed her arms, and shook her head.

"As my Pops always says, 'In heaven, there is no beer. That's why we drink ours here.' Time for a drink?" called Donny, waving his arm towards the beer tent. A cheer went up. The bartender looked anxiously at Sarah, who shrugged. He began popping the caps off bottles.

"Well, I guess the bar's open. Glad we're not paying for it. I hope they have a backup supply, or we're going to have a shitload of angry drunks on our hands. I'm going to retrieve our annoying little Pied Piper. You go get Otto's notes," said Sarah calmly then shook Aislin gently. "Aislin? Aislin, snap out of it. We have work to do."

Nick came up from behind them. "I saw what happened. I've called Letty. She's going to the station to wait for Otto. Sarah, I'll get Donny. And then we can have a quick meeting about how we're going to handle this. Okay? Aislin? Are you listening?" Aislin continued to stare blankly at the lineup in the beer tent.

"Donny's drunk and brokenhearted," Sarah called to Nick as he was walking away. "Just sayin'. Okay, Aislin, you stay here, and I'll go get Otto's notes and speak to that poor woman sitting there all alone on the stage."

Aislin did as she was told. She watched Nick masterfully cut Donny from the herd and guide him towards her.

Donny weaved unsteadily. Nick grabbed him just as he was about to topple onto Aislin.

"Donny, you're a hot mess!" Sarah hissed at her brother when she returned with the notes. "What were you thinking? We don't want people drinking now. It's way too early."

"It's my heart. It hurts to breathe. I have looked love in the eye. I'll never be the same," sobbed Donny.

"Thank God for granting us small mercies. Pull yourself together. This is the third time this month your heart's been broken."

Aislin pulled herself out of her reverie. "What are we going to do? Everything's a mess; everyone's getting drunk. And Otto's been arrested."

"Yes, but we have Nick! Right, Nick? You have a commanding presence. Can you help us? We need to get this wreck back on the rails, and no one is going to pay attention to Aislin or me."

Nick grimaced. "I don't know. I'm not good at public speaking. And I don't have a relationship with these people, so I don't think I'll have much luck breaking up the party. Sorry."

Donny straightened up. "I'll do it. These are my people." He staggered over to the stage, tripped on the first step, and fell. He pulled himself up and gave Sarah, Aislin, and Nick a shaky victory sign. The seated young mother pulled her son onto her lap, shrinking into her coat.

"Hey, you guys in the beer tent. Get your asses out here. We're here to say goodbye to our good buddy Twiggy," Donny yelled into the mic. Instant silence.

"Says who?" came a bellowed reply.

"Come onnnn, you guys. My sister and Aislin have worked soooo hard to get this shitshow going. Do it for them. That's them over there. Aren't they beautiful? I love my sister. I love you, Sarah. An' I really love Aislin. I mean, I've loved her my whole life. But she doesn't love me. So I took my shattered heart elsewhere. And I fell in love with Jaylene. I love Jaylene. I love you, Jaylene. But Jaylene doesn't love me either. No one loves me."

Donny's head tipped forward onto his chest. Sobs came through the mic. He wiped his eyes and nose on his sleeve. "I want every woman that Twiggy has ever boinked to come on up here so we can have a great big hug."

The crowd was enjoying the new emcee. They cheered him. Their cheers cheered him up. Emboldened, he yelled, "Here's to our wives and girlfriends: May they never meet!"

The men in the crowd hooted and clapped. The women glared at them.

"Donny Quinn, that's disrespectful. Even for you," yelled Jill. "Get your shit together or get off the stage."

"It wasn't me. Groucho Marx said it. Blame him," Donny yelled back at her with all the belligerent courage he could muster. "Anyway, where was I? Oh, right." He gestured wildly with his arm. "Come on. We want all of Twiggy's exes to come up here and get cozy and comfortable. And bring your brats. Kids. I mean kids."

More cheering. Low-volume cajoling began. Eventually, four women, glaring at each other, reluctantly moved towards the stage, kids in tow.

Donny swayed as he encouraged them to hurry up and take a seat. "Come on, come on. Don't take all bloody day." He focused blearily on one woman with five pale children trailing behind her up the stairs. Leaning in shakily, he said, "Joseph, Mary, sweet baby Jesus, and the wee donkey, how many kids do you have? Are these *all* Twiggy's? Are you sure, honey, that the dearly departed Twiggy shot all that baby batter?"

Blushing, the woman ushered the last of her children into a seat then spun and slugged Donny on the nose. He went down hard.

"Hey, who the hell do you think you are?" asked one of the other women on the stage, stepping over Donny's prone body. "Donny Quinn is one of the good guys."

"Really, Jaylene? You kicked his sorry ass out of your life. We all heard him say that. Just the way Twiggy kicked your saggy ass out of his."

"He didn't kick me out, Liz. I kicked him out. He was about as faithful as a goat."

"Ya got that right," said another woman seated on the stage, arms crossed. "He was never around for long. As soon as I got pregnant, he was gone. Only saw him on Kyle's birthday. We had a wedding all planned until you showed him your tits, Liz."

"Oh, shut up, Sandy," yelled Liz. "You're the biggest idiot of us all. You actually thought he was going to marry you? Ha. What a joke. Twiggy was a lot of things, but man, he was not the marrying kind."

Liz plonked herself down again and crossed her arms. Her children sat as still as ornaments.

Another woman, with three children all older than the others, was quietly crying into a tissue. Her oldest son stood behind her with his hand on her shoulder, his face crimson.

Donny sat up, gingerly feeling his nose, which was leaking a thin trail of blood. "I need a drink. As illuminating as it is, the discourse between you lovely ladies is giving me a massive headache. And one of you tried to break my nose." He gestured to the young boy. "You look like a strong lad. Give me a hand up, will you?" The boy did as asked. Donny leaned heavily on his shoulder. "Help me over to the beer tent, and I'll buy you a beer," he whispered, forgetting he was still wired to the mic.

Another cheer from the audience.

Aislin, Sarah, and Nick were off to one side watching the debacle. As Donny hobbled past, Sarah muttered, "I am going to kill that little bugger," and marched off towards her brother and his human crutch. Donny saw her coming and steered his helper into the crowd.

Aislin turned to Nick, who was grinning and shaking his head. "You find this funny? This is a bloody disaster! I am so out of my depth here. Whose bright idea was it to invite Twiggy's herd of women to all be together on the stage?"

"In hindsight, it may not have been our wisest decision. We were going for a respectful tone, but I'm thinking we neglected to consider the nature of the guests. And who could have predicted Donny getting drunk and insulting one of Twiggy's exes?" Nick choked back a laugh.

"Sarah probably could have called that one. Can't you do something?"

"I am not going up there. No one in their right mind is going to wade into that," Nick said, pointing.

Liz and Sandy were in each other's faces, yelling. The other two women were watching warily. The tote with the toys was tipped over, and three little boys were fighting over a brightly coloured spaceship. Two young girls were engaged in a tug-of-war over a stuffed dog.

The audience lost interest in the yelling match and was moving like a school of fish towards the beer tent. Sarah and Donny were nowhere to be seen.

"I'm going to look for Sarah. She's the event manager."

Nick grabbed her arm. "Hear that?"

"Shit! It's the bikes." Nick ran across the grass towards the parking lot where the first bikes were pulling in. It was 10-Gauge. Leader of the pack. Behind his bike was a trailer with Twiggy's bike, his vest draped and dripping over the seat. Such a sad sight. Aislin thought of military funerals with a riderless horse, boots reversed in the stirrups. She thought it ironic that bikers should borrow a tradition from the military.

The air filled with the deafening roar of hundreds of Harleys. Panic flooded Aislin. She had never heard anything like it. Her first instinct was to flee. To drive away. Far, far away. Away from the noise and chaos.

Sarah ran up to her. "Who gave 10-Gauge the green light? We need to settle down Twiggy's women. Come on." Sarah dragged Aislin by her arm.

"Do you have a plan?"

"I am going to sic Jill on them. No one argues with her."

But Jill was way ahead of them. She was taking off her apron as she stomped up the steps, her face thunderous. She stepped between Liz and Sandy, spoke quietly to them, and watched as they meekly sat down far from each other. Jill then went over to the squabbling children and pointed to the toy box. Seven of the children quietly put everything back in the box, two ran straight to their mothers, but one little fellow defiantly put his toy behind his back, glaring at Jill.

"You're not the boss of me!"

Hands on hips, Jill silently glared right back. His bravado evaporated in seconds. He threw the toy down and fled to his mother.

Before leaving the stage, Jill surveyed her handiwork, eyeing each familial cluster. No one on the stage moved a muscle. They looked like a still-life painting.

Aislin and Sarah both gave her the thumbs-up sign. Jill veered towards them.

"So, girls, I have a lot riding on this in terms of food costs and reputation. If you want to continue doing business with me, you will consider that. It's time to earn your keep. Get this shitshow back on track."

"How do we do that?" mewed Aislin. "We've got a stage full of pissed-off women, a whole pack of soaked-to-the-skin, miserable bikers, our emcee is in jail, our replacement emcee is drunk and disorderly, and guests are all getting drunk before the event begins. This means we may run out of alcohol, and I don't even want to think about how that will end."

"Thanks for looking on the bright side," replied Jill. She sized Aislin up before turning to Sarah. "It's obviously on you to step up. I suggest you talk to 10-Gauge, give him a summary of the situation, and ask him to take over as emcee. He can get these people to settle."

She turned back to Aislin. "Why don't you make yourself useful and find out how things are going for your grandmother's lover over at the jailhouse. If that's not too stressful for you."

Aislin burned with shame. "Who died and made her God?" she muttered as Jill strode away. Sarah elbowed her and shook her head.

"Don't go there. Let's get to work. You call Letty. We do need to find out how things stand with Otto. I mean, he could be in serious trouble if he spills the beans. We could all be in serious trouble. He looked too damn happy to be in the back seat of a cop car. Who knows how far he'll go to fulfill his badass fantasy."

"That's a terrifying thought," said Aislin.

"Speaking of terrifying, Nick's waving us over to join him and 10-Gauge. Call Letty after we find out what's up. Hopefully, our client has the recipe for the secret sauce to cure this insanity," said Sarah.

10-Gauge was stepping out of his wet leather chaps as they approached. The two men he was speaking to were those who had ridden with him the day he turned up in their garden and charmed Letty and Sarah into going along with this crazy gig in the first place. His voice was taut, and he was choosing his words carefully. Nick looked more than a little anxious. He grimaced at Aislin and Sarah.

"Now, I need you two morons to get back on your bikes and pay a visit to Weronika and make sure she feels respected. Listen to her sob story, take her out to dinner or whatever. Just keep her the hell away from here. Pretend you understand. Pretend you give a goddamn. Go."

He glowered at Sarah. "What the hell is this? We hired you to run a funeral, not a three-ring fucking circus." Before he could continue, a woman's voice came through the mic.

"Hello, people? My name is Weronika Czekoj. I am widow of Aleksy Czekoj. I will tell you about lovely Aleksy."

"If she's here, who's running hell?" called Donny from the beer tent. His fans cheered.

"Goddamn it. What is she doing here?" 10-Gauge snarled at no one in particular. "I'll take care of this."

10-Gauge turned off his angry-biker persona and turned on his charm. Turned it way up. He moved with nonchalant ease across the grass, waving at a couple of people, patting others on the shoulder, giving quick side hugs to others. Weronika watched warily. Aislin, Sarah, and Nick watched anxiously.

He didn't bother with stairs but jogged a couple of steps and leapt up, then turned and bowed as the beer tent occupants clapped. He slipped an arm around Weronika's waist, whispered something that made her blush. He deftly took control of the mic and the stage. Now flushed with anger, Weronika took a seat with Twiggy's women.

"Who's here for Twiggy?" He waited for the noise to die down. "We just finished our memorial ride to celebrate our fallen comrade. It was such an honour to ride with our brothers from other chapters. It's been a long time since we've done a memorial ride. And that's a good thing, right?" More applause. The bikers shouted in agreement.

"Pardon me if I stumble. I'm winging it. Emcee was not my role, but circumstances beyond my control prevailed. Those of you who know me know that I am the shy, retiring type," he said, flashing his high wattage smile—lots of heckling and laughter. One happy mourner called him a rooster. Donny took it further and yelled that 10-Gauge was as sexy as socks on a rooster. The mood was far from funereal.

"Well, we can relax, right? Our third emcee of the day will prance around and ooze charm all over everyone. Don't know about you, but I feel redundant," said Sarah. "Jill's guarding her food like an Anatolian shepherd guards sheep. The beer tent is open. Our guests are enjoying the entertainment. Not exactly what we planned, though. Not even close. Is this the norm for a biker funeral? I wonder if Twiggy would be pleased?"

"Can we be sued? How tight was the contract you signed? 10-Gauge is not happy with us," said Aislin. "Maybe all the attention he's getting will put him in a better mood. And now that the big cheese of the local biker gang is in control, no one would dare mess things up, right?"

Nick interrupted. "I don't think we're out of the woods yet. Weronika is a wild card. 10-Gauge may think she's eating out of his hand, but I wouldn't count on it." He lowered his voice. "Weronika has her suspicions, and she isn't going to just drop them. I expect she's shared those suspicions with the cops."

"I don't want to think about that. That's why they picked up Otto. Right? And we're going to be next." Panic swelled within Aislin.

Sarah hugged her. "Hey, it's all going to work out eventually. Stay calm. Breathe. We're just going to focus on getting through this."

Chapter 20

"I have to call Letty. Excuse me. I'm going to find a quieter spot." She saw Jim Brownlee approaching as soon as she stepped away from Nick and Sarah. She turned and went in a different direction, hoping he would take the hint.

She counted the rings, knowing Letty's voice mail kicked in on the sixth. No answer. She tried Otto's. Same result. She called Letty again, thinking her grandmother may have missed the call because she had to fish through her purse for the phone, but still no answer, so she left a message. And followed that with a text. Aislin hesitated briefly before calling Otto again, and then she texted him, too. She called Letty one more time. Just in case.

Was Letty not answering because the reception was terrible in the station? Aislin quickly dismissed that as ludicrous. If any building in town had reliable reception, it would be the RCMP detachment. Did she not answer because she, too, had been detained? If they were questioning Letty, it was only a matter of time before they were all hauled in. 10-Gauge had been grilled earlier in the week.

Aislin wandered through the crowd. Her internal monologue stopped when she overheard a jean-clad, heavily built, middle-aged man say, "I hear there's some suspicion about just what happened to that broad's husband. She's gone all over town telling people he was murdered, and now it sounds as though the cops think she might be right. They paid a visit to the Dogs' clubhouse while the boys were away on the ride. Logical, even for this bunch of Keystone Cops."

His companion nodded. "Yup, heard about that. 10-Gauge is not very happy with his lieutenants for how they handled the situation. Shit's coming their way."

"Isn't this the craziest goddamn funeral you've ever been to? Most entertaining, too. That Donny guy is a riot. I bet he knows more than he should. 10-Gauge better hope he keeps his mouth shut."

"Donny better hope he keeps his drunk mouth shut, too." Both men chuckled. "But, from what we've seen, there's a snowball's chance in hell of that happening." They clinked bottles.

Aislin looked wildly around for Nick and Sarah. They had moved closer to the stage. 10-Gauge was eulogizing Twiggy. Weronika wore the look of someone who still had something to say.

"Any way we can get her off the stage?" asked Aislin. "She looks as though she's going to blow at any moment. And neither Letty nor Otto is answering their phones. So, where are they? Have they both been arrested? Or is one or the other or both in the emergency ward? There is no logical answer for them to not be answering their phones. I am desperately trying not to freak out."

Nick put his arm around her shoulder and gave her a quick side hug. Then abruptly pulled away. "Don't go there. They're fine."

"Yes, they're fine! Probably having 'made bail' sex in the Behemoth," said Sarah absently, her eyes on the crowd. She was not at all engaged in the conversation.

A soft mist filled the air. Umbrellas popped up accordingly, shielding people from the moisture and each other. The beer tent was emptying, the drinkers drawn to the entertainment on the stage.

10-Gauge was prancing back and forth with all the zeal and passion of an evangelical minister pumping up the flock to donate their life savings. He was telling colourful stories. Some even included Twiggy. And he was oblivious to the growing irritation of the women sitting behind him.

But Weronika was not. Every time he mentioned himself, she turned to the women still seated on the stage with their children and imitated gagging. She had them. Kindred spirits. They began to snicker, and the children, quick to know when their mothers were distracted, slipped away to play. Weronika stood up behind 10-Gauge and began to do the same to the crowd. They lapped it up. 10-Gauge, believing he was the source of their appreciation, kept the hype flowing.

"Whatever this is, it's completely off the rails and completely inappropriate," groaned Sarah to Aislin and Nick. "I have no idea how to get it back on track. And I thought weddings were train wrecks waiting to happen."

"We need to figure out something or abandon ship and flee. And who are all these new people? 10-Gauge said to expect eighty to a hundred max. And our permit is for a hundred. So what's going on?"

There was indeed a flood of people entering the park. They all seemed to know one another, and they all seemed to be texting as they walked.

"That one is a client," said Nick, pointing to a young woman. "I think I'll just go have a quick word with her."

Aislin felt the green-eyed monster rise. The woman was gorgeous. No wonder Nick spotted her. And he sure didn't hesitate to volunteer. She watched the woman turn and smile shyly at Nick. He took her elbow and guided her to a quieter spot. Because she was petite, she turned her face up as he spoke to her. Aislin looked away.

Sarah was off to one side, haranguing Donny. She waved Aislin over. "So, it seems Wonder Boy here put it out to his social media pals that there was free booze and food at Picnic Park. Jill is going to freaking kill us. And we thought the bikers were going to be our problem."

"Donny, what were you thinking!" snapped Aislin. "You came up with the plan for this event! To help us. We trusted you. We relied on you!"

"I'm sorry, Aislin. I'm just a stupid loser. I've been destination fucked my whole life." Donny hung his head and sniffed. "But I can fix this."

"Just like you fixed things earlier? No thanks!" said Aislin. She turned just in time to see the woman Nick was talking to reach out and touch his arm. Aislin spun back so fast she knocked into Donny, who tipped over into his sister, who pushed him away. He staggered forward, just barely keeping his balance.

The sight of Donny, drunk and dejected, pierced Aislin's heart. He was the guy who had always looked out for her and Sarah. Frank called him "Donny on the spot" because Donny would materialize from thin air and extricate the girls from awkward situations.

"Come on. Let's get you some coffee," said Aislin, hooking her arm under his. "Jill has lots, I'm sure."

"Nope, not going near her. She's going to kill me. She said so. And I believe her."

"Okay, well, you wait here, and I'll bring the coffee to you," said Aislin, relieved to have something to do. "Sarah, we need to come up with a plan on how to get 10-Gauge off the stage. And we need to figure out who our fourth emcee is going to be."

Jim Brownlee appeared at her side as she walked to the food tent. She tried to turn away, but he grabbed her elbow. She shook her arm free. "Don't you dare touch me, you small-minded malicious bastard. You creep me out. Always have. I don't know how Frank could stand you. So just fuck off!"

As the final words left Aislin's lips, a hush fell on the crowd. Everyone froze. Jim's face turned purple-red and sweaty. His piggy eyes bulged. And then he collapsed at her feet. Nick ran to him, rolled him onto his back, and began CPR. He barked at Aislin to call an ambulance. Jill ordered people to step back. Nick was pumping hard and fast on Jim's chest. He counted to thirty, then paused to blow air into Jim's mouth. He kept up this pattern until the ambulance pulled onto the grass beside them. The paramedics efficiently took over. Nick gave them a summary of what had happened and how long he had delivered CPR. With one paramedic continuing the CPR, Jim was lifted onto a stretcher and loaded into the ambulance.

As the ambulance departed with sirens blaring, more sirens approached.

An RCMP cruiser drove right up onto the grass. The same two officers as before stepped out and marched to the stage. 10-Gauge smiled at them. Weronika grinned wickedly.

"Good afternoon, gentlemen. Great to see you again. What is it this time? Have I double-parked my bike? Is the license on my trailer expired?"

"Alphonso Albertini, I am arresting you for murder." The officer attempted to read 10-Gauge his rights, but five bikers fired up their Harleys as soon as he opened his mouth.

The officer started again. Five more bikes started. He made one more fruitless attempt to follow procedure. 10-Gauge, smiling broadly, dropped the mic on the stage, made a big show of bowing his head and putting his hands together in the prayer position. He turned his head slightly and winked at the crowd. Then, raising his head, he sought out his lieutenants and nodded to them. They departed at full throttle. As one, the other bikers did the same.

"What were you saying, Inspector Clouseau?" asked 10-Gauge innocently.

The officer read 10-Gauge his rights, finishing with "Do you understand?"

"Not my first rodeo, as you well know," said 10-Gauge, winking again at the crowd. Some laughed nervously.

"Please answer yes or no."

"Yes, Inspector Clouseau, I understand my rights as described. Shall we go?"

10-Gauge's eyes sought Sarah. All playfulness gone. He shook his head at her.

Donny shuffled over to Sarah and draped his arm over her shoulders. "Jesus on a pogo stick, dear sister, this has become a right royal dumpster fire."

She pulled away. "Really, Donny? And why is that?" Nick blocked Sarah's arm, stopping her from slapping her brother.

"Let's not turn on one another. We need a plan, and we need one fast. Aislin? Aislin? *Aislin!* Pay attention," Nick barked.

Aislin looked at him blankly. "I have to call the hospital. To see if Jim is still alive. What if he isn't? What if I killed him? Will I be charged with murder, too?" Aislin's eyes grew as the horror washed over her. "I just wanted him to leave me alone. And I can't find Letty or Otto." Aislin was gasping deeply between each word. Nick took her face in his hands, covering her mouth and pinching one nostril closed. She tried to pull away, but he held her steady and spoke quietly, ensuring her that everything was going to be okay and that she had to focus on slowing her breath. Nick released her nostril then removed his hand from her mouth.

Keeping her eyes locked on his face, Aislin did as instructed. Her breathing slowed. But as the stress left, her knees buckled. Nick caught her and hugged her to him, rubbing her back and speaking softly into her hair. He lifted his head and asked Sarah to run and get some food.

"What the hell is going on? Is that Aislin Fitzgerald? I knew it!" came a voice from behind Nick.

"Not now, Kate. I am dealing with a medical issue."

"Is that what you're calling it? Doesn't look like that to me."

Donny stepped between Nick and his wife. "You, my dear, are making an assumption. I witnessed everything, and it is indeed a medical issue."

"You're drunk, so your observations are worthless. Furthermore, even if you weren't drunk, your observations would be worthless, so just shut up and mind your own business."

"Why are you even here, Kate?" asked Nick.

"I saw on social media that some sort of craziness was happening at Picnic Park. I knew you were here, so we decided to check it out. And I find you hugging another woman in full view of everyone."

"Who's 'we,' Kate? You're here with your new lover, and you have the audacity to judge me for helping out a friend in medical distress. Really, Kate? That's a bit rich, don't you think?" Nick continued to hold Aislin in his arms.

"At least I'm not flaunting it in everyone's face," hissed Kate.

The nausea and unsteadiness had disappeared, but Aislin was comfortable exactly where she was, so she made no effort to pull away. She didn't have the strength to deal with any more drama. She wanted Kate, drunk Donny, all of Twiggy's women, everyone, to disappear so she could just stand there and inhale the scent of Nick. She burrowed in further.

Sarah was jogging back from the food tent but slowed when she saw Kate. She circled behind Nick to see if Aislin was up for air. She tapped her on the shoulder.

"Kate's here!" she whispered. Aislin nodded.

"I brought you a snack. You should eat it. And you should probably stop hugging Nick. Just sayin'." Aislin shook her head.

"Forgive me for what I'm about to do," Sarah whispered.

"Nick, I can take over with Aislin while you and Kate find somewhere private to continue your discussion." Sarah pried Nick's arms off her friend. "Aislin, let's go grab a seat on the stage."

Aislin avoided looking at Kate as Sarah steered her to the stage. They picked their way through the sea of small toys and children and found seats beside the shy woman who had first climbed onstage. She blankly watched her son colouring with chalk from the toy box.

"Hi, how's it going?" asked Sarah as she peeled the wrapper from the muffin and broke off chunks for Aislin. "My friend here had a bit of an anxiety attack. I mean, why not? Right? Everything that could go wrong has gone wrong. Spectacularly. But on the bright side, the bikers have all buggered off, so our fear of a turf war breaking out has been put to rest. No bullets zinging by. No blood pumping from open wounds. No heads or hands chopped off for crab bait. So all good there. But we did have a heart attack, so we may actually have a body count. Too soon to know. And it looks as though we now have a domestic dispute blowing up. No idea how that will end," Sarah commented as she fed Aislin.

The woman beside them began to sob quietly. She picked up her son and turned to Aislin and Sarah. "This whole thing has been a disgusting mess. The man I loved, the father of this little boy, is gone. Forever this time. And I came here to say goodbye. But it's been one disaster after another. This is the worst day of my life! You two should be ashamed. I hope you go straight to hell."

Aislin took the last half of the muffin, broke off a piece, and fed it to Sarah. "She seemed nice."

Jill appeared from within her food tent. She took stock of the crowd, pausing on Nick and Kate, who were still arguing, then swung her gaze to where Aislin and Sarah were sitting and let it hang there just long enough to make them squirm. She waved them over.

"Some of Twiggy's women will need help getting plates for all their kids, so you two are going to get in there and make yourselves useful. For a change. And when you've done that, you're going to talk to the bartender. See how much stock he has left. When he runs out, we're shutting this shitshow down."

"Food's ready," she yelled. "Women with kids first, and if there's any food left, you boozehounds can have some. Lineup starts here. No pushing." Jill remained in place, arms crossed.

After helping the mothers get their children settled, Aislin and Sarah slipped into the beer tent, which was nearly empty, as everyone had shuffled over to line up obediently in front of Jill.

The bartender's face glistened with sweat. There were large moist patches under his arms. "Would have been nice to have some help in here. I couldn't keep up. Way more than the eighty we were told to stock for. Where did they all come from? And what the hell happened out there? Someone said the emcee was arrested and that some guy died of a heart attack. I've never worked an event quite like this. This isn't close to what my boss said it would be. He said it was an outdoor celebration of life. Who's in charge of this gong show?"

"Jill is in charge," said Sarah quickly before Aislin could speak.

"Good to know. She's one scary woman. I won't be complaining to her, that's for sure, and will warn my boss to be careful."

"Mm, wise of you," replied Sarah. "Jill wants to know how much more beer you have and how long you think it will be before you run out."

"I've got almost half a vanload left; enough for another couple of hours. That's the other thing. I've never seen so much beer ordered for a funeral. But people seem to be slowing down, and once they eat, they'll get sleepy and want to go home."

"Thanks, we will pass that info on to Jill." Aislin and Sarah contained their laughter until they were well away from both tents.

"Oh my God, that was brilliant," gasped Aislin. "You've always been good at dodging responsibility."

Chapter 21

Aislin had successfully avoided looking directly at Nick and Kate, but when Sarah left, she indulged herself. Kate was throwing her arms around dramatically, as she had always done. Nick looked resigned. There was no sign of the young woman who had arrived with Kate. Nor was there any sign of Donny.

Her spidey senses suddenly went on full alert.

"There you are," said Theo Thunberger, suddenly so close to Aislin she could feel his breath.

"Theo? Why are you here?" she asked, stepping away.

"I want to know what you know about why the cops, including forensics, combed The Maples today. Right in the middle of a funeral for the same guy you're supposedly having a celebration of life for. Think of how his family felt. They were trying to send off their son minus the taint of the life of crime he obviously led. Extremely inconvenient.

"And I've been thinking about the timing of your mysterious visit, mysterious illness, and the equally mysterious statement that you wanted to go on a date. I knew you were up to something. Now, I want you to tell me exactly what's going on."

"I don't have to do any such thing. Why would I know anything about why the cops were at your place? I don't know what you're talking about. And I was not up to anything." Aislin hoped her indignation covered her shock and fear.

"I just find your sudden and short-lived fascination with me interesting. Why exactly were you there? It's all very suspicious. And believe you me, the cops are very interested in that time period. Otto's abuse of protocol in terms of record keeping was also of great interest. I couldn't answer their questions because I have no idea what he's done. The records are a mess. It will take months to sort out. Senile old bastard." He took stock of the scene as he spoke. "Where's your darling Otto? Oh right, I heard he was arrested."

Trying to balance himself, an overloaded paper plate, and a beer, Donny watched this exchange. With exaggerated care, he selected a mini quiche from his plate, found his mouth, inserted it, then with equal care, folded his plate and put it in his pocket. Patting the pocket, he staggered over to Aislin.

"Is this guy bothering you? He looks like he is." As Donny spoke, small, moist particles of pastry sprayed Theo's face and jacket.

"Get away from me, you filthy drunk! You're disgusting."

"You can't talk to Donny like that, you twerp. Get lost." Aislin shoved Theo so hard that he staggered backwards and couldn't keep his footing on the wet grass. He was up almost as fast as he went down, but the damage was done. The seat of his pants was damp and dirty, his face angry red. "You're a crazy bitch."

"Okay, everyone take a few steps back," ordered Nick, stepping between Aislin and Theo. Glowering at Theo, he said, "And buddy, don't you dare say anything like that again."

"There you go, rushing to the defence of poor Aislin," snarled Kate, joining them. She yanked Aislin around to face her. "You milked the sad little orphan role for all it's worth. Everyone felt sorry for you. You could do no wrong: Aislin Fitzgerald, the paragon of perfection. But I knew you wanted Nick. You made no secret of it in school, and as soon as you came back, you started on him again." Kate spat on Aislin's shoes.

"That's enough!" shouted Nick. "Get your girlfriend and get lost. I'm just so fed up with you."

"Well, your mother isn't! She agrees with me."

"Kate, stop talking and *go away*! *Now!*"

En masse, the crowd dropped conversations midsentence and turned towards this new source of entertainment. Jill diverted their attention by giving the last call for food.

Nick led Aislin back to the stage and sat her down. "You stay here while I go get us some real food. I haven't eaten for hours, and it looks as though you are in much the same state."

Aislin did as she was told. From her vantage point, she scrutinized Kate. In high school, Kate dressed to accentuate her curvy body, blatantly flaunting her sexuality. She was sexy, edgy, beautiful, brilliant, and artistic. And she knew these attributes gave her power. A big fish in a small pond. Everyone craved her attention. Aislin recalled how Kate had breezed down the hallways with her entourage of chosen ones in tow.

Kate dressed now as she did then, but neither her power nor her edge had transitioned well to being a small fish in a big pond. Her formerly long, curly, blonde hair was now short, spiky, and multicoloured. She looked awkward and desperate. Aislin dug deep for compassion, but the shovel came up empty. In school, her envy of Kate had been borderline hatred. She no longer envied her, but the wellspring of hate readily bubbled up.

Nick slid into the chair beside her, placing a plate of food on her lap. They ate in silence. The clouds scudded away. Droplets of moisture on the trees and shrubs sparkled, and the sunshine drew people from the food and beer tents.

Sarah lugged Donny onto the stage and dumped him in a seat. "Keep an eye on him while I get him some food to soak up all the booze."

Donny, winking at Aislin, carefully pulled the folded paper plate from his pocket. She leaned over and gently took it from him. "Here, let me take that. Your sister will bring you something a bit more appetizing."

The four of them sat in silence, watching the crowd while they ate. As her blood-sugar level rose, Aislin reflected on her recent behaviour. The harsh light of self-assessment was unkind.

"I have to apologize for being a useless, high-maintenance, needy twit. And for causing Jim's heart attack. And for pushing that twerp onto his ass on the grass. And for having a meltdown. And for losing Letty and Otto. I actually haven't done a damn thing to help."

No one offered any correction. Not her partner and not Nick. Not even Donny. She expected Nick to jump in and say something.

Anything. Not just sit there chewing. Resentment began to brew within. And confusion. She could not get a handle on his feelings for her. She looked sideways at him and realized with a rush of relief that he was not listening. He was intently watching Theo, who had been cornered by Weronika.

"Whatever they're talking about can't be good for us," he said, pointing with his head. "Who wants to go find out?"

Sarah nodded in Aislin's direction. "Aislin's the Theo-whisperer. Just try not to resort to violence," she said, grinning wickedly. "And for the record, none of us have done much. We all just stood back and watched the horror unfold. No way we could have anticipated any of this. I mean, we had visions of gunfire and bodies piling up, but not two of our emcees arrested, exes fighting, or someone having a heart attack. At least with a wedding, you get a dress rehearsal, so you kinda know what issues need active management. The only blame I can lay at your feet, Aislin, is coming up with the idea of us being funeral planners. And if I do that, then I have to accept my role in landing us this gig. I fell for the charming biker, which was exactly his plan. He pegged me, not you, as the one most likely to swoon. And like a love-struck teenager, I fell under his spell."

Donny nodded sagely. "Yes, dear sister, you have always been attracted to bottom-feeders. It's a singular failing of your otherwise sterling character."

"Don't you dare talk to *me* about going with bottom-feeders! You are the one who went sniffing around one of Twiggy's scummy exes."

"Jaylene is not scummy. She's the keeper of my fragile heart."

"Right. Last month the keeper of your fragile heart was a 1985 Chevy truck. I suppose we should feel heartened that your object of affection is human this time. And younger than you."

"Okay, you two, break it up," said Nick. "We need to figure out how to bring this to a close."

Sarah pulled out the itinerary, Otto's speaking notes, and eulogy. "According to this, we should be wrapping up the slideshow and handing out the keepsakes. But the keeper of the keepsakes is currently detained, so I guess we can skip that part. Such a shame, as I was looking forward to seeing small children run around with bullet keychains engraved with their father's name. Such a touching sight."

"Then let's run the slideshow. That way, people might remember why they're here. And the technician can earn his keep because he has had nothing to do so far. When it's over, one of us will go up there and thank everyone for coming and send them home," said Aislin. "Donny, you have the memory stick, right?"

After a moment of blankness, Donny smiled and patted his pocket. Aislin groaned. "Say it isn't so, Donny. Not the pocket you put your food in."

He pulled out the stick, examined it slowly at eye level, then with equal care, put it in his mouth and sucked forcefully on it.

"You bloody idiot!" yelled Sarah. She yanked the memory stick from his lips and shook it, unleashing a slimy cascade of saliva and bits of potato salad. Aislin cringed and quickly wiped her face while Nick flicked potatoes from his jacket. "Damn your eyes, Donny Quinn, damn your drunk eyes. Why are you such a mess? Why do you always screw up?"

Nick handed Sarah a napkin. As she wiped down her coat, he said, "Moving right along, we can go straight to the eulogy. But which of us is going to deliver it? And Donny, that question does not include you."

Aislin moved her chair closer to Donny and put her arm around his shoulders. "It's okay. We all still love you, don't we, Sarah?"

"No, we don't. But, back to the important question, who the heck can we ask? We're pretty much at the bottom of the barrel."

"Jill," sobbed Donny. "She loved Twiggy."

Aislin smacked Donny on the chest. "You're right! She did. She told Otto and me she would always love him. Donny! You're brilliant. Thank you."

Sarah rolled her eyes. "I wouldn't go that far, but it's a good suggestion. Who's going to ask her? She's pretty disgusted with us. Except you, Nick. Jill still likes you."

"Ahem. Mind providing some context for your last statement, Sarah?" asked Jill, joining them on the stage. She stood with her hands on her hips, surveying them. "I've been waiting and wondering when you were actually going to deliver some vestige of what was planned. So far, you've done next to nothing but flap around like a bunch of chickens. Now, what did I just walk in on? What's going on?" Jill looked to Nick for the answer.

Nick said, "We need you to read Twiggy's eulogy. It should be read by someone who knew him. Cared for him."

"Loved him," corrected Donny. "You're the only one who should do this. It should have been you all along." He and Jill looked at each other.

"Amanda, get me a beer," yelled Jill. "Make it two. No, bring six." She shrugged. "It's been a hell of a day, so I figure we all need a beer. Even you, Donny."

"No, thank you, I am turning over a new leaf. I'm going to live a life of temperance and celibacy—no more drinking, no more dames. I shall wrap myself in a shroud of abstinence."

"Really? I can't wait for this phase. At least I won't have to worry about you corrupting Fitz. He wolf-whistled a woman while out with Pops the other day. Pops's head nearly exploded; he put it down to hanging out with you, brother dear," said Sarah, twisting the cap off her beer. She held up the bottle to admire Twiggy's vest on the custom label. "The brewery did a good job on this. At least something went well. Cheers."

The group sipped in silence. Aislin's first sip turned her legs to rubber. The beer, her sleepless night, and a day of minimal food and maximum anxiety immobilized her. She looked at the wet, muddy grass, the groups of dishevelled drinkers, the wrung-out mothers, the small herd of noisy kids.

An observation flitted through her mind, which she spoke as soon as she thought it. "Did Twiggy breed with every woman he met? From here, it looks as though he was a one-man population explosion."

Nick and Sarah looked at their phones. Donny looked for his. No one spoke.

"What? What's wrong with that question? I'm just curious. Blame it on my journalist background. We ask questions."

Jill replied quietly, "Not every woman." Her tone snagged Aislin's attention from the squabbling children. Aislin read Jill's face, from the raw pain trapped in her eyes to the weight of grief pulling at her skin. She wished she could look away, retrieve her glibness, her petulant judgments of Jill's moods. Instead, she willed herself to hold eye contact and acknowledge Jill's heartbreak. She flashed back to the scene in the Mugshot when Jill hugged the box with Twiggy's ashes. How could she forget that? It was such a poignant moment. Aislin put her right hand on her heart and mouthed, "I am so sorry." Jill blinked hard, shrugged, and looked away. Aislin was on the verge of suggesting she look up to stop the tears but refrained.

"Anyone got a pen?" asked Jill. "Otto did a pretty good job because of his decades of listening to eulogies, but it needs more of a personal touch."

Chapter 22

Aislin and Sarah watched with growing concern as Jill steadily drank beer after beer while she muttered and edited Otto's eulogy. After four beers, she stood up and read over the revised version as she wandered around the stage.

"Okay, I'm ready," she said. "Let's get this over with so we can get this day over with. Just give me a few minutes to sort out useless Amanda so she can pack up without screwing up. And one of you should shut down the beer tent."

Aislin's phone vibrated, and she answered without looking. "Where are you? I've been worried. Are you okay? Were you taken in for questioning, too?"

"What do you mean, was I taken in for questioning?" asked Elaine. "I've been trying to reach your grandmother all morning. What's going on over there? I hear you gave Jim Brownlee a heart attack! You're lucky it wasn't fatal."

"Elaine, for the record, I did not give Jim a heart attack. He happened to have a heart attack while we were, ah, talking."

"That's not what I heard. I heard you swore at him and he was so shocked his heart stopped."

"That's ridiculous. The man was one Twinkie and a beer away from a cardiac arrest. It was just a matter of time. He's lucky Nick was here to do CPR."

"Your cavalier attitude is shocking and disturbing. What would

Letty think? And why did you think she was being questioned? What have you dragged her into?"

"Ask your gossip-mongering friends," Aislin said, ending the call.

Sarah looked at her with admiration. "Way to tell off that old windbag. Impressive. I gather she's looking for Letty and has heard about Jim? It must be eating her alive to be on the outside of all the action."

"I feel a bit bad for being rude to her," said Aislin. "There's just something about that woman that's triggering for me. I used to be able to keep a lid on it."

"She is pretty annoying. Just don't give her a heart attack, too."

"Not even close to being funny."

"Let's go save Amanda's life by dragging Jill off her. That should balance your books."

Jill was standing in the disarray of the food tent. A bottle of Scotch in one hand, a shot glass in the other, she yelled orders at Amanda. Amanda's demeanour was that of a prey animal resigned to its fate.

"Hi, Jill, you about ready? The sooner we get through the eulogy, the sooner we can all go home," Sarah said cautiously.

"Give me a minute, okay? Amanda, don't forget to disconnect the propane before yanking the tank. Okay, one more for courage, and then I'm good to go." Jill dispatched the shot of Scotch, then walked unsteadily over to Aislin and Sarah. "Let's do this."

Nick shook his head as he watched their approach, Jill supported between them. "Wow, two arrested and two drunk emcees in a day. That has got to be a record. How about I call people to gather for the eulogy?" he whispered to Aislin.

Tight-lipped, she nodded as she guided Jill to the front of the stage. She removed the rolled-up eulogy from the back pocket of Jill's jeans and smoothed it out as best she could, then Sarah gingerly fished out Jill's glasses from their perch in the deep V-neck of her shirt and cleaned them before handing them to Jill.

Jill straightened up, took the mic, and began to read. She made it through the first lines before giving in to her grief. A sob punctuated every second word. She handed the mic to Sarah while she blew her nose. Apologizing, she started from the top. She did not get much further on her second attempt. It was like watching a car with bald summer tires trying to get up an icy hill.

Sarah gently took the now damp pages from Jill and slipped an arm around her shoulders. Aislin hesitated briefly, then did the same on Jill's other side. Sarah began to read in her strong, clear voice. While in school, Sarah was cast in leading roles in every play. From a young age, she knew instinctively when to lace her words with just the right amount of emotion. Besides landing leading roles, she used it to full effect when talking herself out of trouble. Frank could be relied upon to cave as soon as she began to emote. She had not lost her touch.

The jolly atmosphere evaporated. The partiers from the beer tent straggled out, blinking in the sun, drawn to the tone and timbre of Sarah's voice. Twiggy's former lovers gravitated towards each other. They listened, arms linked, some openly weeping, others stoically dry-eyed. The children stopped playing and stood with their mothers, looking up at the three women.

Aislin did not want to stand there on stage with Jill and Sarah. Unlike Sarah, being on stage made Aislin's skin crawl. She tried to force her mind to settle and focus on the passion, the grief, the heartache, the love Sarah was so beautifully portraying. As Letty had reminded her many times over the past few weeks, it was not all about her. Her intense discomfort was impacting her breathing. She was on the brink of another anxiety attack. On stage, in full view of everyone. She inhaled deeply and slowly, but as she exhaled, the tiniest of snickers bubbled out. She froze. She cast her mind for a distraction. It landed on Jim and his purple face as he collapsed. A snort escaped. She forced herself to think of his wife, Delores, and how scared she must have been. If he had died, would Delores have asked them to organize his funeral? A louder, wetter snort escaped. Sarah paused to look at her. Aislin nodded, biting her bottom lip, to the unspoken question. Yes, she would behave.

But out of the corner of her eye, she saw Weronika with her arm around Donny. They were sharing what looked like a bottle of vodka. Weronika, who had a good six inches on Donny, was resting her head on his. Donny, eye level with her ample bosom, was grinning lovingly at her cleavage. Maniacal laughter took over the controls of Aislin's entire being. The harder she tried to control herself, the harder she laughed. Aislin's face contorted with the effort to gain control. Tears flowed down her cheeks and dripped off her chin. Sarah motioned for her to leave.

Aislin unhooked herself from Jill and stumbled off the stage, grabbing her coat as she passed. She ran to her car, fumbling for her keys. She heard Nick calling her but ignored him. She drove home, laughing so hard she could barely steer or see through her tears.

Her laughter stopped abruptly when she pulled up to Letty's. She braked hard and stared. The gutter on one side of the garage was dangling. The corner of the lawn was a mudhole of tire tracks. The trunk of Letty's car was completely bashed in. The Behemoth was gone.

Filled with dread, Aislin ran up the steps and through the door, not stopping to lift the mat. There was a stillness that empty houses have. Even so, she called Letty's name as she raced up to Letty's room, pausing at the open door. Some drawers were open and empty, and her suitcases were all gone. There was no point in checking the bathroom.

Aislin trudged slowly down the stairs and stood on the front porch staring at the spot formerly filled by the Behemoth. She sighed and turned back inside and spotted the corner of an envelope poking out from beneath the mat. She lifted it and saw two envelopes. One with her name scrawled in Letty's spidery handwriting and the other with Nick's name on it, presumably written by Otto.

She picked them both up and went into the kitchen. She sank into a chair. The breakfast dishes were still on the table, the dishwasher half unloaded. It had been such a long, emotionally erratic day she didn't know if she could handle what she knew awaited her.

She felt chilled, so she reached for Letty's gardening sweater. As she wrapped herself in it, her grandmother's scent wafted up. The dam burst, her anguish so acute the sobs hurt her throat.

"Aislin. Can I come in?" Nick asked.

His voice startled her. She glanced at him, then turned away, wiping her face. "I guess so."

"I got a voice message from Otto that you had something important to give me." He pointed to the envelopes. "I'm assuming it has something to do with those and the absence of the Behemoth."

"Probably." Aislin found a relatively clean tissue in Letty's pocket, shook out the dirt and fir needles, and wiped her nose. "I don't know what's going on. Why did they leave? Without saying goodbye." She started to cry again. "Sorry. I can't seem to stop."

"It's okay, Aislin. Don't worry about it. But if you keep it up, I'll start crying, too. And I ugly cry."

Aislin choked out a laugh and looked up. "Thanks, I needed that." She pointed at the envelope addressed to her. "I don't think I want to open that. I don't want to know what it says."

"I have a feeling I know what's in mine. A few years ago, because Otto doesn't have any relatives, he asked me to be his power of attorney, and I agreed."

Nick sat down beside Aislin. "I can stay while you open your envelope, or I can leave. I'm guessing Otto left mine here because he didn't want you to deal with the shock on your own."

Aislin's waterworks returned. Sobbing, she said, "I *am* on my own. Again. Letty's gone, and she's my only relative. I've messed things up with Sarah and she's never going to forgive me. I can't stay here, but I have nowhere to go."

"Why do you have to go anywhere? Why can't you stay here? In your home? You aren't alone. You still have Sarah." Nick paused. "And me." He stood up and walked over to Secretariat's tank. "My marriage is over. It actually ended years ago. Kate and I—we've been going through the motions, neither of us having the motivation to fix it or end it. Then she met this woman, and well, that was that." He turned back to Aislin. "So, new beginnings for both of us, right, Moe?"

Aislin glanced up then quickly looked away. She didn't trust herself to process what Nick was saying. Her emotional bandwidth was on life support. She looked out at Letty's garden. It looked the way she felt—abandoned.

"What do I do with all of that?" she asked, pointing. "I don't have a clue. And if I don't keep it immaculate, Letty will be furious. If she ever comes home." She stifled a sob.

"Well, I can help you there. I pretty much grew up working in this garden with Frank," Nick replied softly.

"Thanks, but no thanks. You have your clinic and your mother's place to look after. I'll figure it out."

"Aislin Fitzgerald, you can be exceptionally hard-headed. I am not offering because I like the sound of my own voice. I am offering because, believe it or not, I care about you. And believe it or not, I want to spend time with you. And if helping you with the garden is my gateway to being with you, then that's what I'm going to do. The question is, do you want to spend time with me?"

She didn't trust herself to respond and risk exposing her deep well of neediness. She fiddled in silence with the envelopes.

"Aislin, I am going to pour a beer for myself and a glass of wine for you and we are going to go outside and sit in those chairs, and we are going to open these envelopes. Got it? So, go sit outside."

Aislin bristled slightly at being ordered around but reined in her instinct to snap back. She picked up the envelopes, pausing before opening the door. "Thank you," she said in a small voice.

She settled in her chair and looked around the garden. The late afternoon had always been Letty's favourite part of the day. For the first time, she sensed the stillness Letty loved.

Nick joined her. They clinked glasses solemnly and picked up their respective envelopes.

"Okay," he said, "here we go. And, when we're finished reading, if you show me yours, I'll show you mine. Deal?"

Aislin turned to him. His face was a map of the stress and exhaustion of the day. She smiled into his tired eyes. "Deal."

About the Author

© Bertrand P. Smith

Growing up on a tiny isolated island off the coast of Vancouver Island, Juliet Domvile spent her early childhood in a world where books, a couple of corgis, and a pet sheep were her constant companions. She has had a varied career ranging from counting nudists on a public beach, to grooming racehorses, to freelance writing articles on a host of topics with which she had no experience, to ghostwriting nonfiction books, one of which is a national bestseller. In 2020, she followed her lifelong dream to write a novel. When she is not writing, she rides a large horse over small jumps and is mostly successful in keeping the horse between her and the ground. She and her husband live on Vancouver Island, have two grown sons, and have shared their lives with a series of corgis, sheep, cats, and chickens.

CPSIA information can be obtained
at www.ICGtesting.com
Printed in the USA
BVHW080139010922
645878BV00001B/3